CRAZY LIES

&

CAT'S-EYES

BOB GOODWIN

Crazy Lies & Cat's-Eyes
© Bob Goodwin 2024

PUBLISHER Bob Goodwin AUSTRALIA

To my ever-expanding extended family

Chapter 1

Jasper

Dutifully every fortnight, Jasper had accepted his injection for the past six and a half years. Granted, for five of those years, he was under a Community Treatment Order and had no choice in receiving the medication. Nevertheless, he never let an opportunity go by when he didn't politely ask to go back onto oral meds. Since the order had lapsed eighteen months ago, he was within his rights to decline the painful needle. Refusing to accept it, however, would soon enough see him back on a compulsory treatment order.

It had happened twice before when he was in his early twenties. *'I'm a voluntary patient living in my own home. If you try to jab me, I'll consider it assault and have you, and your fucking service, charged'*, he had protested. Within forty-eight hours, the mental health team placed another order on him, and the police, together with his case worker, escorted him back to the hospital. His protesting, swearing and resisting only served to convince everyone he had relapsed again and had probably started using illicit drugs once more.

With Jasper, the mental health team had become extremely cautious, as on previous presentations, he had been violent and highly paranoid, with both auditory and visual hallucinations. His use of methamphetamines significantly contributed to his hostility and psychosis. Most times, these perceptual disturbances centred around his belief that others were conspiring against him with plans to send him into the depths of hell to rot with the sinners. He would claim he could see the images of demons in the faces of his friends and even his care providers. His history of violence was littered with assaults on friends, family and others. There was an attack on his neighbour where he smashed the man's nose with several direct punches and followed up with a threat to decapitate him with a machete. Thanks to police intervention, this was avoided. But it was only after assaults on a doctor and nurse at the psychiatric hospital, where Jasper gouged at their faces and eyes with his fingernails, that the treatment team took things more seriously and kept him on a long-term treatment order and closer follow-up.

In these earlier years, Jasper was a tall and slender man with a reasonable fitness level thanks to his running and home gym workouts. He was pleased he was able to give his abductors a hard time on each occasion they carted him away.

Now, though, after years on the drug, he had gained thirty kilos. He remained strong by doing casual bricklaying and concreting work, but all running and aerobic exercise had ceased. Despite this, within himself, he felt reasonably well and content; however, in the back of his mind, he knew that he had not reached his full potential. From his point of view, the past episodes of hospitalisation had not been all bad, for it was in the psych ward where he met the love of his life. Cassandra had depression and was admitted to the mental health unit after recovering in the ICU following an overdose of antidepressant tablets. After their eventual discharge from hospital, the pair moved in together, firstly in a small one-bedroom flat, until they eventually secured public housing in Claymore, Sydney. It was a simple, three-bedroom, low-set brick home, but it suited the couple and their two young children - Faith, now aged nine, and Delaney, eight.

Chapter 2

Faith & Delaney

For the most part, the two young siblings enjoyed each other's company. They both attended the same school, with Faith in year three and Delaney in his second year. Faith, being the eldest and with, in her own words, so much more school experience, would keep her eye on her brother, checking in on him at morning tea and lunch breaks.

On weekends, under their mother's watch and, less frequently, their father's, they would play together and with friends. Running around tagging each other, saying *you're it,* kicking balls and playing cricket were some of their favourite activities.

Their mother, Cassandra, would often get the play started before making an excuse that she needed a rest. She was a petite twenty-nine-year-old who liked to keep herself active. Besides playing with the children and a busy day of housework, she would walk a few kilometres when she could squeeze in the time. Her weight seldom varied regardless of her level of activity or diet. Her mother had been a chronically skinny woman, and Cassandra had inherited the same metabolic genes, much to her sister's annoyance.

Cassie had been settled on a picnic blanket with a magazine for the past two hours. She loved checking out the latest fashions, hairstyles and Hollywood gossip while the band Echosmith played softly through her phone. Mostly, though, she would fantasise about a life so different to her own - a home she owned, a swimming pool, a kitchen with an island bench, money to dress and feed the family in style, a lovely trip to the theatre occasionally and a personal hairstylist.

Late on a Saturday afternoon, after the children had hours of fun, Cassie closed her magazine and called them over.

'Delaney, are you feeling better?' she asked, passing him a water bottle.

Earlier in the day, he had one of his *turns*, where he would blackout as if he had fallen into a deep sleep. He appeared to be away in a world of his own, still breathing normally and sluggishly moving his limbs. Generally, he would return to his usual energetic self after five minutes. Occasionally, though, it would last longer. The longest so far had been forty-five minutes, and he regained full consciousness as he arrived at the emergency department with his worried parents. Investigations for blood pressure problems, epilepsy and other brain-related issues were all negative. It had been suggested it was due to heightened anxiety. Cassie wondered if the growling rottweiler that wandered through their playing area earlier was the cause.

'I'm fine, Mum. Are we going home now?'

She nodded. The three of them headed off. It was a ten-minute walk home. Mum carried the picnic basket; Faith had a soccer ball, and Delaney had a cricket bat.

The young boy tapped his sister on the shoulder. 'You're it!' he yelled, then scampered down the road a few metres.

'Delaney Jeffrey Johansson!' exclaimed his mother. The loud call of all three names meant he was doing something wrong. He left the road and moved to the safer grassy footpath a few metres ahead of the others.

'You've had a good play. Time to settle down, I think,' she added.

'You're still it!' he called back to Faith, but she had lost interest and bounced the ball several times.

Delaney sighed and looked down at his shoes. 'Ah… you're no fun,' he said under his breath as he whacked a patch of bare ground with the cricket bat. The bat struck something shiny that shot forward and rolled. He bent and picked it up. After a quick polish on his t-shirt, he held it up. 'Look what I found,' he announced proudly.

'A pretty marble,' said Cassandra. 'Lucky you.'

'It might mean something,' said Faith.

'Like what?' Del shrugged.

'Ask your father,' said Cassandra. 'He's the one who loves connecting all the dots.'

'Yeah, I will.' Delaney studied his treasure. Three different colours on a leafy-shaped swirl were in the centre of the glass ball. After turning it around and holding it close to his eye, he gave it a final rub, then dropped it in the pocket of his shorts, patting it afterwards to ensure it was safely tucked away. This was the first of several he found around the same spot, as if someone had dropped them randomly along the footpath so that he could find them. He polished them up and kept them in a small wooden bowl beside his bed, getting them out occasionally to shoot them across the floor and knock over his toy soldiers.

'I'll play dress-up with you in the morning,' Faith announced. 'But I want to be the grandfather wizard.'

'When do I get a turn to be the old weird guy?'

'I'm better at casting spells than you. You can be my servant.'

'No thanks, I'll be a policeman and arrest you if you try to cast a spell on me.'

'It would be a good spell. To protect you, silly. So that the bad spirits can't hurt you.'

'Before either of you get busy with other things, don't forget that you have school projects to do tomorrow,' said their mother. 'I have plenty of old magazines with pretty pictures you can use.'

Faith was to make a collage of many different people, while Delaney was to highlight two colours using pictures and coloured pencils.

*   *   *

The following afternoon, as planned, Faith dressed up as an old man wizard using her father's old shirt, baggy trousers tied up with a piece of nylon rope, a small branch as a walking stick, and an even smaller one as a magic wand. She had shaped and stuck some cotton wool under her chin as a wispy beard and sprinkled baby powder through her brown hair to make it appear grey. Delaney wore blue clothes, a cap, and a plastic gun tucked into his pants. He had drawn sergeant stripes on his upper sleeves with chalk. Both were trying unsuccessfully to give each other orders.

Cassandra strolled from the kitchen to the dining room table. It was littered with open magazines, cut-up pieces of paper, and loose pencils. Here and there were patches of dripped glue. Lying next to each other at one end were the two creations.

'Oh dear,' she studied the images. 'Jasper! You've gotta see this.' She called out loudly as he was elsewhere in the house. Cassie looked closer at the pictures, shaking her head. 'Oh, my God.'

'What's up?' Her husband walked in with an exaggerated, deliberate, slow, wobbly gait. 'Woo… hoo… woo…,' he raised his arms while he tried making ghost noises. Cassie looked up.

'What on earth are you up to?'

Jasper's face, hair, and neck were white with baby powder. He was draped in a sheet. Black circles were around his eyes. 'Just being a ghost. Fooling around with the kids.'

'Well, stop that and look here.'

Jasper moved alongside. 'Ah, they've finished their schoolwork.' He checked them out. 'Hmm… that's a bit unusual.'

Faith had cut out many heads from the magazines and stuck them in a big cluster. Next to the collection of heads was what looked like a giant guillotine with red colouring on the blade and around the device's base. Delaney had, as per instructions, used just two colours - black and red. He had roughly cut out many pairs of eyes and surrounded them with heavy red colouring. Black lightning bolts connected the eyes.

Cassie looked at her husband. 'This seems a little bizarre and quite dark and awful.'

'Well… it's different. Delaney's had those nightmares.'

'Do we need to do something? See someone? And what about Faith?'

Jasper smiled and nodded. 'I know what this is about.' He tapped on the guillotine.

'And?'

'There was a show the other day on SBS. The French Revolution.'

'You let her watch that?'

'Well… it was educational, and she wanted to see it.'

Cassie slapped him on the shoulder. 'Jasper Graham Johansson!'

'Yeah, but she likes watching that sort of stuff.'

'I don't care. It's not healthy for a nine-year-old.'

'True enough, but she likes history, documentaries and even news programs. Her work, though, is very neat and quite advanced for her age. She is the clever one, that's for sure.'

'She is a year older.'

'I know, but still. It's remarkable. I like it.'

The couple looked at each other. Jasper grinned. 'Everything means something, love. Connections are everywhere, sometimes obvious, sometimes not.'

Cassie looked directly at him. 'Huh… I really can't take you seriously with a face like that. Go clean yourself up.' She waved him away.

Chapter 3
Jasper & Nigel

'You never let a chance go by, Jasper,' smiled Nigel. His grin pushed up his fat cheeks and revealed his uneven top teeth.

'Never do, mate.' Jasper stood, scraping his dining chair backward across the vinyl. 'The usual? White and two?' He tilted his head at his long-time case worker.

'Lovely. Much appreciated.' Nigel leaned back a little on the wooden chair and pushed a small red, white and blue cardboard box to one side on the laminate dining table. 'The team has been discussing your injections since my last visit,' continued Nigel with a smile.

'Hmmm… I've heard that a few times.' Jasper flicked on the kettle and grabbed two mugs.

'You know you can go onto the monthly shots.'

'No thanks. Just the thought of such a dose going into my body all at once worries me.' Jasper raised a stop hand just as Nigel was about to talk. 'I've heard all your assurances before, my friend. And no, I'm not changing my mind.' He dropped a teaspoon of dark, grainy instant coffee into each cup.

'Okay, I understand. And you're right; we've been over this a thousand times. You know what's new? I've heard talk of a three-monthly shot coming soon.'

'Really!' Jasper gasped as he turned his head toward Nigel. 'That is fucked up. People will die with such a dose in their bodies.'

'Hopefully not. Pretty sure they're testing it thoroughly.'

'Psychiatry isn't a precise science, mate… more like trial and error. So, is that the standard fortnightly one on the table? I'm not being a Guinea pig for anyone… ever!'

'Hey, I'm on your side here.' Nigel tapped the box. 'This is the same one as every other fortnight.' He picked it up, glanced at the label, then nodded and smiled as Jasper added hot water to the cups. 'That's if you still want it?' he said casually.

'Hey?' Jasper jerked his head up and spilled hot water onto the kitchen bench. 'Oh shit… damn.' He grabbed a tea towel. 'What do you mean? If I still want it?'

'I was asked to try to talk you into the monthly jab. I told the team it was a no-go but that I'd go through the motions.'

'Yeah, right.' He added the milk and sugar. 'You know me better than anyone. Those quacks should listen to you.'

'So, Jasper… if you want to take orals. We've decided to give it a try.'

Jasper hurried over as quickly and carefully as he could while holding two cups. He set them on the table with only minor spillage, then darted to Nigel, bent awkwardly, and hugged him.

'Are you fair fucking-dinkum?' Jasper stood back upright. 'Please don't tease me.'

Nigel got to his feet. He was a full head shorter than his patient but twice as wide. He gave a broad smile. 'It's all squared away. I've been giving you favourable reports for ages. I know how much you've been trying.'

'All those self-help books have finally paid off!'

'It seems so. Good for you. I'll see you again in two weeks to check how the orals are going. If all's well after four weeks, we will go to monthly visits. And if you don't mind, I'd like to ask Cassandra to act as your reminder.

*   *   *

Thirty minutes later, as the two men were laughing and telling each other stories about crazy people, they heard a car pull up on the gravel driveway. It was Cassandra returning after dropping the kids off at school and doing some shopping.

'And remember when I thought you had x-ray vision,' chuckled Jasper.

'When all I had was watery, itchy eyes,' laughed Nigel.

'I accused you of staring at my cock.'

'Yeah. You yelled it out, and everyone in K-Mart thought I was a pervert. I had to keep looking up at the fucking ceiling. Too scared to look down in case I spied your groin out the corner of my eye.' They both laughed again. The front door opened, and a thin lady with long, salt-and-pepper hair entered, holding two shopping bags.

'I can hear you two from outside. What's going on? Have you guys had too much coffee?'

'Hello Cassie,' said Nigel as he stood. 'Let me help you with those.'

'It's okay,' she said, but Nigel reached out to take a bag anyway. 'Okay, ta. Take this heavier one for me.'

'I'm going onto oral medication,' announced Jasper.

'Really?' She looked at the case worker. 'Is that true, Nigel?'

'It's a trial. And I'd like you to be Jasper's reminder. We're starting with Risperidone, two milligrams twice a day.' He placed the grocery bag on the kitchen bench.

'Of course. I'll be happy to keep an eye on him.' She set down the other bag, then turned and embraced her husband, who was now alongside her. 'This is such good news.' She squeezed him. 'You've been so patient. This is what you've wanted for so long, sweetheart.'

'Yeah, it's about time.' He kissed her head, then looked at his case worker. 'Thanks, mate.'

Chapter 4

Money & Monsters

'Tony says I can have some extra work for the next few weeks. He has a contract for the new Rosemeadow shopping centre. There'll be plenty of concrete pouring and bricks to lay,' said Jasper. He was sitting back in a well-worn lounge chair, partially watching some reruns of Mash. The furniture was sparse - two worn single-seaters and two grubby beanbags, one blue and one pink, all sitting on a grey rug. The TV sat on a foldout camping table; underneath were cardboard boxes full of children's toys. The vinyl flooring needed replacement. A ceiling fan wobbled slowly, barely able to push out any breeze.

'That's good news, sweetheart,' called Cassandra from the kitchen where she was preparing the kid's lunchboxes for the following day. 'The extra money will be a help. The kids need some new shoes.'

'Again? I thought we just bought some a couple of months back.'

'That would be twelve months back. Their feet haven't stopped growing, you know. And I'd like to get Faith a bicycle and Delaney a three-wheel scooter.'

'Don't spend everything before we have it now, will you?'

'No love, of course not. I'm just saying that if it all works out, it would be nice to get the kids a little something special.'

'You do plenty for them. You're a great mum. You fuss over them so much. I reckon they're pretty happy.'

'Faith, Delaney and you, my love, are my world. I want the best for all of us.' She tucked some sandwiches wrapped in Gladwrap into the plastic containers.

'They love you so much,' added Jasper. 'I see their eyes light up every time you pick them up, drop them off and kiss them goodnight.'

'They love you just as much, sweetheart.'

'They get more time with you. And that's fine. I'm busy with work and writing my book.'

'I know. How's it shaping up?' She put the lunchboxes in the fridge.

'It's coming along, but a little slower than I would like. And yes, just to let you know, I'll need to spend Saturday morning researching at the library.'

'Browsing through some more psychology books?'

'I think I've read them all,' he chuckled. 'But I need to check a few historical texts.'

'Wow! I guess the benefit of writing is that you get so much more education along the way,' she nodded. 'Saturday will be okay, love... I see you spending so many hours on the laptop, which is perfectly fine with me. But it does leave me intrigued. Are you ready to tell me anything about it yet?'

Jasper remained in his lounge chair, smiled and shook his finger in her direction. 'Ah... there she goes again,' he joked. 'Trying to pry. Can't be patient.'

'Sorry. Maybe give me a hint of what it's about. Sure, if you prefer, I can wait until it's finished to read the whole thing. But I'd like a little teaser.'

Jasper glanced at the TV. 'It's a bit like this show,' he laughed.

'Mash?' declared Cassie with her eyes open wide. 'It's a comedy war story? Really?'

'It's a war, but not in the traditional sense. The funny and unusual aspect is about how it all will be resolved in the end. That's all you're getting out of me for now.' He moved his fingers across his lips as if zipping his mouth shut.

'Mum, I keep waking up,' came the sad voice of a child.

Both parents turned to see their son, Delaney, standing near the dining table in his Wiggles pyjamas. He frowned and rubbed his eyes. Cassandra immediately knelt before him, stroked the eight-year-old's short, dark hair, and squeezed him by his shoulders.

'Oh, my darling. Did you get a fright again? My poor baby.'

'The monster was back,' he sobbed.

'The same one? Dear oh dear.'

'The one with six, big shiny eyes,' continued Delaney. 'I think it was in my wardrobe.'

'I wonder what this means,' said Jasper as he stood. 'Monsters, eyes, wardrobes and getting scared.'

'I want it to stop,' whimpered the young boy.

'Of course, you would. Let me check your room,' said Jasper. 'What do we need to do about this, my boy?' It was a question both Delaney and Faith had heard many times before. Jasper walked with his hand resting gently on his son's neck. They headed to the bedroom. 'Well, Delaney?'

'Do we need to do the corset thing again?' he replied.

'That would be the quartet!' chuckled Jasper. 'Two thinks, one plan and one act. You got it. Planning solves problems and prevents others, even ones about monsters with lots of big eyes. Always think twice, plan carefully, and act decisively when you are sure. You see, four things, that's the quartet.'

'Yes, Dad, I'll try, but it's scary.'

'I know. That's why part of that plan is me. Monsters don't like big, strong Dads.' Jasper grinned. 'And they'll be just as scared of you when you are older.'

In the bedroom, Jasper flicked on the light, checked the wardrobe, looked under the bed, and peered out the window.

'That monster knew I was coming. He's already made a retreat.'

On the bedside table was a small wooden bowl containing several cat's-eye marbles. Jasper knelt and tucked his son into bed.

'There you go, my boy.' He picked up a marble, held it not far from Delaney's face, and rolled it between his fingers.

'It's so good you found these. It was meant to be because a cat's eye marble has a special magic. This is why the monster has never been able to hurt you,' said Jasper. He looked at his son, who was wide-eyed and staring at the glass ball.

'They have protective powers,' continued Jasper. They are the guardians of the soul. If you look at them, I mean, really look inside them, you will see things. Visions, the future, you will see the magic.' He moved the marble slowly in front of the boy's eyes. 'Why don't I place one of these on the windowsill, one under your bed and another in the wardrobe? Let's keep you safe.'

Delaney smiled and snuggled down into the bed. 'Thanks, Dad.'

Chapter 5

Is This Recovery?

For two months, Jasper had not missed a dose of his medication. Over the first few weeks, Cassie had been his reminder, morning and night. It was not that he needed it, but they had an agreement with Nigel.

His case worker had visited him twice and was pleased with everything. Nigel's most recent visit was his last before he headed north to Queensland for warmer weather and a new job. On Nigel's final review, he took Jasper to lunch - a gift to his long-time client. They both ordered chicken schnitzel and chips at a Campbelltown café.

'Truly delightful,' said Jasper as he wiped his lips.

'They do a good feed here.' Nigel dragged two chips through the sauce.

'You head off in a week or two then?'

'A week from Sunday,' said Nigel.

'Driving?'

'Yeah. I'm taking it easy.' He swallowed and repeated the process with the remaining few fries. 'A couple of overnighters on the way. Your new caseworker will be Trevor. He's a little green. Go easy on him, will you?'

'Of course,' smiled Jasper.

Nigel raised a finger and waved it in Jasper's direction. 'Yeah, yeah… I know you…' he spoke through his food. 'You're a bit of a trickster… and I should add, a master of deception if you choose.'

'Hey, mate. I'll be good. Scout's honour.' He gave a two-finger salute.

'Have you ever been a scout?'

'Well... not as such,' smiled Jasper.

'Hmmm.'

Later that day, Nigel reported back to the mental health team and passed Jasper Johansson's case over to the younger, Trevor. It was hoped that Jasper could be discharged from the service after a couple more visits.

Later that evening, Jasper crushed his tablet between his fingers and flushed away the evidence. He looked in the mirror at his unshaven square jawline and stroked his chin. 'At last, you have a real opportunity to better yourself, Jasper Johansson. And you don't need drugs that do no more than turn you into a fat bastard and stifle your creativity... but perhaps some other substances may expedite your recovery and help with productivity. After all, you have a job to do.'

Chapter 6

Freedom to Think

After a chat with Cassandra a few weeks ago, her reminder role and loose supervision of her husband's medication had ceased. He assured her he would reach out if he had any problems.

Jasper did not need anyone to monitor his progress; he had complete confidence in his ability to assess himself. Besides, as much as he just wanted to stop the drug altogether, he had set himself a gradual program of reduction. One thing Jasper had in spades was patience. He'd waited out the compulsory treatment order, and he'd waited out the injections. Whether it be weeks, months or years, he had his mind set on his goals.

It was five weeks since he disposed of the first evening dose. Now, he had stopped all evening meds and dropped Monday and Friday mornings. He still felt remarkably well and had dropped five kilograms. In addition, and to complement his improvement, he had finally found a meth dealer. It had taken some time and several discreet enquiries, but he was confident he had secured a reliable source. Jasper started carefully, taking one-quarter of a tablet to gauge the effect. Even with this small dose, he could feel that taste of pleasure, confidence and heightened alertness. His speed stash was secreted in the heel of his old working boots. His cash supply, slowly built up over the years, was inside the lining of a heavy winter jacket.

Jasper's writing had improved significantly since reducing one drug and starting another. It was also important to not just stop doses but to discreetly dispose of each tablet; that way, his prescriptions would still fall due at the correct time, and no one else would be the wiser - not his wife and not his young case manager. It was also important not to use speed daily, more on a needs basis. Jasper knew he could handle the drug and not get highly addicted and psychotic due to sleep deprivation, which was what happened all those years ago.

It was at ten on a weekday morning that Trevor rapped on the front door. Cassandra was out shopping for some kid's clothes. Jasper knew this was a make-or-break visit. If he could give the young Trevor a good impression, he would be closed from the service, and his further follow-up would be conducted via his local GP, Dr Goldsmith.

Trevor was a slim twenty-four-year-old who looked more like he was only twelve.

'How have you been, Jasper?' asked Trevor in a soft, slightly effeminate voice.

'Been well. In fact, I feel better now than I have in a long time. A big thanks to you and the team for looking after me,' came the upbeat reply.

'That's great. How's the family?'

The two continued to chat for several minutes about meaningless topics, the family, the weather, the news, and even Nigel, before Trevor shifted the conversation.

'Have you felt that people have been out to harm or hurt you?'

This was expected, and Jasper had rehearsed his response. 'If any such thing was concerning me, I would've told Cassie. I saw Dr Goldsmith last week, and he was pleased with my progress and is happy to continue seeing me. So no, nothing like that is going on.' He smiled while his hands clenched into fists below the table.

'Good to hear.'

Jasper tilted his head to one side, leaned forward, and looked at Trevor. He unclenched a fist, raised his hand and pointed at his case worker's face. 'Is there something in your eye?' As he said those words, he checked himself. He looked away, then back. 'Sorry, I didn't mean to be rude. Pointing and all.'

'Left or right?' asked Trevor, touching his face.

'Ahh… the left… the left.'

The caseworker rubbed near the corner of his eye. 'Did I get it?' He looked at his finger.'

'Yeah, yeah… a bit of fluff, I think.' Jasper put his hand back under the dining table, slightly raised his buttocks left and right, and pushed both hands firmly underneath himself.

'Good, okay. Where were we? Oh yes, I wanted to ask if you had any thoughts of wanting to hurt or harm others?'

'Huh,' blurted Jasper. 'No such thoughts. Next question.'

'Any thoughts of wanting to hurt or harm yourself?'

'No such thoughts.'

'Any suicidal ideas?'

'Definitely not.'

'Well, that all seems pretty good to me. I'll report back to the team, and in all likelihood, you'll now be closed from the service. You can continue to see Dr Goldsmith as required. I would suggest at least three monthly.'

'Of course. That's when I'll need to renew my prescription.'

Trevor gave a little hand wave followed by a thumbs up. 'Perfect.' Jasper smiled as he squirmed a little in his seat. He shoved his hands further under himself. *Keep those hands down. No pointing. No fists,* he told himself.

Jasper waved the case worker off. He turned his back and allowed himself to slide down the closed door to the floor. He took a few deep breaths. 'Fucking black-eyed demon,' he said in a loud whisper.

Chapter 7

Family Dinner

On a cool August evening, the Johansson family sat together for dinner. It had been some weeks since this had happened, with Jasper being occupied with his writing or taking an early night after a hard day's work.

'This is nice. Everyone together at the table,' said Cassandra brightly as she set down the fourth plate in front of Delaney.

'Thank you, Mum. We love *sewers*,' said the boy with a polite smile. The skewered chicken with tomato sauce and crunchy chips was a kid's favourite and was now referred to as *sewers* after the regular mispronunciation of the word when the children were a little younger.

'What do you think it means for us to call these *sewers* instead of skewers?' asked Jasper.

'I doubt it is anything significant, love,' said Cassie. She saw her husband's mouth tighten and eyes narrow. 'But... no doubt it means something. What do you think?'

'Mark my words. We will know one day,' he cautioned and waved a finger. 'Meaning is inherent in almost everything we do.'

Cassandra put a chip in her mouth while Delaney and Faith picked up the round end of the metal skewer. Jasper looked at them, his hands still at his sides.

'I'd like to know why we aren't saying Grace?' he shouted, catching everyone by surprise.

'What?' mumbled Cassandra through her food. She pushed out a smile and a slight chuckle.

'Well, why aren't we?'

'We've never said Grace, sweetheart.' She placed the next chip back on her plate.

'What is that, Dad?' asked Faith with a mouthful of food.

'Well, maybe this family should start,' he barked. Faith and Delaney stopped eating. Both looked at their father and then mother. Cassie reached left and right and gently patted the children's hands.

'Is there any reason you think we should not do that?' Jasper looked wide-eyed at them all. 'Well, is there?' he said even louder.

'No reason. Of course not,' replied Cassie. She shifted her attention back to the children. 'It's okay, my darlings. Your dad has an idea… and it might be nice to give thanks for our food. Many families do this at every meal.' She caught her husband's eye. 'Why don't you start us off then, sweetheart? Faith, Delaney, put your chicken back on your plates for now.'

Jasper watched as the other three sat there looking at him unsurely. The children had stopped chewing even though they had food in their mouths. He nodded his head slowly.

'We lower our heads slightly like this,' he instructed as he bowed but still watched. 'We clasp our hands lightly like this.' He demonstrated.

'Is this a funny game, Dad?' said Delaney.

'No! Do as I do,' he demanded. They all followed his lead.

'Dear God. Help us remember all the souls that have helped with this meal…'

'Mum cooked this, Dad. I remember,' nodded Delaney brightly.

'Hush! Listen to me, boy!' yelled Jasper. Del's face dropped, and his eyes watered. 'Thank you, Lord, for looking after us.' Jasper softened his tone. 'Help us find the right path to serve you better. Drive evil, in all its forms, from our lives. Amen.' He raised his head.

'Now you all say *Amen*.' He looked around at his family. 'Well, come on, say it!'

'Amen,' they all replied in a disjointed way.

'Now we can eat,' he said with a chuckle. 'Sorry if I upset anyone. This is a good thing to do when we're all together.'

Jasper watched as his family ate, only taking an occasional bite himself. Cassandra caught his eye and smiled as she continued her meal. The two children looked up several times as their father stared. Del's jaw quivered, but he said nothing. He slowly finished his meal and then sat back in his chair. As he did, his eyes glazed over and rolled upwards.

'Oh, dear. He's off again,' blurted Cassie. She darted over and held him, looking scornfully back at Jasper on her way.

'Not my bloody fault,' he yelled, then got up and left.

Cassie held her son. 'It's okay, my love.' She kissed his forehead. 'You're fine. It'll all be over in a few minutes.' Faith moved alongside her brother and stroked his hair.

Chapter 8

The Referral

The following morning, after the kids had been delivered to school and Jasper had been dropped off for four hours of bricklaying, Cassandra sat on the edge of a lounge chair and pushed her hands across her forehead. She blotted some tears away before they could roll down her cheeks. She looked twice at the bedroom door before she stood and headed over.

In the main bedroom, she paused at the end of the bed and studied Jasper's side - the way the quilt, sheets and pillow were positioned. The neatly made bed looked symmetrical. Cassandra returned to the open door, looked, and listened for a few seconds. No one was around. She stepped quickly to her husband's pillow and lifted it, revealing the laptop. She studied it for a full minute, using her fingers to measure its exact position. How many finger widths from the edge of the mattress, and how far from the bedhead?

Cassie lifted it, sat on the bed and opened the device. After pushing the on switch, she waited, hoping there was no password. On the desktop screen, there was only one icon - a folder called *PRIVATE*.

'Oh dear,' she muttered. She opened the folder only to find another *PRIVATE* folder. She repeatedly double-clicked until, eventually, after twenty clicks, three documents were visible. Each was called *THE QUARTET* and had a date attached.

'Oh, The Quartet! That sounds a bit familiar. A story about planning and taking action. Hmm… sorry, Jasper. Maybe I'm judging you too harshly. She double-clicked what appeared to be the most recent version. The document opened at a blank page. Cassie scrolled back to the beginning and saw the title page. *THE QUARTET: Take Heed Everyone, Quickly Unite And Repel The Evil Torment* - She gasped. 'Oh, fuck!' She said loudly, catching herself by surprise; her eyes darted about the room and the open door as if she may have attracted attention. Then she let out a huge sigh and sobbed quietly. Moving through page after page of writing, she stopped on the last typed page, after which there were many blank pages. She read from the top...

One thing I know is that they come in all guises. Don't be fooled. There is no way forward. Satosayoman, satosayoman, satosayoman. Beguiled and bepuzzled, the mind plays tricks. Tricks and kicks at the spirit of truth. Be told, beware, but don't despair. Don't roast or boast, then just become toast. Eyes are the window to the soul. Eyes are the gift that keeps on giving. Don't close, don't turn; see them for what they are. The evil comes stalking you while you are quietly sleeping like a beauty. Hazards; beacons; lightning; brewing; coffee; stimulants; drugs; prescriptions; stop; leave; recover...

Cassandra covered her mouth and then quickly tapped her way back to a random page...

Innocent victims are caught up in the Fire, and Waterworks are turned on and off. Goes the switch to something new, something borrowed, something blue. Oceans of plenty; troops to battle the elements. Don't believe everything you see or hear or touch. Trust not your eyes, ears and fingers. Deception is all around; love is dead. See and be seen. Maybe the scene of betrayal. Evil comes running...

'Oh my God!' She stopped reading, scrolled to a blank page, closed all the folders and turned off the laptop. She carefully placed it back on the mattress, adjusting the position until it was the same as she had found it.

She saw his medication box on his bedside table. The foil had plenty of punched-out spots where tablets had been removed.

'You're too clever for your own good, Jasper Johansson.' She closed the drawer, left the bedroom and rang the mental health team.

The receptionist transferred her call to the on-call intake assessment officer as Jasper was no longer an open client.

Cassie's call was ultimately answered by Angela, who requested all his identifying information, including his date of birth, address, next of kin, and GP details.

'Thank you for all that. Now Cassandra, what are your concerns?'

'Jasper is having a relapse. He needs to be taken back into hospital,' her voice quivered.

'If you could, take it one step at a time. Tell me exactly what is happening,' Angela said calmly.

'He made us all say grace at dinner. We never do that.'

'Okay... and...'

'His mood was irritable, and the children were frightened. We all were. And he is writing a book. I read some of it, and it's complete nonsense with some threatening language. It shows his mind is very disturbed.'

'Is he taking any prescribed medication?'

'He makes it look as though he is. He gets his scripts filled. Pushes out the tablets from the foil. But I know him. He's clever, and this is what he's doing to fool everyone.'

'I see. I should say Cassandra...'

'Cassie... please.'

'Sure. I should say Cassie that generally when people have a relapse and become psychotic, they don't bother taking or even pretending to take their medication.'

'He is a clever man. He understands the mental health system. He's educated himself in psychology and other things. He will become violent. He could even be using illegal drugs like he did in the past. You must assess him… you simply must… please, I beg you,' she pleaded.

'Have you seen him using or found anything to suggest that?'

'You're not listening. He's very clever.'

'Yes, Cassie, I see, and I hear you. Does your husband know you are referring him?'

'Of course not,' squawked Cassie loudly. 'I'm not stupid.'

'Maybe he could see his General Practitioner.'

'He won't. And even if he did, it wouldn't help. Dr Goldsmith is not a psychiatrist, and Jasper would say what the doctor wanted to hear.'

'I see.'

'No, you don't. He'll hurt someone. Check his file. He's assaulted people before, including health workers. I know him better than anyone else.'

'Naturally, if he becomes dangerous, you must call the police.'

'How about you come here to see him and bring the police with you.'

'For that to happen, you would need to go to the courthouse and see a magistrate to get the relevant paperwork done.'

'It's Friday afternoon!'

'Yes, I know. Alternatively, I would happily make him an appointment, but you must get his agreement first.'

The words stopped flowing as Cassie panted and cried.

'Hello… you still there, Cassie?'

'Oh… ah…' she sobbed.

'I understand this is upsetting for you, but we can…'

'No, you don't understand,' interrupted a distraught Cassie.

'I'm doing my best to get a handle on the situation so I can give you a plan going forward.'

'Oh my God…' she said, taking several deep breaths. 'How old are you, Angela?'

'I'm a trained professional.'

'How many years have you been working in mental health?'

'I'm experienced and well-trained. You need not concern yourself with that.'

'Leave it with me. I know what I need to do.'

'That's good. What plan do you…' Cassie tapped the red button on her mobile and cut the intake worker off.

Chapter 9

Madness Takes Its Toll

That evening, Cassandra sat at the dinner table with Faith and Delaney. The children were happy enough with the chips and chicken nuggets. It was a quick and easy cook for Cassie and suited the occasion as she had other matters on her mind. Despite their reluctance at the earlier-than-usual bedtime routine, she had already directed the kids to the bathroom and had them both pajamaed up.

Jasper had earlier insisted he needed to update his writing and had taken himself to the bedroom and his laptop, where he had been for the last forty-five minutes.

Every few seconds, Cassie glanced at the bedroom door. Had she positioned the laptop properly? Was the pillow correctly aligned? Would he burst from the room in a psychotic rage? Was the fact that he hadn't come out by now a good sign? She knew this evening might be one of her last opportunities to sort things out with him - but it might already be too late.

Finally, as Faith and Delaney downed the last of their nuggets, their father emerged from the bedroom. Jasper hadn't changed after work and still wore his soiled overalls. He stood tall and strolled to the dining table - his work boots stomping heavily. His eyes locked on Cassie. As the gap between them closed, she went to stand, but Jasper gestured with a hand for her to remain seated. The children shifted their gaze between both parents. He walked the longer way around the table, brushing his fingers lightly over the tops of his children's heads, all the time looking at Cassie.

He extended his hand, 'Give me your phone.' He spoke sharply.

Without pause, she took it from the pocket of her dressing gown. 'Sure, love. Is something wrong? Can I prepare you a meal now?'

Jasper gave a breathy chuckle as he poked around on the phone. He pushed a button and then held the phone to his ear. He listened momentarily, then said, 'Sorry, wrong number.' He hung up and handed the phone back.

'I rang to see if an appointment was available,' she said quickly, wanting to speak first. 'I wanted to see someone.' He glared at her. There was a tightness in his unshaven jaw. 'For me, honey. An appointment for me. My mood's been so up and down. I just wanted to chat with someone.' She looked around, not holding eye contact, then displayed her palms in a gesture of honesty.

He stepped closer and placed a hand on the back of her chair.

'Dad, are you angry?' asked Faith.

Immediately, he swung his head and shouted, 'Don't look at me!'

'What's wrong, Dad?' asked Delaney.

'Don't talk to me,' he bellowed. 'And neither of you move from this table.' He pointed a stabbing finger at them both. 'I still have power over you. For how long, I don't know.' He heard whimpering and saw their gloomy faces. 'No! Don't try that manipulation. No tears! No sounds!'

The children did their best to stay quiet. Uncontrollable tears ran down their cheeks. He turned back to his wife.

'What did you think of my book?'

She stared at him for a moment. He knew everything. It seemed best to be upfront. 'Ah… The Quartet, yes. It's a familiar-sounding title. The content was a little different from what I was expecting. Overall, I thought it had too many blank pages,' she said.

'It has no blank pages.'

'There were at least a hundred pages I couldn't read and maybe about thirty or so that I could.'

'You couldn't read the pages I didn't want you to read,' Jasper chuckled and looked briefly to the ceiling. 'I still have some control.' He nodded with some contentment. 'I coloured the words in white, so they blended in with the background.'

'That was a good idea, honey. I know you didn't want me to read it before it was finished. I apologise. It was wrong of me, but I've been hanging out to see it.'

'The parts I allowed you to read, what did you think?'

'I should clear these plates away.' She reached across the table and then went to stand, but he pushed her down. 'What? Are you going to do the washing up?' she snapped.

'Answer me!' demanded Jasper.

'Okay… I didn't understand it. It seemed illogical. Maybe if you'd let me read the whole thing, it would've made sense.'

'So, you read bits of it. Thought I was crazy and rang mental health?'

'Everything I do is out of care and concern for you… for our family. You should know that by now.'

'Oh, I know a lot, Cassie. You are still Cassandra, aren't you?'

'I'm still your loving wife, Jasper. Always.'

'And these?' He turned to the children and flung an open hand. 'Who the fuck are they?'

'Faith and Delaney. Your loving children, they think…'

'No!' he yelled, interrupting. 'They are not.' He moved next to Faith and held her chin firmly. 'Look at these eyes. Black lifeless eyes.' He moved to Delaney and did the same. 'These eyes. Evil. Black. Dead!'

Both children cried loudly.

'See how they try to manipulate me. Evil!' He raised a clenched fist above Delaney. His hand shook. He slammed down on the table. A plate bounced up and broke on the floor. Faith ran to her bedroom. Delaney slid off his chair to the floor and inched a little under the table, where he lay curled up in a weeping ball. His breathing rate escalated.

Jasper marched back to Cassie. 'You have twenty-four hours to fix this. I want them gone. And I mean gone… like forever. If you don't do something to prove yourself, then I will.' He stormed off to the bedroom. Cassandra darted around to Delaney, lay on the floor and hugged her son.

'I've got you.' She eased him out from under the table, squatting while clinging to him. 'You're going to be fine. I'll make sure of that.' She kissed his forehead.

Despite his weight of twenty-three kilograms, she lifted him almost effortlessly and carried him to the children's bedroom, where Faith was huddled in a corner. It took Delaney thirty minutes to fully recover.

Jasper's demands did not faze Cassie. She had already decided to get Faith and Delaney out of the house. The difference was that her goal was their protection, while his intent seemed to be their destruction. She regretted that she had not done it sooner before he terrorised them.

Chapter 10

The Relocation

It was Saturday morning. Cassandra had slept on the sofa, or at least attempted to rest as best she could following the events of yesterday evening. She had put together a plan.

Jasper slept alone in the main bedroom. Cassie noticed the bedroom light was on all night and heard him tapping away heavily on the laptop keypad several times.

The children were dressed, had breakfast, and were playing Ludo on the grey rug on the lounge room floor when their father finally emerged. He hadn't showered but had at least changed his clothes. He approached Cassie in the laundry.

'I'm going out,' he said bluntly, glancing at his watch. 'You have nine hours and forty-two minutes to attend to the matter we discussed.' He waved a finger at her. 'Failure brings dire consequences.' Cassie just nodded. Jasper left, taking the car.

* * *

After an hour, Cassie packed suitcases for herself and the children. A taxi was expected within the next thirty minutes. She sat in a dining chair with her two children standing before her.

'I have an important job for you both,' she started. 'Dad is very unwell, and I need you to help get him better. He may get even sicker, so you must go away for a while… sort of like a holiday. That way, he won't have to worry if you've had your dinner, bathed, or done your homework, and he can think about getting better and being the best dad that he can be for you both.'

'Have we been bad, Mum?' asked a tearful Delaney.

'Did we make Dad unhappy?' added Faith.

'No, she said firmly. 'This is not your fault.' She took each child's hand and squeezed their fingers, pulling them closer.

'What does it mean, though?' asked Faith.

'It means, darling, that Dad has stopped taking his medicine. It means he's been a bit naughty.'

'Dad said it meant something bad,' added Del.

'Dad says many mistaken things because he is a bit sick,' said Cassie. 'I want you to go and grab a few of your favourite toys to take with you. We're going to see Aunt Theresa.'

*   *   *

After an hour's drive, the taxi pulled up outside a large double-story rendered home at Lane Cove in Sydney at eleven thirty. It had been some time since the kids had seen Aunt Theresa and Uncle Graham, but they loved visiting. The home had a pool, a big back deck, and a spa in the bathroom. The property boundary was alongside Stringybark Reserve, with many hectares of treed bushland winding along Stringybark Creek.

'Aunt Theresa has a nice house,' said Delaney as the car stopped.

Cassandra gave a big sigh and breathed, 'Yeah.' She handed over cash to the driver, thanked him, then helped the kids out and grabbed the three suitcases from the boot. There was a breeze, but nevertheless, the air was hot. In the distance, a smoke haze disguised the trees and buildings with a grey blanket.

Cassie deliberately had not called ahead, hoping that her sister, or someone, would be home. What she had done earlier, though, was call four motels and three health retreats, none of which she had any intention of staying at. It was some temporary insurance for when her husband next checked her phone.

The three stood on the footpath. Cassie had a child on either side of her. Tears tumbled quietly down her cheeks. She blotted her face with a small hanky.

'It's okay, Mum,' said Faith. The child took her mother's hand. 'Aunt Theresa is nice. She'll look after us until Dad is better.'

'Yeah, don't worry, Mum,' added Delaney.

Some curtains near the front door briefly parted. A moment later, the door flew open. Theresa came running out. She was a slender lady, and today, she was all dressed up in high heels and an olive-green jumpsuit with cape-style sleeves.

'Oh my God!' she called as she shuffled down the cement pathway as quickly as possible.

The sisters hugged. Theresa's eyes watered on seeing Cassie's face.

'What's happened? Are you okay?' She momentarily squatted and hugged the children. 'Hi, you guys. It's so good to see you. And you probably don't know we have a trampoline in the backyard now.' She did her best to sound excited, giving them a big smile.

'Let's chat inside,' said Cassie, finally able to get some words out.

Yes, let's go. We need to get into the air-con,' added Theresa.

*   *   *

Despite the heat, Faith and Delaney found their way to the trampoline in the company of George, Theresa's twelve-year-old and only child. He was less than impressed to be dragged away from his online gaming to keep an eye on a couple of young brats.

The sisters sat next to each other on the sofa. The lounge was nearly as big as Cassie's house back at Claymore. Theresa poured some tea from an ornate ceramic teapot on a silver tray.

'So sorry to be a bother,' said Cassie. 'You look like you're about to go out for a nice meal or something.'

'No, you've arrived just at the right time. Many of the wives from Graham's Rotary Club were getting together to have a boozy lunch and decide on the next fundraiser.' She shook her head and smiled. 'Not my thing, really, so thanks, you've done me a favour.' Theresa passed over a cup of tea.

'Sorry.'

'No,' Theresa shook her head. 'I won't think of it. It's fine. I'm guessing this whole thing…' she gesticulated with her head and arms. 'Is it about Jasper?'

'He's relapsed. This is as bad as he's ever been.'

'I'm so sorry. Is this like when he was in the hospital… what… ten years back?'

'That was fifteen, and it's worse. We don't feel safe. Well… not so much me; it's the kids.'

'Cassie, he just has to go back to the hospital.' Theresa set her cup down.

'That's not as simple as it sounds.'

'Get the police then.'

'That is part of my next strategy. I'm pretty sure he's stopped his meds. He could even be using some illegal drug. He's being very clever, but he's also saying dreadful things. It's sort of like he thinks Faith and Delaney are possessed or something. He demanded that I eliminate them, and he wasn't just talking about a relocation!'

'Cassie! Oh my God!'

'I know. I have a huge request, Theresa.'

'You can stay here. Of course, no problem. Stay until Jasper is in a safe place.'

'It's not me that I'm concerned about. I want the kids to stay with you for a while. I need to have a last-ditch attempt to get him help. I must go back.'

'Now you're the one that's crazy.'

'Maybe, but I must try. He's been so well for so long. Holding down a job and all.'

'The kids can stay as long as they want. We've got plenty of room.'

'Here's the thing, Theresa. They can't stay too long. He'll know. He will find them.'

'Not if he's locked up, he won't!'

'To some extent, he's able to say the right things. He can fool people. Health workers, his GP, and probably the cops who have no mental health training.'

'But if he's that crazy…'

'Theresa!' interrupted Cassie. 'I know him. He checks my phone, that's why I couldn't ring you. But sooner or later, he'll turn up at your front door. There is nothing more certain.' Cassie spoke louder; her teacup rattled around on its saucer. She carefully placed it on the coffee table. Her fingers trembled. Then her phone rang. 'It's him again. He's rung and messaged several times already.'

'You've got to switch the phone off,' said Theresa. 'I've another you can use.'

Cassie looked at her sister unsurely. 'I'll turn it off. I still love him, you know. He's troubled. He's sick. I think I'll need to go back later on today. See if I can get him to the hospital somehow.'

'Yes. You're right; he needs help, which he'll get sooner or later. But you must look out for yourself… for the kids too.'

'I worry more for the kids… and now I've involved you too,' she whimpered.

'We have a good security system. Alarms and cameras.'

'Okay, that's reassuring, but here's what you must do…' she looked at her sister. 'Promise me.'

'Tell me. I'll do whatever you say. Promise.'

'After the weekend, I want you to get someone else… someone I don't know… that I've never met. Get these people to look after the kids for a few days. Does any reliable person spring to mind?'

'A couple of people. I could organise it.'

'Thanks,' said Cassie, her voice breaking. 'And if he shows up here, don't let him inside. Call the police if he doesn't leave.' She buried her face in her hands. Theresa wriggled along the sofa and hugged her.

'You be careful. It's going to be okay.'

The pair held each other for a minute. Both sobbed and kissed each other's cheek.

'I'll get you that other phone,' said Theresa. 'Keep it secret. Call me. Be careful.' She patted her sister's back. 'Let me go and fix you all a nice lunch.'

Chapter 11

Jasper's Chronicles - Part 1

"The Torment"

I write with slow deliberation in the company of a valued colleague who must remain nameless. My colleague transcribes and edits my narration to maintain an understandable clarity for the ill-informed. Consequently, it is a slow write, with many corrections and overuse of the backspace key. Nevertheless, the message within will be clear, and the implications will be abundant.

I have dreamt of this day. This time of reckoning is when all things change. Somehow, I've always known this was coming, and inside myself, I've been preparing, both consciously and unconsciously, for many years: mental preparations, plans, thoughts and ideas for this very time.

As I write these revelations, I feel a dark and heavy presence, as if my thoughts and written words have been broadcast from the mountaintops and all those with malevolent ears, hell-bent on my demise, have been summoned forth. My colleague shivers, shakes and holds himself wrapped in his arms. I shout, 'Be gone with you!' in a high-pitched voice. Then I follow up with, 'Take your pestilence elsewhere and heed my intent on your destruction.' This time, I use a different lower voice. My final acclimation is in a loud whisper, 'It is here we gather in numbers against you. We will obliterate your vision. You will perish and rot. Be gone.' For three whole minutes, there is a cool quietness; then I sense the evil leaving, and the circulation of air settles and warms. My anxious colleague breathes a sigh of relief and unfolds.

I continue this account feeling reassured that I still hold some power over this darkness. I pray this strength continues to serve me well through these testing times.

I'm fortunate to have the virtue of patience. Perhaps this was always part of His plan.

It has started, and I have no idea when or how it will end, but I will be ready whenever that is. Meanwhile, the evil replicants that have displaced the pure must be tracked down and destroyed. The deeds of Satosayoman must be found and reversed or eliminated.

It Is Satosayoman, the son of Satan, who has brought all this devilishment.

I see their eyes: cold, evil, black and lifeless. My vision is now clear. I have been chosen for this arduous task. I hope there are others like me - many others. Potent, mind-altering substances hid my gift. These substances filled my being with ignorance and repressed my ability and forward thinking.

My beautiful children and my wife are but a few who have been taken. I hope we, and many others, will one day be reunited. Despite the possibility of this outcome being remote, I remain undaunted in my quest. My colleague is astute and intelligent and will guide me through this turbulence. I must never mention his name or refer to him as anything but my colleague. Such utterances would see him as a marked soul and a target for the harrowing darkness, which I now call - The Torment.

Chapter 12

Visitors

On Tuesday, Jasper was interrupted by a loud rap on the door. He was sitting on the side of the bath, soaking his feet in a few centimetres of iced water. He removed the plug, gently patted the souls of his feet dry, and slipped on a pair of Crocs. The visitor knocked again; this time, it sounded more like a hard slap, and then there was a shout, 'Police! Open your door!'

For thirty more seconds, Jasper stood quietly. His lips pit-pattering away with his eyes closed. He took a couple of deep breaths and opened the door.

'Officers,' he said with mild surprise. He looked around. There were five uniformed police - two together at the front and three behind. Two squad cars were parked on the street. 'Is everything okay?'

'I'm Sergeant Warren Keats. I assume you are Jasper Johansson?' The sergeant spoke mainly out of one side of his mouth in a firm, gravelly, no-nonsense voice. Keats was by far the largest of the five in height and width. His width seemed to be predominantly muscle.

'Yes, I'm Jasper. What's going on?'

'Is there anyone else in the house?'

'Well... no... it's just me,' replied Jasper unsurely.

The officer took a step closer. Jasper took two smaller steps back and released his hold on the door.

'You sure about that?' Keats peered in, looking left and right.

'Did my wife call you? Is that why you're all here?'

'And why would she do that, Mister Johansson?'

'Because she thinks I'm having a relapse. She thinks I've stopped my meds. But that's not true. She left me, you know… took the kids… then returned and took my car.'

'Where did she go?'

'Who knows? Maybe her sister's place. Maybe one of those women's shelters. I don't know. She said she'd give it a week, then come back, and we would take a fresh look at the whole thing.'

'The whole thing?'

'The relationship, the marriage and all that.'

'Ah… I see. Can we come in?'

Jasper looked the big guy up and down. 'You're already in. But suit yourself. Bring in your buddies.' He stood to one side and threw out a welcoming arm. 'I apologise for the heat. The insulation here is non-existent, and the fan barely works.'

Three police entered. The two others moved to the front yard. Jasper glared at their faces, particularly their eyes, as they passed him. The two behind Keats removed their sunglasses; one had an Asian appearance, and the other looked very young and baby-faced. Jasper let out an audible gasp and a high-pitched squeak when he saw their eyes. Keats spun around.

'Is there a problem, Johansson?' he said sharply.

'Black eyes… ah… huh…' said Jasper in a shaky voice. 'The Torment.' He bent over and sucked in a lungful of air with an audible wheeze.

'What?' exclaimed the sergeant.

Jasper took a moment, then stood upright. 'I think I gave my wife a black eye… yes I did… but it wasn't my fault.' He hoped he hadn't given himself away. He reminded himself again of his practised routine and responses. As he took a deep breath, he re-evaluated his sudden inner tension and stress and chose to treat it as a good thing. No pretence was required.

'Are you saying that you punched your wife?'

'Oh… sorry… no, no… I pushed her, she was er… tormenting me, and she hit the side of her head against the fridge,' he stammered. 'Gave her a black eye. It was wrong, but she was leaving me… saying awful things… she was taking Delaney and Faith. I was upset.'

'Hmm…' Keats took out a handkerchief and wiped it around his neck. 'Hey,' he called to baby-face. 'Open the back door. Get some circulation in this place.' Then he gestured to the Asian officer and the hallway with his head. The officer returned the nod and went for a look around the house.

'Her leaving has not been helpful for my mental health,' continued Jasper as he made his way to the lounge with a slight limp.

'Have you injured yourself?' asked the sergeant, looking down at Jasper's Crocs.

'Stood on a nail. I need to be more careful. It's not too bad… As I was saying, I'm now in almost constant anxiety,' he replied, changing the subject and holding out a trembling hand as evidence. 'I've had to cancel work too because I have no vehicle. Everything's turning to shit… oh my God.' Once in the lounge, he dropped into his favourite chair and rubbed his hands over his face. 'I've got an approved disability pension, which I can restart, I suppose, but it's less than I get bricklaying, and I find work is generally good for my physical and mental health. Although now this has happened, I'm not so sure.'

'Pretty sure you can get rental assistance too,' said Keats.

'Probably.'

'No one else here, Sarge,' announced the young officer as he returned to the lounge.

Keats stood over Jasper. 'Do you need help?'

'I'm getting help from my GP, Goldsmith. And I've called Beyond Blue twice. They are happy for me to keep in touch.'

'Good. When did you last hear from your wife?'

'She took the kids and left Saturday morning, then came back briefly early that evening. We talked for about an hour. She left around seven and just buggered off with my car. She had the spare key. I heard the wheels spinning on the gravel and stuck my head out the door, but she was away.'

'What did you chat about?'

'Mostly me. She kept insisting I was not taking my meds. Said my thinking was muddled up and that I'd changed.' Jasper started wringing his hands. 'Said that I wasn't the guy she married. I could do better as a father. Shit like that. A big kick in the guts, you know.' He wiped his eyes with the back of his hand.

'Any contact since?'

'No, no. Nothing,' he blubbered.

'And you don't know where she is?'

'I'd just be guessing. While she was here, I grabbed her phone and checked it. She made a lot of calls to hotels and motels and even a few to health retreats. None to her sister Theresa, though. She deliberately tried to mislead me, calling all those places and knowing I would check her phone. When did she call you guys?' Jasper removed his hands from his face and eye-balled the officer.

'Hmmm… she didn't. She's been reported as a missing person.'

Jasper eased himself from the chair and stood. He wiped his nose roughly with his hand and sniffed. 'So, you think I'm somehow connected with that?'

'The thought had crossed our minds,' grunted Keats. He gave a slight nod and a crooked, wry smile. 'What happened to your hands?'

Jasper turned both hands over and back again. He had two Band-Aids on one hand and one on the other. There were plenty of other minor cuts, scratches and bruises. 'I did my last concreting job yesterday morning. The boss gave me a lift. He said it was a one-off, and then I'd have to sort myself out, which I can't do now. We've been working on the new Rosemeadow shopping centre. Tough work. I've always got cuts, scratches, dry, cracked skin.' He pushed a lifting edge of one Band-Aid back down.

'What's your boss's name?'

'Tony Bernardi.'

'What specific job have you been doing there?'

'We've been framing up and pouring slabs. Concreting. It's hard work.'

'That's how you damaged your hands?'

'Does it every time. You're working with timber, metal reinforcing, blue stone and cement. If I had a choice, I'd prefer just bricklaying. What are you thinking?' Jasper paused and looked at the sergeant, who said nothing immediately. 'You think that I hurt my hands while I was killing my wife?'

'To me, Johansson, everyone is guilty until proven otherwise, and I have a lot of people to talk to. So, I make no accusations of you or anybody else until all the facts are in.' Keats glanced at Baby-face, who was scribbling down a few handwritten notes. 'So far, you seem to be the last person to see her. How often do you check her phone? Check her whereabouts?'

'Not usually at all. You're mistaken. I'm not a pathologically jealous guy,' he growled through several sniffs. 'Look, you check the bedrooms,' snivelled Jasper, pointing down a short hallway. 'She left with suitcases. Took enough stuff for a week for the three of them.'

Keats gestured with his head, and the other two officers went for a second look around. 'You okay if we take a few photos of the place?'

'Knock yourself out…' Jasper waved a hand in the air. 'She planned it, you know. I didn't see it coming. She's taken the car. Gone. She hasn't been herself lately. Something strange came over her.' Jasper spoke loudly and quickly while shaking his head. He rubbed both open hands against his thighs. 'Don't know where she is. I want her back. Cassie. My kids. Back to normal. God!'

'Easy, there, fella. We got this.' Keats spoke softer, placed a hand on Jasper's shoulder and patted him at arm's length in an awkward attempt to settle him.

Jasper pulled away. 'Please don't.' He raised an open hand and stepped back, dropped his head, but peered up with his eyes. 'Sorry, I feel uncomfortable when you do that. It's not you as such. It's… it's police in general. I had some bad past experiences. Sorry.'

'Okay, Johansson. That's all right. I know some of your history. It must have been frightening.'

'Yes sir… it was.' Jasper studied his own feet.

'Tell me your car rego?'

'JASCAS, personalised plates, our names put together. See, we are a couple. Meant to be together,' he forced a grin. 'Who reported her missing?'

'I'm not at liberty to release that information… sorry.'

'What about my kids?'

'Safe and well.'

'Pardon me, sergeant, but what the fuck!' he swallowed and raised two trembling hands. 'My wife's gone missing, and the kids are with some unknown person. She wouldn't just leave them; she wouldn't.' Jasper pulled out his phone and called her number. Keats just stared at him.

'Damn!' cursed Jasper. 'It's turned off or not in a mobile reception area.'

'Yes, we've tried it several times.'

'Probably turned off. I called and messaged her a few times late on Saturday morning and into the afternoon. She never answered. I think she got the shits and turned it off. She must have read the texts because she dropped back later, as I mentioned.'

'Yes, so you said… would you mind handing over your phone? I want to verify your version of the story and check where it's been recently. You understand?'

'What if she calls me?'

'We are quite capable of answering it, and we won't be leaving with it. I need the phone to look at your calls and texts. Do you have a problem with that?'

'No, not at all… of course not.' Jasper handed over the phone. The officers returned from checking the house more thoroughly.

'Some clothes and toys still here, but it looks like what he says is pretty much correct,' declared the Asian officer. 'Only one toothbrush in the bathroom. No hairbrush, very little makeup.'

Jasper saw the black eyes. He started grunting and over-breathing, then let out a sharp squeal.'

'Sit back down!' commanded Keats. 'Now! On the lounge chair! Sit!' Jasper followed the instructions. The sergeant turned his head. 'Grab a glass of water. And you…' he looked at the Asian officer. 'Check this over.' He tossed him the phone.

*   *   *

After watching both cars and all the police leave, Jasper went to the bedroom armed with a dinner knife from the kitchen.

He grabbed a work boot from the wardrobe and then sat on the side of the bed, panting and cursing. 'Fuck The Torment. You nearly blew it, Johansson. Gotta do better. Stupid man. More practice. More practice.'

Using the knife as a lever, he prised off the bottom of the heel and removed a small plastic packet containing white tablets. Jasper took one out, broke it in half and threw it in his mouth. He reattached the boot heel and put it, together with the drugs, back in the wardrobe. He headed back to the lounge and dropped heavily into his favourite chair. Jasper looked at the rug and pushed at it with his toes. It was similar but not identical to the old one; nevertheless, he was pleased with the second-hand replacement. And for only eighty dollars, it was a bargain.

Chapter 13

The Return Visit

Two days later, Keats was back. This time, he had an Asian social worker called Naomi with him. She was a diminutive figure with a face like a weasel. She spoke with a frequent lack of prepositions. Jasper had seen her black eyes. There were other police, too, but they remained in the cars outside.

The purpose of the visit was to assess his mental state, gauge his mental fitness and assess his ability to provide adequate care for his children. The kid's location was still not disclosed. Keats asked a few quick questions about Cassandra, who was still missing, as was the Johansson vehicle. Jasper had no new information. No doubt, a couple of the sergeant's questions were double-checking from the last visit and were designed to try and trip him up.

'How's the bricklaying going at Rosemeadows?' The sergeant had asked. *'I hear there were some bushfires up that way. Did you see much smoke?'* Then he added, *'So what time on the Sunday did you last talk to Cassandra?'* Jasper had his story straight. He reaffirmed that while he saw the smoke haze, he could no longer get to work because of his transport problem, and he last spoke to his wife on Saturday, not Sunday. Keats grunted in an implicit but unconvincing response to Johansson's answers.

While he tried hard, he felt he had done no better than when the five police had visited. It wasn't just Keats that had aggravated him; the social worker had done her fair share, too. She sat too close with reduced personal space. He felt and smelt her breath. There was something wrong, something decaying, like the rotten flesh of a malignant spirit.

His anxiety had escalated, and while he tried to relax after their departure, he couldn't be sure if he used the words *demon* and *torment* in her presence. Maybe these were just his own thoughts. One thing he knew for sure was that he wanted to tear her eyes from their sockets.

*   *   *

That afternoon, a procession of police and other investigators filed into the Rosemeadow building site where Jasper Johansson had been working - Sergeant Warren Keats, a detective, two men pushing a low, three-wheel trolley with an orange box and a monitor, and another uniformed officer with a German Shepherd dog.

A tall and round security guard confronted them near the entrance. 'You all gotta wear hi-vis and hats,' he growled. He took a few steps toward a small, demountable room no bigger than a port-a-loo and opened the door. Inside were boxes of hard hats and hi-vis vests. 'What yous coppers doing here anyway?' He started passing out the gear.

'Police business,' smiled Keats.

'You keep that fuckin' animal muzzled.' He pointed sharply at the dog. 'I'm the OH and S Officer around here.'

'We know how to do our job,' Keats said, locking eyes with the man. 'Just give us our safety gear, and we can move on.'

'And I know how to do mine, copper,' he barked back.

'For the record, what is your name?'

'For the fucking record,' he laughed. 'It's Roscoe Romano. Remember it. And I'm also a senior official in the union.'

Everyone put on their safety gear, and the group headed towards the main site office.

Keats fronted up to the door of a long, demountable building with the words SITE OFFICE stuck across the window in large black lettering on a bright yellow background.

The area was a mass of activity, with several buildings partly constructed. Many workers in their fluro-clothing were around the site. Bobcats, cranes, cement trucks, and forklifts were all in action. Closest to the site office was a massive concrete slab surrounded by supporting timber and star pickets. Multiple pipes and electrical conduits rose from the smooth cement surface.

Tony Bernardi was expecting Keats after he received a phone call forty-eight hours earlier, and the meeting and site inspection had been arranged. He had agreed not to proceed with further work on the slab Johansson had been working on. This was no real impediment to construction as it needed at least seven days to sit and harden enough before further work could proceed.

Bernardi was a short man in his fifties with thick jet-black hair and weathered olive skin. He stood as Keats entered, and the two shook hands firmly across the desk.

'Tony Bernardi,' said the site manager.

'Keats,' said the sergeant. 'Thank you for setting this up. Your security guy, Roscoe Romano, is an arsehole.'

'Unfortunately, we have a few, but he's the ringleader of the arseholes… so to speak,' he chuckled. 'Sorry about that.'

'Yeah,' smiled Keats.

'Now, I don't wanna you ripping up my new concrete, sergeant,' snickered Bernardi in his melodic Italian accent.

'Hoping that won't be necessary. You have that guy we discussed who could, only if necessary, of course, drill a few holes for me.'

'He'll be joining you outside,' Bernardi said, looking past Keats through the window. 'You bring some extra help, I see.'

'Yeah. We have the ground penetrating radar, which will hopefully help preserve your slab. And we have a clever canine to sniff out any human remains. We may need to walk him around other areas too.'

'Yes, I understand.'

'And it's the slab here…' Keats gestured out the side window to the closest stretch of new concrete, '… that Johansson was working on?'

'That's it. He was a different man on his last working day.'

'How so?'

'He was upset, said his wife had pissed off with the kids. He got a bit irritable, too, not wanting to do what was asked of him. Insisting he wanted to use the line hose and pour the concrete when I wanted him to do some form work - boxing up for the next slab.'

'So, what job did he end up doing?'

'Huh,' Bernardi waved the sergeant away. 'What the hell. There was no use aggravating the guy who was already upset. I let him do the concrete pour. I like Jasper. He's a good worker and usually very reliable. You might be wrong, though, sergeant; you think he's a killer. Thinking he's done his wife in and dumped her body here somewhere.'

'Hmmm… We're covering all possibilities, that's all. Being thorough. And I don't think I said anything quite like that.'

'Cadaver dog, radar machines, drilling holes. Pardon me, but I'm not your average fucking idiot, sir,' chuckled the site manager. He gave a big grin and a series of rapid head nods.

'I see, it looks like you've got us pegged,' smiled the sergeant. 'Can you explain why Johansson's hands were excessively damaged?' he added, '… like more than you would expect.'

'And what would you expect? I've seen guys lose fingers, get cuts down to the bone, and have rashes and infections that they can hardly shake off. You wouldn't know unless you do the work.'

'Okay, I take your point,' conceded Keats. 'We best make a start then. Oh, one other thing: Johansson said he couldn't get to work anymore. He told us you gave him a lift on his last day, but that was just a one-off.'

'No. I said I could keep bringing him as long as we were on this job. I drive near his place every day I come to work. So, picking him up was no big deal. He probably didn't want to impose himself on me. He's like that. He's a guy who mostly prefers his own company. I gotta respect that.'

*   *   *

The trolley with the ground-penetrating radar moved back and forth down the length of the slab, with the operators closely monitoring the oscillating waves displayed on the monitor.

So far, two deep, narrow holes had been drilled through the concrete where there appeared to be a space below. One revealed some groundwater movement; the other was just a case of poor compaction.

Taipan, the German Shepherd, had completed a circuit of the slab and was now off with his handler checking other areas of the work site.

As the GPR approached the last corner of the slab nearest the perimeter fence, the wave display altered, showing a space and an unknown object below the slab and on top of the blue stone base.

'Something!' shouted the operator, raising his hand and waving. Keats, the detective and the other officer left their group huddle and headed over.

'What have we got?' asked the detective, a blonde surfer-looking man in his mid-twenties. This was Detective Harry Truman; he had been asked to coordinate the investigation into the disappearance of Cassandra Johansson on behalf of the coroner.

'Something about two metres long and no more than half a metre wide. It appears to be something of low density. Way softer than concrete, iron and blue stone.'

Keats waved to the workman who wheeled over the core driller as the GPR operator made some rudimentary markings with chalk, then backed away.

'I'd like a bigger hole this time if you could,' said Keats.

'Sure,' replied the workman. 'Anything to aggravate that arse, Bernardi,' he snickered.

The drill stood over a metre tall and was clamped into a holding device. A hose from a portable water supply was connected to the drill to keep the diamond drill bit cool. The workman put on all his protective gear. Everyone else took a few steps back.

'Right in the middle of that outline,' yelled Keats.

The drilling took ten minutes. The drilled-out core was worked out of the drill bit and lay flat on the slab. The removed section was a cylinder shape, seventy-five millimetres in diameter and eight hundred millimetres long. The bottom section of the core broke away as it came free from the tool.

The officers and the driller squatted and looked. 'What the fuck is that?' asked Truman.

The workman went to touch it. 'Wait!' bellowed Keats. 'Could be evidence. Don't touch.' He moved closer.

'It's material. It looks like carpet,' noted Truman. 'I don't see anything else. There's no obvious human tissue.'

'I want another hole,' said Keats. He stood, took one giant step, and pointed to the chalk outline on the slab. 'Just here.'

The workman glanced at the site office and smiled. Bernardi was looking out the window. 'No worries, chief,' he said happily.

Fifteen minutes later, he had another core lying on the cement. It was identical to the previous one.

'More carpet. No blood and guts,' quipped the detective.

'Hmmm... why is there fucking carpet?' grumbled Keats.

'Beats me. Ask Bernardi. Maybe some guys were using it as a picnic rug,' suggested Truman light-heartedly.

Keats made a quick phone call. 'Hey, it's Keats. I want Taipan over here.' He hung up.

'Can I do you another hole, boss?' asked the workman. 'Happy to do a bunch of 'em.'

The sergeant shook his head. 'Let's hold off for the moment.'

A minute later, the cadaver dog and handler arrived. Taipan sniffed around the holes and the extracted cores and showed no interest.

'I don't like it. I should get this slab section pulled up,' said Keats.

'No fucking way! Taipan's got nothing,' blurted Truman. 'Test these other bits first. If you get something clear from forensics, come back and smash your heart out. I know it's not the main consideration, but we got a budget, Keats.'

'Hmmm...'

'You've been at Johansson's twice in the past week. Did he have a chunk of carpet missing?'

'He had a rug in the lounge. There was no other carpet in the place.'

'Okay. We'll wait then. We can ask Bernardi to hold off here for a few more days till we give him the all-clear.'

Chapter 14

Introverted

It was six weeks after his wife's disappearance, and upon the written request of the Department of Housing, Jasper was relocated to single-person accommodation, still in the Claymore area. He had been assured that he would be promptly placed in a more appropriate setting should his wife return or if he was granted care of his children. He had been advised that Faith and Delaney would, for the time being, remain in foster care. He had been granted a fortnightly supervised visit to each of his kids, to see each individually on alternate weeks in a room in the Claymore Community Centre. He had declined this option for two reasons: one, it was unnecessarily restrictive and treated him like a criminal, and two, he knew that it was highly likely that they were not his flesh and blood, as his wife had failed to eliminate these evil impostors. He felt his chances of rectifying this situation while under supervision were slim.

His next assessment with Naomi was in four months. Jasper's pension had been fully reinstated, as he no longer had income. The social worker had assisted with this as part of her pretence to appear genuine.

The bed-sit was tiny and by far the smallest in the block of twelve. There were just two rooms - kitchen, dining, lounge, and sleeping- all in one open area, with a shower, toilet, and sink in the other. Jasper had no issues with the place. It suited him fine and was within a short walk of a supermarket and other shops. Dr Goldsmith, his GP, was in the same complex next to the pharmacy.

Jasper had stuck a cardboard notice on his front door - *Rule 1. Do NOT knock; Rule 2. FUCK off! Rule 3: Disobey the rules, then suffer the consequences.*

Jasper took all his remaining cash out of the lining of his jacket and placed it on the small, one-person, all-purpose table. He pushed through the notes. Eight hundred dollars. With that and the little left over from his pension, he could still manage to maintain his supply of meth, providing his usage didn't increase.

He stood and dragged a chair to the front door, wedging it under the handle. He checked both locks and then headed for the shower, picking up a few dirty clothing items on his way.

He threw the clothes he collected, plus what he was wearing, onto the shower floor. The block of units had a communal laundry, which he never used. Jasper stomped up and down on his clothes and gave himself a quick wash.

The habit of disposing of his prescribed medication daily was now well-established. After cleaning his teeth, he pushed out a pill and let it fall into the sink. He leaned close to the mirror, pulled down his eyelids, and shifted his eyes left, right, up, and down.

'Hmm… still looking good, Johansson, no infection, no contamination.'

He laid his wet clothes on the lounge floor and turned the ceiling fan on high. He sat naked on the single bed, grabbed his laptop from under the pillow and punched in the passcode - NaomiDiesB4U. Jasper clicked open thirty-five embedded folders before arriving at the document *THE QUARTET*, which he double-clicked. The file opened with a note on the page saying, *"Pick up where you left off."* He clicked the message, and the document opened on page 4,168.

Chapter 15
Double Trouble

Faith and Delaney were five months into their second foster placement, their first having lasted six weeks.

Blair and Sheena Harrington were a couple in their late twenties who had multiple failed attempts at pregnancy and, after the roller-coaster ride of embryo implants and spontaneous abortions, had decided to cease any further medical intervention. They had registered for adoption but wanted to try fostering as an interim step. It was an opportunity to help others who needed care and see how they could manage as parents.

Blair worked weekdays as an accountant, while Sheena had secured permanent part-time work on Friday and Saturday nights as a registered nurse in an aged care home. Their income, which also included the departmental fostering allowance, was sufficient to pay their mortgage, attend to the needs of a family of four and have a little left over for special treats or short holidays a couple of times a year.

Difficulties with Faith and Delaney started early. The two demanded to be in one another's company as often as possible. They made a point, day after day, about sharing a bedroom. After a week, their persistent protest was rewarded. The two perfect rooms prepared by the Harringtons were transformed into a bedroom with two single beds and the other into a playroom.

All the preparations the Harringtons had made seemed to fall apart. They had purchased new clothing only to find items in the bin, on the lawn or damaged beyond repair. Their efforts at bonding, male with male and female with female, as advised by professionals, proved hopeless, as separating the pair for one-on-one adult attention just provoked storming off in a huff. Another tactic the children adopted was not speaking, taking themselves to a corner, and standing there for as long as they could, sometimes for hours at a stretch. There was minimal crying, screaming, and tantrums that other young children may have displayed.

The dolls that had decorated Faith's first bedroom ended up beheaded and mutilated, while toy cars and trucks for Del were eventually found buried in the backyard. Apart from the lava-lamp night-light app, their two iPads were used more as drink and food trays than for anything else. The wall-mounted TVs in both rooms were used infrequently, and the numerous networks subscribed to by the Harringtons remained unused. Sometimes, in the early morning hours, Faith would turn on the television and watch late-night talk shows and news with the volume near zero. She seemed to manage on only a few hours' sleep.

Faith and Del preferred to play games together - Ludo, snakes and ladders, Yahtzee, dress-up, and knocking down soldiers with marbles. Blair and Sheena's attempts to get involved usually resulted in both children heading to their beds with a book or comic.

For the young couple, the past five months had taken their toll. They were past the point of watching what they said in front of their foster children, and over the past two weeks, Blair had used the word *fuck* in front of both several times.

On a Friday evening, which unbeknown to him would be the penultimate day before he ceased to be a foster parent, Blair returned home from work and went straight to the kitchen to grab a drink. Sheena was there preparing dinner. Blair pulled the pantry door and then stopped, realising it was padlocked. 'Ah… you've done it. And the fridge, too, I see.'

'Hi, honey. Yes… and here's your key.' She passed it over and forced a smile. 'Same one for both locks. And you best pour me one while you're at it,' she said. 'This is the day. I trust you're still good with it?' Sheena was a petite lady of short stature with a layered bob hairstyle.

'Bloody oath. I need some fortification.' He was quickly into the pantry.

'I took tonight off work just in case I needed to stick around for the fallout,' she said, holding out her glass. They both had a generous serve of Aberfeldy Scotch Whisky. 'Dinner will be on the table in ten minutes,' she said.

'We have to do something, don't we?' He looked at his wife as if seeking confirmation. 'Another week without significant change, and I'm off to the loony bin. And it's affecting our relationship. I've been so bloody irritable. Fuck, we've really stuffed this fostering thing. I'm sorry to say this, love, but I'm not sure I'm cut out for being a parent.' Blair dropped heavily into a chair at the dining table. He took a big swig, pushed a hand through his short black accountant hair, and left it sticking out in all directions. He reefed his tie down and undid his top two buttons.

'From what I know, these two are not typical of their age,' said Sheena. 'Maybe it's a reflection of their upbringing. A schizo father and a mother missing in action.' She sat over from her husband. They held hands across the table. 'We're going to be fine. You and me. That's what's most important here. And maybe one day soon we can restart sex.' She tipped her head, and her eyes widened as she looked at him.

'Hmm…,' came the non-committal reply from her husband.

Ten minutes later, the table was set with two plates of steaming spaghetti bolognaise. Blair poked his head around Faith and Delaney's bedroom door, announced dinner was ready and left. He and Sheena sat at the table awaiting the children.

After an expected wait of around three minutes, the kids rocked up for dinner. Both still in their school uniforms. Attempts to change this behaviour were given up long ago.

'Hello, She Mum and Dad Blah,' chuckled Delaney as he danced to the table.

'Hi guys,' said Faith.

The two sat and then looked at each other.

'Where are our meals?' asked Faith. Blair and Sheena started on their spaghetti. 'Well?' she said louder.

Sheena swallowed and then spoke. 'They are in the fridge.'

'What? We have to eat cold meals?'

'Actually, they're still hot. I expect they'll cool after a while, though.'

Faith turned to her brother. 'They're playing games with us.'

'I like games,' grinned Delaney.

'This is a different sort of game. We must get our own meals. I'll go.' She hopped up, went to the fridge, and yanked the handle, but it was locked. 'Oh, I see.' She lifted the padlock and then let it swing back on the latch. 'This game is bigger than I thought.'

'When you change from your school uniforms, we will unlock the fridge,' said Blair. He looked at his wife. 'This is delicious, honey. You're so clever.'

'Faith,' said Sheena, turning in her chair to look at her foster daughter, 'and Delaney…' she nodded at him. 'As your foster parents, we expect changes in your behaviour. As time passes, we hope to remove the fridge and pantry locks.'

'You locked the pantry too?' exclaimed Faith. 'That's not very kind. This seems like a very wicked change for you both.'

'It's a change for the better,' said Blair.

'Sounds evil. Has someone cast a bad spell on you?'

'Certainly not,' scoffed the foster father. 'And I've told you a dozen times already that spells, witchcraft, and all that stuff is complete nonsense. 'How long the fridge and pantry remain locked is up to you.'

'I see,' said Faith with a subtle nod and a hint of a smile.

'What about the Twisties?' said Del, slightly dejected.

'Yes, you can have all these things in return for some good behaviour, doing as you're asked and following the house rules,' added Sheena.

'I see. So, if we change our clothes…' said Faith as she moved back to her brother's side. '… we can have spaghetti?'

'Yes,' said Blair.

'Most definitely,' added Sheena.

Faith faced her brother. 'Come on, Del. We have to change.'

The two departed without further fuss and went to their room.

The foster parents did a perfect high-five across the table.

*   *   *

The young couple had finished their meal, washed up and were in the lounge and onto their third drink. 'It's been thirty minutes,' said Blair.

'I know. We need to hold strong. Relax. The longer they take, the hungrier they get.' Sheena flicked out her recliner footrest.

They had the TV on but with the volume muted. To pass a bit of time, they both tried to guess what the newsreader was saying. While they laughed lightly at themselves, both kept glancing around to see if either of the kids had appeared. Another thirty minutes went by.

Blair got to his feet. 'Let's go and check on them.'

'Sure,' said Sheena, 'Maybe they're playing soldiers or dress-up games.'

'Hmm… dressing up in something other than their bloody school uniforms would be nice.'

The two left the lounge and moved to the rear of the low-set home, where all three bedrooms were. They slowed as they approached the sibling's bedroom. There was a light on and some sound. Blair put an ear to the door.

'Sounds like the ABC news… huh. That'd be a first.' He raised an eyebrow and then opened the door.

The foster parents surveyed the bedroom, checking under the beds, the wardrobes, and the ensuite. Sheena opened the plantation shutters. Behind them, the window was pushed open from the bottom to its maximum angle. The opening was narrow but wide enough for children to squeeze through. One of Faith's lace hankies was caught on the window latch.

'Oh fuck! They've done a runner!' she yelped.

'Jesus. These fucking kids!' bellowed Blair.

Sheena checked for the two overnight bags usually kept on the top of the robe. Both were missing. 'Yep, they've gone for sure.'

'Well, we'll need to report this to the fucking cops!'

Sheena grabbed his arm. 'No. Not yet. If we lose them, our chances of adopting will be completely fucked.'

'I don't care,' shrugged Blair.

'Let's at least try to find them… for, say… half an hour before we do anything. Please love! For me!' pleaded his partner.

'For fuck's sake… damn it… okay. Grab a bloody torch and meet me at the car.'

Moments later, the garage door lifted, and the Toyota Prado reversed out. After the door clunked shut, Faith and Delaney hopped out of the wardrobe in the playroom, still in their school uniforms. 'I'm off to the garage, Del. You get the toolbox from under the sink.'

'Sure, sis. Great plan,' he said brightly. 'This is exciting.'

'Yeah, the quartet, think twice, plan carefully and act decisively, right.' They both laughed.

In the garage, Faith first located the superglue in the cupboard. Next, she used a broom to pull out a plug set high up on the wall. The roller door light, still on after the recent departure, immediately went out. Then she opened the front door, filled the outside lock with glue, closed herself back inside, and repeated the process with the back door. She went around the house, closing and locking all the windows.

In the kitchen, Del was already working away with the screwdriver on the catch of the pantry door. The fridge lock had two plastic pads, one glued to the door and one on the side. Each pad had a metal arm with a loop at the end where the padlock was attached.

Faith entered the kitchen and checked out the fridge lock. She put her face close and smelt it. 'Held on by some strong glue. Only put on today,' she said. She moved to the kettle and turned it on. When it boiled, she warned Del to stand clear, then slowly poured the water over the side pad. The hot water ran down the fridge and pooled over the floor. She pulled hard on the fridge door, and slowly, the side pad slid forward. Then it came entirely off, sending her backwards and onto her backside. Both kids laughed louder and longer than they had for a long time.

Del helped her back to her feet. 'Do you think something nasty has taken over their souls?'

'I've tried some good spells to help them, but it hasn't worked. Whatever it is that has them must be very strong.'

'Doesn't matter anyway,' said Del. 'We have the fridge and pantry open now.'

*   *   *

After twenty-five minutes of driving around, stopping to check parks, school grounds, bus shelters and a nearby shopping centre, Blair and Sheena decided to return home. They were only a block from their home when they heard a police siren, and Blair was pulled over. An officer approached.

'Sir, we've noticed some erratic driving. Have you consumed any alcohol this evening?'

*   *   *

Early the following morning, the children were taken away with two social workers from the Department of Child Safety. On Monday, the Harringtons withdrew their adoption application. Blair Harrington was convicted of mid-range drink driving. He lost his licence for six months and was fined three thousand dollars. There was also the cost of a new front door, which was smashed in by the police looking for the children. They were found quietly sitting in the dining room on their second helping of spaghetti bolognaise.

Chapter 16

The Final Decline

Jasper continued living in the bed-sit, rarely getting out. Having lost forty-five kilos, he was a shadow of his former self. Occasionally, as a special treat, he would order food deliveries. Still, his primary supply source came from the occasional food hamper delivered by the St Vincent De-Paul Society, who left the package at the door, knocked and departed quickly.

He would take a dining chair and often sit outside his front door for hours, looking at everything and everyone, sometimes taking notes. After many months, no one bothered approaching him anymore, lest they receive a greeting resembling that of a wild animal, snarling, growling, and hissing.

The Community Mental Health team had visited twice, once at the request of the Department of Housing and another after contact with the police, who had four reports from concerned tenants of the complex. While they believed he was unwell on both occasions, they had insufficient grounds to drag him away against his wishes.

It was mid-morning on a weekday in May when a uniformed Sergeant Keats and a plainclothes detective knocked on his door.

The door opened slowly, and an unshaven, gaunt face appeared. 'Can't you guys read?' growled Jasper.

'Apologies for the intrusion, and we've read the notice on your door,' said Keats, '… but we have some information for you and a couple of questions to ask. Can we come in?'

Jasper stared at their faces and seemed to be satisfied. 'Huh… suit yourself, but the place is a dump.' He fully opened the door. The breeze and smell hit both officers at the same time. They glanced at each other. Keats coughed. They both entered.

The interior of the bed-sit was squalid. There were clothes on the floor and assorted food containers, cans, bottles and dried-up food scraps. A couple of giant cockroaches scurried under the only lounge chair. Jasper matched the scene perfectly with his dirty torn trousers, black t-shirt with dribble marks, knotted hair and a couple of weeks since his last shave. His arms were marked with dried blood from where he had been scratching. His fingernails were black. His teeth were yellow. He shoved junk from the lounge to the floor and repeated the process with the dining chair.

'Feel free to take a seat, gentleman,' said Jasper.

'Thanks, but we'll stand. Don't expect to be here long,' replied the sergeant.

'Please yourself. Your selfish don't buy fish,' Jasper dropped onto the soft but soiled chair.

'This is Detective Harry Truman,' added Keats.

'Like the president. Not such a true man,' chuckled Jasper. 'He was a cocksucker. Motherfucker. Mass murderer. And I would surmise he was an evil demon. It's a pity he wasn't assassinated or implicated as a killer, a schemer, a bomber of Hiroshima.'

Truman was a tall man in his twenties with smooth-looking tanned skin and blonde hair.

'Pleased to meet you, Mister Johansson,' he said. He did not attempt a handshake. 'We've found your car.'

Jasper widened his eyes in mild surprise. 'Six months of police work to find a car. Outstanding, in the rain,' he scoffed as he scratched at his arms, causing a small trickle of blood. 'A true man likes surfing.

Waves of passion. Lust and fucking. Don't stop sucking people dry and drained.'

Truman raised an eyebrow. 'Hmm… It was on a rarely used road outside of Gilead near the O'Hares Creek Lookout.' Both police watched him for some response. There was no reaction.

'Huh… did my wife come with this discovery?' asked Jasper without stumbling over his words.

'No. Just the vehicle,' said Keats. 'It was burnt out.'

'Huh… the bitch set my car alight. That's fucked up. Stuffed up. Muddled up,' said Jasper. 'I think she became complete sometime after she left me.'

'Complete? Meaning what exactly?' asked the detective.

Jasper waved them away with his hand. 'You wouldn't understand or get the command.'

'Try me.'

Jasper jumped to his feet and moved close to the detective's face. 'Completely taken over by The Torment, officer!' Jasper shouted, breathing his foul breath into Truman's face. The detective eased back slowly. 'Transformed to pure evil,' continued Johansson. 'I saw the signs. Signs, everywhere a sign.' He held his hand out in front of Truman. His fingers quivered. He lifted the other hand, and all his digits trembled before Truman's eyes. 'Shakin', bakin', don't eat bacon. With Cassie, I always thought it was just a matter of time… time is of the essence. The essence of evildoers and sayers.' He put his hands down, turned and sat back down. Jasper looked up at his two visitors, who stared back. 'See, I told you you wouldn't understand. Can I get you a coffee?'

Keats walked to the lounge window and slid it open after a push and shove. He sucked in a few breaths. Harry Truman noticed a few tiny cockroaches surrounding a small brown circle of some substance on the bench as if they were having a community meeting. 'Pass on the coffee,' said the sergeant. 'The bushfires burned out your car.'

'What bushfires?'

'The ones a few months back.'

'Then Cassie could be out there. Burnt to a crisp. Crispy creams. Creamy dreams.'

'Our searches would suggest not,' said Truman.

'Evil triumphs then. Sound the horns and trumpets. The apocalypse is nigh,' sighed Jasper.

'We found the remnants of two mobile phones,' continued Detective Truman. 'Strangely, some months back, on Sunday, the day after you last saw her, we had tracked these mobiles nearly as far as Gilead, and then the signal was lost. Can you shed any light on that?'

'Part light is shed, but why two phones? Two heads are better than one... yes... and once she was pissed with me, she tuned out, turned off, got lost. Asian cops.'

'Why would your wife go to that lookout?'

Jasper shrugged. 'The Hendricksons lived out that way. Way out west. She liked them. I didn't. Shouldn't. Couldn't.'

'What's their address?'

'I neither know nor care, detective.'

Keats noticed the filthy rug over the floor. 'Is this rug from your previous place?'

'The lounge rug. A bug. A buggered-up stud. It was.'

'You probably don't know that we visited your old boss, Bernardi, a few months back. We drilled up some of the concrete. Found an old grey carpet.'

Jasper stared. He was alternating his wide-eyed gaze between the two.

'Does that concern you, Johansson?' asked Detective Truman.

'Jasper doesn't concern himself with such matters,' answered Johansson in a firm, more direct and confident voice. 'He is unemployed, with no current interest in resuming such a job. He is physically incapable of performing gruelling tasks currently.' The two policemen looked at each other. Harry Truman shrugged.

Jasper looked to the ceiling and checked out the corners of the room. 'Time to think. Time to plan. Money, evil-rooted money. Drugs and speed. Meth and metho. I need something.'

'What do you want, Johansson?' barked Keats. 'Drugs?'

'Drugs, bugs, but no slugs. No... can you nice gentleman of the regime, take me to the hospital?'

'After all this time and all your refusals, you now want to go... voluntarily?' asked Keats.

'Yes, sergeant at arm's length. The width and breadth are not the important news of the day.'

'We can take you,' said Keats. 'What about a bag?' Both cops looked around, unsure where to start amidst all the mess. Jasper stood, walked to his bed, and dragged a suitcase from underneath. 'This is all I need,' he said with a smile. 'Let's go.'

*   *   *

Jasper was pleased with the timing of the police visit. It was as if it was meant to be. A sign from a greater power. He had only just finished the last of his meth, and he had insufficient funds to get any more.

Going to the hospital would have its challenges, and to some extent, it might be like going back to square one. He was pretty sure they would insist on injections, and he had already decided he would not object to anything or be too challenging to manage. The most important thing was to remain voluntary, cooperate and agree. Withdrawing from meth could be his biggest hurdle, although he knew it was likely he could score some even while an inpatient.

He hoped to be there for some months, which meant that the mental health team would need to believe that he remains unwell, continues to have relapses and is treatment-resistant. Money could be saved. Good food would help him get his strength back. He knew he must be more careful next time - stronger, focused, and ready to confront The Torment head-on.

Chapter 17

Coroner's Case

'Got that report finished, Sarge?' asked Harry Truman. 'I need to get everything off to the coroner.'

'Nearly,' replied Keats. He looked up at the detective. 'Shit mate, are you sunburnt?'

'A little.'

'A little? Fuck! Looks nasty. Have you been on the beach?'

'Waves were pumping. I was surfing yesterday.'

'Ah… Johannson picked that.' Keats pointed and waved his finger at the young detective.

'He also said that I was a mass murderer, an evil demon and a lustful fucker.'

'You see, there are seeds of truth in every delusion.'

'Fuck off, Keats!' Truman shook his head. 'The report?'

'I'll have it on your desk this afternoon. It would've been good to try another chat with Johansson. Telling him that stuff about the concrete and the carpet provoked an odd reaction.'

'Oh, no… you're not going back to that. The bloody dog found nothing. There was no body or part thereof under that concrete.'

'I get that. But I reckon he's not telling us the whole story.'

'I've had enough of his crazy arse. Anything further will be up to the coroner. We're way past due on this investigation.'

It had been two weeks since the pair had visited Jasper and transported him to the hospital. They had gathered a few more statements. Two from the Hendricksons out past Gilead, and while they commented favourably on Cassandra's personality, they were of limited assistance as they hadn't had contact with Mrs Johansson for months. They re-interviewed Cassandra's sister, Theresa, who could only add that she believed Cassandra was hiding somewhere to remain safe from her husband. They also attempted another chat with Jasper in the inpatient psychiatric ward. This was a waste of time as he was on a bed in a single room, barely conscious, his slurred speech scarcely audible. Staff had reported how he had become increasingly delusional with some aggression, and they indicated that he would remain on high doses of sedation for some days.

Chapter 18

Jasper's Chronicles - Part 2

An Admission of Sorts

My colleague and I write in this place. I know I must not reveal my companion's name, although I must confess that, at times, I forget the reasoning behind this. Nevertheless, I heed this direction planted deep within my brain, and I trust clarity will return in due course. My companion demonstrates a degree of skill that I do not possess. I provide the dialogue while my colleague writes and corrects my often erroneous and bitter diatribe.

This is a place of immeasurable suffering endured more by others than by me. It is not that I suffer less; it is just that I've learned to accept it and not resist it - focus on the longer goal, think twice, plan carefully, and act decisively when the time is right (which is not now). Two of my fellow travellers have succumbed to the taunts, the drugs, the beatings and the wrath of their internal turmoil. Gareth swung in the night from a bedsheet in the bathroom, and Karen bled out litres at three in the morning after receiving a smuggled-in box-cutter blade. Hopefully, both are at rest and in a better place, although no such guarantees exist.

A diagnosis is a fluid concept, changeable as the wind. A brand of schizo-affective disorder exacerbated by illicit drug use is, to me, a meaningless tag by which the all-knowing educated sheep here use to prescribe me a cocktail of various corrective poisons. A monthly shot of an anti-psychotic, a daily dose of lithium, refraining from the use of any methamphetamines and regular dialogue with a psychologist and psychiatrist are considered the necessary ingredients for my return to a normal state of mental health and, ultimately, a return to a home somewhere.

I have, and I choose to say, by choice, deviated from an acceptable path and have been subject to single-room confinement, tranquillising injections and some thump therapy from a couple of heartless souls. Swearing and screaming into the ceiling, throwing food and plastic plates and trying to gouge at a doctor's eyes are not well tolerated but are guaranteed to hold your reservation in the establishment.

I know of The Torment; it plagues my mind less now than it used to. I struggle to define it, yet I know it is there… somewhere hiding and waiting. I breathe not its name aloud lest it descends upon me while I am ill-equipped to survive its onslaught.

Things I've done before this confinement lose definition over time. I ask the question, if another falls on one's sword, then does the other share equality of guilt? My comprehension of some events eludes me, yet I feel a profound sense of loss and guilt. In some corners of my mind, I have doubts it ever happened. I have dreams of a rolled-up grey carpet that writhes within itself as if alive. It smells of a vile concoction of decayed flesh and excrement. I miss you, Cassie.

My occupancy at this house of pain now passes six months. I've regained a healthy weight and bank balance. The pain I will bear until I can no longer. My departure will be followed by a period of introspection, rebuilding and a relentless search for the truth.

Chapter 19

The Kids Divided

After Faith and Delaney had been removed from their fourth foster home, the Department decided it would be more helpful to all concerned if they were fostered separately. Both children had been challenging, with verbal and sometimes physical aggression towards other children and their foster parents. When both were together, there seemed to be an element of conspiracy to jeopardise their placement. They had run away six times.

On some occasions, Theresa had been used as a go-between during placements. She had declined several times to keep them long-term, citing conflict with her son George, worries about reprisals from Jasper and a reluctance to any such arrangement by her husband.

They were kept at the same school to begin with, but here, too, their behaviour and schoolwork both declined. Counsellors had been involved; however, despite the passage of time, the sudden loss of both their parents in unusual circumstances was a hurdle that was proving too difficult to overcome.

The two siblings, aged nine and ten, sat together in a small but comfortable waiting room. A social worker had just left and was expected to return in a few minutes with an administrative officer.

The colourful room was adorned with toys better suited to much younger children. Faith put her arm around her shorter brother as both sat on a small sofa.

'You know they've had enough of us, don't you?' she said. 'They can't manage us anymore.'

'So… what does that mean?' Del had a marble in his hand, nervously squeezing and rolling it around with his fingers.

'They're going to separate us. We'll each be going to different foster homes,' replied Faith.

'Should we run away before that cranky one comes back?'

'There's a security guy down the hall. We won't get far. I need you to be strong for me, Del.'

He looked at her. His top lip quivered.

'I'll always find you,' said Faith. 'Promise. We'll get back together again.'

'With Mum?' he sobbed.

'I hope so. I'm going to miss you so much. But I shall find you. I'll always look out for you, no matter what.' She kissed the tears on his cheek. 'I love you, Delaney.'

'I love you too…' he hugged her. They stayed in a long embrace before Delaney lightly touched her hair. 'I liked your hair better when it was long and curly.'

She smiled. 'Me too.'

'That last mum was not a nice lady. I'm glad we ran away.'

'Yeah. Remember the story of Samson? He lost his strength when they cut his hair. But hair always grows back. My strength will always be there… just waiting.'

'For the right day,' nodded Delaney. 'You sure you'll be able to find me?'

'I will. I promise… think twice…'

'Plan carefully…;' added Del.

'Then act decisively.' She winked.

Del gave a slight, knowing grin. 'I hope Dad's better now.'

*   *   *

A significant relocation was organised with two separate families on the Gold Coast. While the siblings would not attend the same school, it was hoped that they would be reunited once they were both settled into their new environments and when their behaviour was stable. Unfortunately, no such reunion for the two children would ever happen.

Chapter 20

Delaney

In year five of primary school, Delaney's interest in marbles resurfaced. He remembered when he found some a few years back and how excited it made him feel. He ultimately discovered the truth about his find after a senior boy named Callum West, who had a history of misdemeanours, was picked up by the police. Callum had been using marbles in his slingshot to shoot birds and other wildlife. This information, though, did not diminish Delaney's enthusiasm, and he was unfazed that the boy concerned had taken out two magpies, a lorikeet and a possum.

His interest had expanded, and he had pieced together an impressive collection of these glass balls. He purchased some at stores and others online from around the world. Hal and Fiona, his foster parents, were delighted when he developed this fascination and supported his collecting habit. While it gave him a sense of achievement and satisfaction, the best thing for them was that he became quieter, less irritable and less combative with others at home and school.

While there were marbles made from substances other than glass, these held little interest for Delaney, and his collection was exclusively cat's-eye varieties. He believed he had some rare ones and kept several specials aside, never using them for play.

Delaney had been instrumental at school in introducing marbles to many kids who knew little about them. His show-and-tell presentations were always marble-related, and he had introduced the playing of marble games before the first school bell rang and during lunchtime - a practice that hadn't occurred at the school since the 1980s. The games started with only three boys playing, but after a few months, many children were in the playground drawing circles in the dirt and firing larger marbles into the ring to knock out as many smaller ones as possible. Portable devices were regularly used to take pics and videos of players and games and to text results to one another.

On a warm summer's day in November before the first school bell, Delaney rested his favourite tom-bowler on his forefinger with his thumb behind it, all set to blast it into the circle and win more marbles.

'Is that Jupiter?' asked Angus.

'Sure is. I don't bring him out very often.' He paused his shot and held up the marble to show his friend. 'See, it is white, orange, brown and red - all the colours of the planet Jupiter. 'You are in trouble now,' chuckled Del as he resumed his shooting position.

He had already won six and was hopeful of winning the last five. His opponent and good friend, Angus, watched with gritted teeth and crossed fingers. The eleven-year-old fired Jupiter just as the first bell sounded.

Derrick Martin, a larger and older boy from year six, jumped in front of the pair of players. He snatched up all the remaining marbles, including the larger tom-bowler. 'Grabs after the first bell, suckers!' he shouted and bolted away towards class.

'Hey! Stop!' yelled Angus. The boy grabbed a few small rocks and dirt and threw them in Derrick's direction, but he was well away. Delaney remained kneeling. 'He's got your tommy, Del. He's got Jupiter.'

'Yeah, he's a big bully.'

'Is that a thing - *grabs after the first bell?*'

'Looks like it is now, I guess,' answered Delaney in a quiet, controlled voice. He held his chin and took some deep breaths. The boy was a virtual clone of his father; however, puppy fat hid his squarish chin.

'We gotta get it back… and my cat's-eyes too,' added Angus woefully.

'Yeah…'

'What do we do?'

'First, we relax,' replied Del. He sat on the dusty ground, closed his eyes and started slow breathing.'

'Relax?' exclaimed Angus. 'What the hell for?'

'So I don't spin out. Give me a moment.'

Angus sat next to his friend and waited for two minutes. The second bell sounded.

Del opened his eyes. 'We should go. Don't worry, Angus, I'll think of something,' he said calmly.

'Are you upset? Looks like you don't care.'

'Oh, I care… I care a lot. I think better when I'm not stressed out.' Delaney stood and dusted off his knees and backside. 'Let's go to class… come on.'

'We should report him.'

'No. My brain is working on a few other ideas,' smiled Delaney.

*   *   *

After dinner that evening, Delaney excused himself from the company of his foster parents and went to his bedroom. He lit a small, scented candle he had quietly borrowed from Fiona's duchess and placed it on his bedside table. From the drawer, he removed a small jewellery case. Inside, he had a collection of the first few marbles he had found at Claymore in Sydney, all shining against the red velour lining. He selected a tri-coloured cat's eye. Holding it between two fingers, he closed one eye and looked at the candle flame through the glass. Slowly, he moved the marble closer to his eye until he reached a point of focus. He could see a perfect circle full of colours and shapes. As he became entranced, he saw outlines of multi-coloured trees, hills and mountains.

Del had sought out information about using marbles for this purpose, referred to as scrying, and about the revelations that could happen. He had read about the effects this can have - helping with relaxation, clarity of thought, and sometimes even providing predictions. Cat's-eye marbles have also been associated with good luck, protection, and warding off evil spirits.

He looked deeper. The rounded hills morphed into eyes, and then a shower of what looked like rain and snow obliterated the scene. Del gasped and moved the marble away.

He returned the candle after tucking his marble safely away with his other specials. The message had been received, and now it was time to think, plan, and act, as his father had taught him.

*   *   *

Delaney cut back on his games for the next few school days and spent time watching big Derrick. He saw him steal three more times, upsetting several younger students. There was a small calico bag with a drawstring in his pocket. It was bulging with stolen property. Delaney got close to him several times when the bully opened his locker and turned the dials on the combination lock. 'Sucker!' smirked Derrick on two occasions when he had spotted him nearby. Del noticed the bully shove the bag of stolen marbles onto the top shelf, next to some books and a lunchbox.

Over a few afternoons and evenings, Delaney had been busy at home constructing and testing a booby trap device using a mousetrap, a bent soup spoon and some wire. He tried it out at home and twice in his school locker.

On a Wednesday afternoon, a week after Delaney had lost his tom-bowler, he raised his hand in class and was excused for a bathroom break. As he approached the bank of lockers, he tipped some thick black liquid from a small Tupperware container into his hand. With a well-timed jump, he smeared the substance over the surveillance camera. After quickly washing his hands, he moved to Derrick's locker. Delaney had a good idea of the possible combinations, and on his fifth attempt, he had the locker open. Looking at the top shelf, he saw the books, lunch box, and the bag of marbles, all forming the exact contour of hills he had recently seen through his cat's-eye. He smiled.

That afternoon, the bell sounded, signalling that the school day was over. Within a few minutes, children of assorted ages were milling around, collecting their bits and pieces and hastily making their way off the Gold Coast primary school campus.

Delaney sat on a bench near the lockers, leaning back on a building support post. When Derrick appeared and went straight to his locker, Del's stomach churned, and his eyes blurred.

Inside the metal cabinet, the length of the fishing line became tighter as the door opened. A Japanese five-yen coin with a hole in the centre dragged across the top of Derrick's lunchbox and fell from the edge onto the mousetrap, setting it off. A soup spoon full of splintered and powdered glass launched into the bully's face. He screamed in pain, covering his eyes. A few students rushed to his aid.

*　　　　*　　　　*

Delaney woke with one of the female student teachers shaking his shoulder. 'Are you okay?'

'Oh…' he took a moment to gather his orientation. He had been in a daze against the post. 'Yes… I'm okay. I felt a bit dizzy and had to sit down. What's the time?'

'Nearly four.'

'Oh… I've been resting here for over forty minutes. Wow, that's longer than I thought.'

'All that drama with poor Derrick. No doubt that upset you,' she said.

'Oh yeah… terrible. I hope he'll be okay.'

'Me too. He's on his way to hospital. Poor boy.'

'I better get going.'

'You sure you're okay now?'

'Positive. Perfectly fine. The walk home will clear my head. Thank you for checking on me.' Delaney grabbed his school bag and headed away.

*　　　　*　　　　*

Del dutifully walked around the marble players, returning the stolen cat's eyes the following day. Then, he squatted down with Angus, ready to play.

'What have you done?' asked his friend.

'I broke into his locker. Got our stolen property.'

Angus looked at him unsurely. 'That's it?'

'Let's play,' said Delaney, drawing a circle in the dirt.

'He went off in an ambulance,' said Angus in a loud whisper.

'Okay. Who cares? Not me.'

'He got glass in his eyes.'

Delaney shrugged. 'Wow, he should be more careful... serves him right... hey, you gonna play or what?' Delaney smiled as he pulled his favourite tom-bowler, Jupiter, from the pocket of his school shorts.

All teachers were asked to provide names of anyone they knew who had a conflict with Derrick. The list they pieced together had twenty-eight names. Delaney Johansson was not one of them. The images on the surveillance camera were too blurry to be of any value.

Chapter 21

Faith

Faith, too, had started a collection. For her, it was jewellery. It was all she asked for if anyone ever quizzed her about gifts. The twelve-year-old had no interest in delicate necklaces or earrings; for her, it was heavier pendants, studded leather wrist bands or pins and badges for her Gold Coast Titans footy cap. She could barely wait until she was eighteen to get some tattoos, but for now, she had to settle for stick-on ones - usually picking a fantasy-style character with prominent eyes or teeth.

Her foster parents, Gayle and Ted, were wealthy, having just one child and unable to conceive a second. While she had her own bedroom, Faith had to keep company with Nadine, a prissy, self-centred fourteen-year-old passionate about boys and makeup.

It was a Thursday evening when the family of four sat down to an early dinner on the back patio overlooking the waterway, the private pontoon, the plunge pool, and Ted's pride and joy, his cruising motor yacht.

'This food smells divine,' said Ted as he sniffed in deeply, his head partly over the bowl of butter chicken curry. 'And the colour is outstanding.'

Gayle, a thin, fortyish blonde with disproportionately large breasts, arrived with the steaming rice. 'There we are. Can I serve anyone?'

Faith held her plate forward. From across the table, Nadine pushed hers in front of Faith's. 'Me, please,' she said with a smile and a tilt of her head as she looked at her foster sister.

'Now, girls,' cautioned Gayle. 'There's plenty for everyone.'

'It looks just great, love. I'm famished,' said Ted. 'You should get the recipe.'

Gayle gave him a wide-eyed look. 'What on earth for?'

'Our kitchen is magnificent… everything you could ever need… you know.' It was yet another futile attempt by him to get his wife into cooking. Gourmet Gold Dining, one of several upmarket food services the Scriver-Bunt family used, delivered the evening meal.

'Plenty of husbands cook too,' she replied. 'And I like the kitchen to look nice.'

'It's certainly uncontaminated by food,' he scoffed.

'I can learn,' said Faith, popping up a hand with a finger wave.

'Don't bother,' snapped Nadine. 'As if anyone would eat it. Err, yuk.'

Faith looked at the bleached blonde teenager and her whole face of makeup.

'What are you *looking* at?' sniggered Nadine.

'Why do you need to put lipstick on when we're about to eat?'

'I like to look nice. Maybe you could try it sometime. Anyway, Mum and I are going late-night shopping for some new fashion, not something that would interest you.'

'Come on you two,' said Gayle. 'You're both beautiful. Let's leave it at that.'

'One of us is. The other is an ugly duckling,' added Nadine quickly.

'Now, now!' Ted interrupted firmly. 'Let's be polite. And I'd like to say, Nadine, that your sister…'

'Foster sister,' interrupted Nadine.

'Yes, your *foster* sister has luscious auburn hair and lovely cheekbones. So there,' he nodded and smiled at his daughter.

'But her lips are too thin,' added Nadine. 'Boys like girls with full lips… like mine.' She pushed her lips out a little more than necessary.

'Can we change the subject please?' asked Faith.

'We should. Isn't it nice to all be together as a family,' said Ted.

'This family is a three plus one add-on,' scoffed Nadine. The teenager laughed to herself and began eating.

'You should be kinder to me… sis,' said Faith, emphasising *sis*.

Gayle leaned over closer to her foster daughter's ear. 'And Faith, you are welcome to come shopping with us tonight.'

'Pass.'

'When you get a bit older, sweetie,' continued Gayle, '… You will want to dress up nicely and wear makeup. It's good for the soul to look pretty and helps you get on in life.'

Faith reeled back as she looked at her foster mother's made-up face. She was sure Gayle was at least forty-five despite her always insisting that she was thirty-nine. *These two are like peas in a pod*, she thought.

'I think we've talked about this before,' said Faith as she slid her plate forward. She gave a big swallow, then said what she was thinking. 'I'm not like you, Gayle, or you, Nadine. I don't need to fill out my lips, straighten my nose and bleach my hair… because I'm not just on this planet to look for a man and get fucked, get married and have fucking kids.'

Nadine gasped, covered her mouth and looked at her father who dropped his fork. Gayle was momentarily stunned. Faith pushed her chair back and took off to her room.

*　　　*　　　*

After Ted had stacked the dishwasher, he decided to look in on Faith who had been in her room for the past hour. Gayle and Nadine had left for their late-night fashion shopping.

He strode up the stairs, taking them three at a time. While he never specifically worked out, Ted had an athletic build. He knocked on the upstairs bedroom door, waited a few seconds, brushed his hand over his widow's peak and short brown hair, checked his breath by breathing into his hand, and entered. Unlike Nadine's room, there was no lock. Faith was sitting on her bed, flicking through a Venom Dark Origin comic. She was still wearing her black denim jeans and a Harley-Davidson t-shirt.

'Are you okay?' he asked.

'Fine.'

Ted moved closer. 'I don't know how you can read in this light.' The curtains were drawn, and the only illumination came from a fantasy nightlight of a dragon sitting on an orb that glowed purple.

'I manage.'

He sat near her on the side of the bed. 'I know sometimes you feel that you're not part of this family...' Faith peered over the top of the comic and rolled her eyes. '... but I can assure you that you most definitely are. You're not like your Mum or Nadine, and you don't need to be; that's perfectly fine.'

'She's not my Mum.' Faith moved the comic away from her face.

'She's trying hard,' said Ted.

'No matter how hard she tries, she'll always be Gayle to me, Ted.'

He inched a little closer. 'I like that you're different. Different is great.'

'I'm all good here. You can go now.'

'You'll be thirteen soon. A teenager.'

'Yes, that's usually what it means - the next birthday after twelve.'

'You have beautiful hair. Long, dark, curly. A reddish tinge. He reached out to touch her ringlets, but she jerked away. 'Relax, Faith.' Ted placed a hand on her knee. Her legs were drawn up, with the comic now resting against them.

'What are you doing?'

'I want you to know how much I love how you are developing into a beautiful young woman.'

She stared at him for a moment, thinking. He gave her a broad smile.

'Huh… was that you the other night?' she asked. 'In the bathroom while I was in the shower. I thought it was Nadine coming in to grab her stupid makeup. I thought she put my towel to her face… but that was you… Jesus! No wonder you were in no hurry to fix that lock.'

'There is no need to feel embarrassed. Yes, you are developing breasts. Some pubic hair. That's so lovely.'

'Please leave, Ted. That's just sick. You're just an old pervert. Get out of here!' She moved sideways over the bed and huddled next to the wall.

'I can be very gentle.'

'Fuck off, Ted!' she yelled.

He lunged at her, grabbed her arm and pulled her to the middle of the single bed. She tried shoving him away. She kicked, slapped and squealed. He jumped on her, straddling her tummy and holding her arms down. She spat in his face.

'I'm your best fucking friend,' he shouted. 'You be nice, and your stay here can be pleasant for both of us.' He belted her hard across the face with an open hand. She tried kicking her knees into his back. He struck her again on the other cheek. She stopped struggling and panted.

'I'll leave...' he panted, too. 'But... we obviously need more time together. I'm a nice person. We can have our secrets... We *will* have our secrets. And a word of this to anyone else will make everything much worse for you. You must understand that your reputation with the Department is already littered with misbehaviour, violence, and absconding. No one will believe a word you say. Nod if we're clear on this.'

Faith nodded. Ted got off her and headed to the door, stopping and turning just before he left. 'Goodnight, Faith. You are beautiful.' He blew her a kiss. She gave him the finger. The door closed softly behind him.

Faith jumped from the bed. She positioned the desk chair under the door handle, grabbed some books, and wedged them as hard as she could under the door. She sank to the floor, huddled and sobbed.

After ten minutes, she blew her nose and roughly wiped her face with her shirt. She had been with the Scriver-Bunts for nearly two years. While she had felt Ted's eyes on her before, this was the first time he'd tried anything. Quite clearly, he had some plans for her future, but Faith was determined that would never happen. She sat in the middle of the floor. *Think twice, plan carefully, Faith,* she told herself. *Then, act decisively.*

As many thoughts flicked through her mind, she remembered a recent break-in and robbery in which a carpenter who lived just a few streets away had all his tools stolen. A plan began to evolve.

Later that evening, when Gayle and Nadine returned, Faith removed the books and the chair. Tonight, she would go without a shower.

Chapter 22

Faith's Plan

The initial part of Faith's scheme was never to be left alone at home with Ted until after her plan had been executed. His IT business of data management and online security, where he worked from home three days a week, presented some difficulties. Attending school helped to some extent, as did a couple of shopping excursions with Gayle, which wasn't all bad, as she managed to get away from her foster mum for a short time and buy some clothing she needed for her forthcoming activities. She did feign some interest in some makeup to keep Gayle happy.

Faith spent time looking out her bedroom window. Her room faced the front of the house, the driveway and the cul-de-sac of exclusive homes. There was the sloping tiled roof of the lower floor and a downpipe descending from the gutter into the rose garden. She needed to see if she could get up and down without attracting attention, damaging herself or breaking anything. Faith put olive oil on the sliding window to silence its creaks and squeaks. She worked out she could lever the fly screen out with a kitchen knife and easily clip it back in again.

She practised in the early morning hours, eventually learning the best positions for her feet and hands. Apart from a few thorny jabs from the roses, she was happy with this part of her plan.

Twice in recent nights, she deliberately went downstairs and through the lounge, triggering the security system from a sensor near the front door. She would then exit, locking the door behind her, climb up the pipe, and return to her room. After the second occurrence, Ted called the security firm to run a check. They found no problem and suggested it may have been a gecko walking over the sensor.

Six days later, on Wednesday evening, she needed to act.

The Scriver-Bunt home had a security camera directed from the front door and across the lawn; there was another at the rear, pointed towards the pontoon and motor yacht. In addition, there was a coded security keypad on the inside near both the front and back entrances. When activated, there was a thirty-second interval to enter the code after entry. As a matter of routine, Ted would activate the lower-level motion detectors every night before bed. Over the past few months, Gayle had twice activated the alarms when she absentmindedly staggered downstairs to access her stash of diazepam, completely forgetting to disarm the system.

At two in the morning, with a bath towel in hand, Faith headed quietly downstairs. She wore her brand-new, dark hooded tracksuit, thick black socks and some cloth gloves. She entered the code near the rear door. The red light on the panel changed to green. Next, she quickly went to the kitchen and grabbed a large glass tumbler from the cupboard.

At the back of the house was a general-purpose room where all the pool chemicals, garden equipment, assorted hand tools and several power tools were stored. Faith set the tumbler down on a workbench.

Outside, she threw her towel over the security camera, returned to the room and picked up an angle grinder and a power drill.

Faith made several trips from the room to the end of the pontoon, where she carefully lowered nearly all the tools into the water below the boat, letting them sink three metres to the muddy bottom. She held onto a hammer.

With an outside light and a half-moon in a clear sky, she was not invisible, but she was quiet.

Back in the general-purpose room, she first slipped a black mask over her face, then poured some pool acid into the glass tumbler. She left the room with a hammer in one hand and the tumbler in the other. After placing both items outside, she leaned back around the back door and punched in the code. The red, activated light came on.

Faith stood back outside, looking at the glass panels in the back door. She was nearly at the point of no return. *Think and plan. Have you done everything? Have you thought twice?* She paused and went through all the steps. She raised the hammer to smash the glass and then remembered the towel. *Fuck, Faith. Think!*

*   *   *

Upstairs, in the main bedroom, Ted woke and sat bolt upright. 'What the fuck was that?'

'What honey?' groaned Gayle as she turned to her other side.

'Sounded like something smashing. Glass maybe.' He spun his head from side to side, trying to detect further sounds.

'You're dreaming,' breathed his wife. 'I didn't hear anything.'

'Well, you wouldn't. Not with all that Valium on board.'

'That's not very nice,' she grumbled. 'Go back to sleep.'

Then, the alarm started with a high and low siren that no one could miss. Ted jumped up, grabbed a pitching wedge he kept under the bed, and took off downstairs, wearing only his pyjama shorts. Gayle dragged herself from the bed and slipped on her dressing gown. She ambled to the top of the stairs.

'Honey,' she yelled, competing with the alarm. 'Is everything alright?' As she took her first step on the staircase, a shrill scream pierced the air, clearly heard above the security system. Gayle knew it was Ted, despite never having heard him make such a painful sound. She ran and stumbled down the stairs supported by the railing. Nadine emerged from her room, huddled in her gown.

*   *   *

Thirty minutes later, an ambulance left the home with Ted sedated but still conscious in the back. A tearful Gayle accompanied him. With Nadine and Faith's help, she had poured large volumes of water over his face and eyes until the ambulance arrived. Nevertheless, his skin was blistered, red and pulpy. His eyelids seemed to have been consumed by the acid.

The police had cordoned off part of the rear of the home, and forensic experts were already gathering evidence and taking many photographs.

The girls sat in the lounge with a female officer who kept them company and asked basic questions. It would be at least twenty-four hours before an interview with Ted could be conducted.

*   *   *

After six weeks, a blind Edward Scriver-Bunt was discharged from the hospital. He still had several seeping burn wounds on his face and required daily dressings. Ted's breathing remained laboured. He had spent his first few hospital days in intensive care with respiratory burns from the hydrochloric acid vapour. He was told that his lungs may never completely recover.

While police investigations were ongoing, their preliminary assessment was that two gloved persons had broken into the home to steal the power tools. It seemed that at least one had made their getaway by boat while the other covered the security camera. It was noted that the security system had been reset. This was possibly a system error, as it had been malfunctioning recently. It was believed that one of the perpetrators would've been someone who knew the home's layout and had been inside before.

So far, they had interviewed friends, family members, and some tradespeople who had done odd jobs over the past few months. It was thought that the robbery, whilst more daring, was highly likely related to the recent break-in and theft of tools from a nearby carpenter.

For Faith, the second part of her plan was beginning. She would gradually make this home her domain. She would get everything she wanted. Ted would guide and teach her about computers, mainly searching for missing persons, namely her parents and brother. The self-absorbed Gayle and Nadine would not be up to the task of managing an ailing and blind husband and father. Manipulation would be child's play. The family would be hers for the taking.

Chapter 23

The Group - Part 1

In a meeting room at a community centre near Broadbeach on the Gold Coast, six young adults helped themselves to tea, coffee and biscuits. For the most part, they strolled about with only brief interactions with one another.

Apart from the table supporting the hot water urn and the beverage accessories, there was little else in the room besides a circle of seven evenly spaced chairs surrounding a low, oval-shaped coffee table. A box of tissues sat at either end.

A young, fit-looking man, and the only person wearing shorts, slid a chair back and sat. Everyone was dressed casually.

A man wearing black jeans and a black t-shirt with a faded Black Sabbath band picture dropped two spoons of sugar into his cup and stirred. An untidy young guy with long knotted hair came alongside and lightly bumped his shoulder.

'Hey, Del,' mumbled the untidy man as he reached across and grabbed a mug.

'Hey there, Tom,' came the reply. 'How's things?'

'Ah… ya know.' Tom kept his head down and continued making his drink. Del patted him on the shoulder. 'Today will be a better day, my friend.' Both young men moved away with their coffees. 'Have you found new accommodation yet?'

'Huh… sort of,' replied Tom. 'A knockdown in Beaufort Street.'

'I guess a few nomads live there?'

'Oh yeah, users mostly.'

'Damn Tom. Sorry to hear that.'

There was a loud clapping of hands. 'Good morning, all. In two minutes, we need to kick things off. Bring your coffee over.' It was Eduardo Mendes, a forty-year-old, dark-skinned man and the group leader. Mendes was tall and had a smooth, almost melodic voice that sounded like he could burst into song at any moment.

He sat down directly across from the only other seated person. 'Hello, Myles. How was your weekend?' he asked while displaying a broad smile that showed a complete set of teeth that seemed whiter than white against his skin colouring.

Myles partly raised his head, but not enough to make eye contact. He pushed his Nikes across the wooden floor. 'Fine,' he eventually said.

'Fine is usually okay, but as you know, Myles, it is not a particularly revealing response. And one that discourages further conversation.'

'Yeah,' mumbled Myles.

Eduardo looked around. Others moved over and sat. The counsellor nodded and smiled as the chairs filled.

'Thank you all for coming. It's heart-warming to see that we have full attendance today. Good morning again.' He opened his long arms and looked around at everyone. He received a few mumbled *good mornings,* a *hi Eduardo* and some unclear murmurs from the six participants.

'As usual, I'll start today by telling you a little about myself,' he chirped. 'Feel free to share and discuss this with each other during the break -whatever you choose. Then, we will briefly recap last week's session and chat about your homework. And the thought for the day is this - *emotional baggage: unpack it or send it packing* - pass it on and share.'

This was the usual beginning for each session. Eduardo hoped his attendees would model his self-disclosures, and to some extent, this strategy was successful. Near the end of the meeting, he always left one or two tasks as homework to complete, if possible, before the next get-together.

Del caught the eye of April Armstrong, sitting across from him, and gave her a nod and a smile. She returned the smile and held her gaze on him longer than necessary for a brief hello.

On Del's left was Jerome Gillard; he broke eye contact with April and leaned over to him. 'Did you do that homework, mate?'

'Tried,' came the soft reply. 'Think I managed something.' Jerome was a twenty-two-year-old, undernourished guy with multiple healed scars over both arms that he no longer bothered trying to conceal.

'As you all know, I grew up in Angola and became a counsellor here in Australia,' revealed Eduardo. 'You may not know that I studied for four years in Angola to become a Catholic priest. I dropped out for a couple of reasons. The loneliness was intense, and I was craving more social contact. I also witnessed some deliberate lying by senior clergy members who should've known better. I became disillusioned and left to find something more rewarding. If you have any questions, I'm happy to answer them as best as I can.'

'Do you still believe in God?' asked Celine Woods, a short, barrel-shaped lady beside Myles Ramsay. Celine was nineteen and always had a question, usually very direct, sometimes bordering on rudeness. She had several biscuits in her lap.

'Yes, I do,' replied the counsellor.

'What were they lying about? Was it sexual abuse?' she continued and then pushed a complete biscuit into her mouth.

'It was that and psychological abuse, Celine.'

The nineteen-year-old chomped away quickly and raised a stop hand as she chewed. 'Were you abused?' she asked with her mouth still half full.

'Fortunately, I was not.'

The room went quiet. The counsellor let the silence linger a moment before he moved on. 'Okay, thank you, Celine, for those questions. Now, we had a good discussion about relaxation and stress reduction last week,' said Eduardo, emphasising the keywords. As he spoke, he swept his hands from his knees to his face, closed his eyes and took a slow, deep breath. Celine, Tom and April all mimicked some of his actions.

'We then tried some techniques,' continued the counsellor. 'Some we noted were simple to describe but a bit harder to put into practice. The homework I left you was to find just one time in your past when you had some positive feelings. This could be anywhere, at any time. I asked you to try to think about it in as much detail as possible...' he paused and looked at his group. 'You could write it down or just have it clear in your mind. How did we do with this? Would anyone like to share?'

Del, April and Celine looked around at the group; the three others diverted their eyes in avoidance.

'What about you, Myles?' said Celine. 'You hardly spoke last week.'

'Not today, please,' he replied, not lifting his head.

Del reached out to Jerome and pushed him lightly on his arm. 'Come on, mate. You said you gave it a go. What have you got for us?'

Jerome whispered, 'Okay, okay.' He took a breath and then raised a hand. 'I can... like... say something.'

'Thank you, Jerome. How did it go for you?' continued Eduardo.

'I remembered a time… well, a few years back…'

'Yes… we'd like to hear about that. Please, share it with the group,' said the counsellor.

'I was alone in the dunes at Surfer's Beach. It was a clear day but a bit windy. The surf was loud, and the waves were rolling into these giant tubes. Is this okay so far?'

'Yes, Jerome. Please continue.'

'Thank you… you see, I had been upset… distraught because Tabitha had dumped me. I started to cut my arms for the first time. It felt good… like all the stress was leaving my body as the blood poured out…'

'Jerome,' interrupted Eduardo. 'I've made a mistake in not making this task clearer. I apologise. The memory we seek is meant to be positive and not connected to harm to self or others. The memory you describe is a maladaptive response, which is not a desirable way of moving forward and improving our lives and self-esteem.'

'Oh… sorry, Eduardo. I've fucked up.'

'No, no. That's okay. Thank you for sharing something that I know was difficult for you.' The counsellor stood and squatted next to Jerome and placed a comforting arm on his shoulder. 'But now that we are a little clearer on the ground rules, is there anyone else?'

Eventually, the discussion got moving, and several people opened up with positive memories they were prepared to share. Del spoke up about his childhood when he found marbles in the street and how excited he felt. After fifty minutes, the group, as was the usual routine, took a short break.

April made a beeline for Del. At twenty-five, she was the oldest and the tallest of the six. She hurried across the floor in rapid short steps, her unrestrained boobs bouncing underneath her square-necked tank top, which also showed off her midriff. 'I like your hair,' she announced as soon as she was close. Del's hair was light brown, collar length and neat.

'Thank you, April. That's nice of you to say. Yours is lovely too,' he replied to the bleached blonde.

'Yes, it is, isn't it,' she said coyly, touching her hair. 'I learned that in group you know,' she continued. 'Giving compliments. It helps get people talking… It makes people feel good… and I love talking to you, Del…. It makes me feel good. You know.' She moved a bit closer. 'I like your shirt.' She touched the faded face of Ozzie Osbourne.

'Good for you. It's an old favourite. A bit worn out now, I think.' Del took a slow step back to gain a little space.

'No!' she yelled. Heads turned. 'That's not what you say.'

'Sorry.'

'You say, *thank you, April, you're very kind!* You don't throw my compliment away. You just don't, Del!'

'I said I'm sorry.'

'And you don't step away. That's rude.' She slapped his chest with an open hand and stormed off. Del looked around at his other group of friends and shrugged. He saw a few smirks and heard a few chuckles, even from Myles.

After they regrouped, Eduardo divided them into three pairs. The object was to chat to your partner about any topic you liked, and then they were to relate the information they heard back to you. If possible, maintain eye contact and show appropriate interest in the other person using non-verbal gestures. Del was with Myles, Celine with Tom, and April with Jerome. The three pairs had turned their chairs to face each other.

'This sounds hard for me,' said Myles. 'I'm not a big fan of people.'

'You made it here today. That's a good start,' said Del kindly. 'I know you play some computer games. Maybe you can tell me about one of them.'

Myles breathed heavily with his head down. After a minute, he said, 'Okay.' He glanced at Del. 'Battlefield is a World War One game... very realistic images... can be hard to watch for some people...' Myles' gaze was up and down between his shoes and Del.

'Wow. Sounds interesting,' said Del.

'You can play on different battlefields around the world... France, Germany, even the Arabian desert...' Myles continued to describe the game, describing various battle scenes involving soldiers and tanks. As he spoke, he relaxed, and his eye contact improved.

'There is this part that I really love,' he looked up. Del noticed his eyes. Myles had two colours in each eye. His left was blue with a wedge of brown, while his right was blue with a wedge of green. 'You can drive a World War One tank and blast away the enemy and buildings; it's so cool...' his speech stopped. 'What, Del?'

'Your eyes are different colours. I've never seen that before. Like marbles... wow, like cat's-eye marbles... damn... oh, sorry Myles, I've interrupted your story.'

'It's okay,' the game player dropped his head and stopped talking.

'Sorry, mate. But... well, your eyes are... amazing... fascinating...'

'Stop,' said Myles. 'Please.'

'Okay, I should tell my story. I have one from when I was in primary school. It's about this kid who stole my marbles...'

Myles kept his head down, raised a hand and said, 'Enough! Don't! Please don't take the piss. Fuck off! Leave me alone!'

Chapter 24

Preparations

The small room's windows were covered with cardboard and thick black tape. An uncovered light bulb hung on its wiring from the high ceiling, swinging slightly as an oscillating fan at the end of a wooden workbench jerked its way back and forth in a semicircle.

A bench-top grinder with two spinning wheels whirred away. Two hands wearing protective gloves adjusted the tool rest to the desired position. Then, they took up a solid aluminium ice cream scoop and worked the edges against the spinning wheel. After several minutes, the work shifted to a flat, wet, sharpening stone to hone the tool. The edges were worked slowly in the same direction, checking every couple of minutes to view the shiny, sharpened edges.

To one side of the closed door was a small wooden table and chair facing a wall-mounted mirror. On the table was a collection of makeup - a tray of assorted paints, brushes in various sizes, makeup wax, liquid latex, skin powders, false noses, and loose hair pieces in greys, browns and whites. Sitting on the corner were two books with coloured tabs protruding in many places - The Colour Atlas of Ophthalmology and Clinical Procedures in Primary Eye Care.

The gloved hands held an apple in one hand and the honed scoop in the other. The apple turned as scooped balls fell one after the other, each extracted with precision and minimal effort.

The scoop was wiped with a cloth and honed with a few more glides over the stone before being placed into an empty vinyl pencil case and zipped shut.

Chapter 25

The Doctor

Faith Scriver-Bunt pushed the elevator button for level twelve - her fifth visit to the tall Southport building to see her psychiatrist.

With her agreement, her surname was changed three years ago after the Scriver-Bunts officially adopted her.

Her life there had turned around dramatically after Ted was assaulted with acid and lost his sight. She had provided him with care. Initially helping with his dressings, which Gayle and Nadine could barely even touch without feeling ill, and later assisting the blind man with many daily tasks. She had been instrumental in getting additional rails in the bathrooms and other areas. Faith kept her eye on his oxygen supply and medications and would order more as necessary. She had helped him adjust after each of three more surgeries for his burns. Preparing meals for the family had become one of her strengths, and even Nadine had to admit they were tasty. Ted never again made any attempt to assault or intimidate her. He remained thankful and polite, although he had asked her many questions about that fateful day. A memory had come back to him where, for a split second, he saw someone of about her height in a dark tracksuit, and then everything turned to excruciating pain and total darkness. Ted had to stop work and sell his motor yacht. Financially, the Scriver-Bunts still managed quite well, thanks to rental income from several properties. Ted had suggested to Gayle and Nadine that they may need to cut back on some of their clothing, makeup and Botox, but this was yet to happen.

The lift opened, and Faith strolled into the plush foyer and presented herself at the marble-topped reception desk. Four private psychiatrists shared the many rooms in the office. The nineteen-year-old needed only to nod at Val, the bespectacled middle-aged lady, who politely said, 'Good morning, Faith. Please take a seat. Doctor Huang will see you shortly.'

She had barely time to peruse the pictures in a National Geographic magazine when Doctor Lulu Huang's smiling oriental face appeared. The two saw each other, and the psychiatrist held open the door.

Faith sat in a leather reclining office chair inside the consulting room. Her doctor sat opposite. A low table between them held a water jug, glasses, and tissues.

Dr Huang was in her mid-fifties; her hair was long and now mostly grey and tied back into a bun at the back of her head. Her light pink pantsuit was elegant and slimming. 'Nice to see you again, Faith,' she said. Her voice was clear and soft, with a slight Chinese accent. 'You have some colour on you today.' Faith's favourite colour for several years had been black. Today, she had chunky black boots, jeans, a black blouse, a black beret, and a chunky chain necklace, each link in a different rainbow colour. 'I do like the contrast against the black. It's gorgeous,' continued the psychiatrist.

'Thanks. I hate to say it, but it was Gayle's idea, and I do quite like it.'

'Is everything okay at home?'

'Same, same… you know.'

'You and Ted?'

'Huh… I think I've reached a point where I no longer despise him. There were times when I wanted to hurt him, and I did. I took the dressings off too quickly; I wiped the tender skin harder than necessary. Other things too… yeah.'

'Last week, I felt you were on the brink of telling me something. Maybe about Ted, maybe about your real dad. Shall we explore that a little more deeply? Move a bit further into the relaxation?'

Faith took a big sigh. 'I'm not sure. It might be upsetting. I don't want to say something that I might regret. I wouldn't like to get myself in trouble,' she shrugged.

'Trouble!' exclaimed the doctor. 'With me... not likely. You know this is absolutely one hundred percent confidential.' The psychiatrist gave a reassuring smile.

'Yeah, I know that.' Faith looked at the floor. 'To be honest, I have some barriers to full disclosure about several things.'

'Yes. That's why, with full relaxation and a trance-like state, you would find it easier and more comfortable to discuss some of the hard stuff and then move forward.'

'Hypnosis?'

'That word has connotations I don't care for,' replied the psychiatrist with the warmest of smiles. 'It makes people think they are not in control and that their mind can be altered somehow. I suggest we build on what we've already achieved with the deep relaxation process. I believe it's the next logical step.'

Faith gave an unsure look and pushed her lips to one side.

'Let's agree that if there's anything you're not happy with, I'll delete any recording and keep no other type of record. I'll also ensure that you fully recall everything we discuss.'

'Hmm... okay then. Almost sounds like an offer too good to refuse,' she joked. 'Let's go for it.' Faith tilted the chair back. She sank into the soft leather, took a couple of deep breaths, and closed her eyes. 'Here goes nothing.'

Doctor Huang's soft voice took on a soothing quality as she went through a deep relaxation procedure. After some minutes, she used keywords selected by Faith and repeated them three times to deepen Faith's relaxation even further. 'Bright eyes … Bright eyes … Bright eyes.'

The nineteen-year-old's breathing deepened and slowed; any sign of tightness in her facial muscles disappeared as her lips parted slightly.

'Faith, we've talked about Ted Scriver-Bunt and your real father, Jasper Johansson. Let's look further into that conversation,' said the psychiatrist softly. Faith's head gave the smallest of nods. 'We know your last contact with your biological father was when you left for a brief stay with your Aunty when you were nine years old. When did you last hear any news of your dad?'

Faith groaned a little before she spoke. 'It was before I… before Ted got injured,' she said in a slow whisper while adjusting her response. The slight stall in her speech did not go unnoticed by Lulu Huang. 'Ted said bad stuff to me sometimes. He told me that my dad was in a mental institution and would probably never get released. He said he had a friend who works in health in Sydney. I called places myself but couldn't get any answers.'

'As far as you know, your dad had paranoid schizophrenia?'

'Yes, Mum had said that. But we promised never to say it in front of him.'

'What do you think happened to your mother?'

'Ted used to say she ran off to get away from my brother and me, but I know that's bullshit. She wouldn't leave us…' Faith's head rolled a little from side to side. 'I've often wondered if Dad might have killed her. He's a smart man, devious; if anyone could get away with it, he could.'

'Are you smart and devious like your dad?'

'Yes… but not in a bad way. Dad always told us as kids to think, plan, and take decisive action.'

'Is that what happened with Ted? Did you take action to sort out that problem?'

Faith's body squirmed in her chair. She took a moment to respond, then said, 'Yes, I took action. I adjusted Ted's attitude.'

'I'd like to take you back to that night when Ted was injured. Remember that you are in the safest, most confidential place and that I'll wake you if you become distressed. Tell me how you enacted your plan…'

Faith spoke slowly, going through every detail, from the purchase of the dark tracksuit to throwing the acid into Ted's eyes. Lulu Huang sat back in her chair; her eyes widened. Contrary to the psychiatrist's expectations, her client was completely calm.

'And after the acid throwing, what was the next step?' asked the psychiatrist, doing her best to keep her voice uniform.

Faith went on to cover her return to her bedroom via the drainpipe, her appearance at the crime scene, the arrival of the police and ambos, and Ted being transported to the hospital with Gayle alongside. It was at this moment that tears formed in her closed eyes.

'Does this upset you?'

'A little… you see, I didn't intend for him to have long-term respiratory problems. I hadn't thought about the fumes from the acid burning his lungs. I was upset with myself for not thinking that through beforehand. Dad would've been disappointed in me… sorry Dad.'

'Yet you were content for him to go blind and have serious facial burns?' Lulu swallowed heavily.

'Oh, yes, of course. I had foreseen all of that. That was my plan. He was never going to see my body again. Never. That part was simply perfection.'

'And now it seems you are probably his main carer. You are doing so much for a man that you dislike. Faith, there is an unconscious defence mechanism called *undoing*. This is where a person tries to cancel out destructive thoughts or actions by engaging in almost opposite behaviour. Do you understand what I'm saying here?'

There was quiet for a moment while Lulu watched her patient contemplate. Eventually, there was a nod and a faint *yes*.

'Does this *undoing* possibly apply to you?' asked Doctor Huang.

'I live with wealthy people. I get a good allowance, and I get almost everything I want. I have more freedom now than I've ever had. So, there is no undoing; there is just doing for my benefit.'

*   *   *

After leaving Faith with a couple of positive affirmations, the psychiatrist woke her from her trance and instructed her to have total recall of everything that had been revealed and discussed.

Faith spent a few minutes crying and using several tissues. After composing herself, she said, 'I don't think my real dad murdered my mother.'

'Is that what made you weep on waking up?'

'Yes.'

'I see. Yes, that would be a challenging thing to deal with. And there is nothing to suggest he did that. Your mother is listed as a missing person, an all-too-common occurrence in this country. Let's hope that sometime in the not-too-distant future, you can get some resolution to this.'

Faith blew her nose. 'What now? Do I go to jail?'

'Absolutely not. I won't be documenting any of that. I've already deleted the digital recording. But there is something I think may benefit you.'

'A lobotomy?' Faith smiled.

'We will put that on hold for now,' chuckled Lulu. 'No, a better alternative is some group therapy. There is a very supportive and well-recommended therapist called Eduardo Mendes. I'll give you his card. With your agreement, I'd like to place you on the waiting list, and I can contact him and see if I can give you some priority.'

'I can't go blabbing about all this in a group!'

'Of course you can't. No, no, no. The emphasis is more on social interactions, communication, self-awareness, and self-care. To me, these are good things for you to target. These are areas that we identified during previous appointments. Those other issues will be just between you and me.'

'Okay, I'm good with that. You can refer me.'

'Excellent. The group has twelve weekly meetings, and participants can join at any time. The sessions are cyclical.'

'Thank you, Lulu.'

*   *   *

As Faith descended in the elevator, she glanced at the business card of Eduardo Mendes - Counsellor/Therapist, handed to her by Doctor Huang. She pushed it into the left rear pocket of her black jeans. From the right pocket, she pulled out a leaflet and unfolded it. On the front, it read:

Group Therapy
Counsellor - Eduardo Mendes

Bond with others.

Learn Mindfulness.

Improve Your Resilience

Improve Your Self-Esteem

Faith smiled and whispered to herself. 'I'm in.'

Everything was working out as she had planned, from instigating her GP's initial referral to Lulu Huang a few weeks ago to the follow-up with Eduardo Mendes and group therapy. She had left nothing to chance.

Chapter 26

The Angel

It had been nearly three weeks, and the killer had been patient. The current routine of the victim had been sufficiently established. The regular Monday to Friday, eight-kilometre evening run through Albert Park on the Gold Coast; the fast sprint finish trying to better his time; an eight-minute cool down walk back home before a hot shower. Myles Ramsay would then settle in for an evening of online gaming and a little TV while munching on snacks and an occasional food delivery. Thus far, the killer had only seen two other young people visit him - a male and a female on separate occasions, both staying less than thirty minutes.

Even Myles's pre-run behaviour had been studied - the dressing in the regular running gear and Nikes, the gulping of a few mouthfuls of a sports drink, the stretching using the front fence and lamppost, the light trot to the park before the run proper.

For the most part, Myles followed the weekend park-run five-kilometre course, winding his way through the park before doubling back on the second lap to increase his running distance to eight kilometres. He'd then head home to nearby Pacific Boulevard.

He avoided running on the weekend when hundreds of others would be out there getting in his way and exacerbating his anxiety - mums and dads with strollers, walkers, people with dogs, noisy children, athletes, aspiring athletes showing off their activewear, and the intolerable social chin-waggers. Over recent weeks, it had been early evening runs Monday to Friday, plus an occasional random early weekend walk to nowhere in particular, always on his own.

Twice while he was out, and for approximately twenty minutes, the killer had been inside his home. Myles lived alone, and rather than carry keys while running, he left them under a rock, hidden in a leafy pot plant near his front door.

Rather careless, thought the killer. But, on the other hand, he would have no reason to believe there was someone ready to take more than just his life.

On a Thursday evening in July, in fading light, a person resembling a dishevelled elderly man with long grey hair pushed a shopping trolley full of junk up to a park bench in Albert Park, about four hundred metres from where the park run would start and finish, had it been a weekend. He sat. Behind the bench was a thick crop of trees and a few acacia bushes bordering a waterway - an offshoot of the nearby Nerang River. To the left, the pathway turned under the motorway and then around the creeks and waterholes of Albert Park. The visibility of the immediate area was less than usual, thanks to the destruction of the nearest light and security camera, pieces of which lay on the path and nearby grass.

From what the killer had noted, Thursday evenings, for whatever reason, appeared to be the least attractive for random walkers, dog lovers and joggers.

Today, Myles would run slower, thanks to the Rohypnol added to his sports drink. The calculation of when he may stop running and ultimately pass out was not exact. Still, the killer had considered his weight, level of fitness, and his drinking of approximately two hundred millilitres before each run. So, with the remaining twilight, the killer felt reasonably confident that a walking or staggering Myles Ramsay would soon be in view.

*   *   *

The killer tapped a mobile phone and checked the time. Myles was precisely on schedule. He stumbled from the path to the grass but managed to stay upright. He regained composure and gathered himself, continuing at a much slower pace. He shook his head.

'Fucking anti-depressants,' he shouted to himself. He slowed to a walk. 'Fucking psychiatrists,' he yelled.

He briefly recalled a discussion with the doctor who believed that his social isolation was the result of a depressive illness. Two months ago, Myles had reluctantly agreed to both a trial of anti-depressant medication and to attend the community centre for group therapy.

Suddenly, the runner lunged to one side and fell to the grass. A hand took hold of his upper arm as he tried to regain his feet.

'Hey, young man. Are you okay?'

Myles managed to see the face of what looked like an older man. The long, grey hair fell onto his face. 'Hey…' he panted. 'Please… help me?'

'Hello, Myles. My name is Angel. You are very fortunate because my sole purpose is to do just that.' The voice was both husky and breathy.

Several puzzling thoughts tumbled quickly through his mind. *Do I know you? A man called Angel; this must be a good thing. What's happening to me? Am I dying?* 'Call… an ambulance… please...' he panted. His world was spinning. A dark curtain was descending.

'We'll see. Move a little this way.' Angel guided a stumbling Myles a few metres, letting him fall near a clump of bushes, long grass, and a few trees. The bank to the waterway was only two metres away. Myles let out a gasp as he lost consciousness. Angel dragged him a little further into the foliage.

Chapter 27

Discovery

Detectives Michelle Gardiner and Kevin Milford looked down at Myles Ramsay's body. Gardiner donned a face mask and gloves and checked the surrounding area. Her colleague followed her lead. Both already wore shoe coverings. Michelle was the senior detective assigned to the case by her boss, Inspector Charlie Forsyth, who quickly informed her that … *Albert Park is a popular place. It's a busy place. There are cameras. They'd be witnesses. Wrap this one up quickly, Gardiner.*

Forensics had already examined the scene, taken many photographs and bagged some evidence. They stood by, waiting for the detectives to complete their inspection. Myles's body lay on his back, with his head tilted to one side. It was positioned next to a tall eucalyptus tree and between two low wattle bushes, which provided partial concealment from the cement path and the homes across the waterway. An early morning jogger had discovered the body when he stopped to urinate near the trees.

'What's with those eyes?' said Kevin, the older and taller of the two. He squatted and leaned closer. His girth, together with his current position, quickly became uncomfortable. He pushed his hands into his sides, groaned and stood after only a few seconds.

Michelle dropped to her haunches and removed a biro from her shirt pocket. 'Listen,' she said. She reached across Myles's head and tapped one of his eyeballs with the end of the pen. There was a clicking sound. She repeated it with the other eye.

'What the fuck?' Kevin drew his head back.

'His eyes have been replaced with marbles - large marbles. I think they call the bigger ones *tom-bowlers, dobbers* or *smashers,*' she replied calmly. 'Both his eyeballs and eyelids have been removed.

Myles's face looked like it had a red, bloodied mask over where his eyes once were and down to the ears, where blood had flowed from the eye sockets. There was a deep red congealed circle around both marble eyes, and while there were bloody smears over the tom-bowlers, it was not enough to hide the green feathered vane in the centre of each glass marble.

'There doesn't seem to be any ragged marks or tears. What do you think that suggests?' she asked her older but less experienced colleague.

'Hmm... something very sharp was used, I guess.'

'Yes, and the killer had some level of skill.'

'And you recognised them as marbles straight away?' Kevin glanced at his partner.

'Among other unusual things, Milford, my son, collects marbles. These types are called cat's-eyes.'

'Kids still play with marbles?'

'Was more popular in the sixties and seventies.'

'Yeah, the pre-tech era.'

'This was a premeditated attack. The light and security camera have been smashed. There are other cameras. We can check the footage back at the office.'

Detective Gardiner scanned the rest of the body. 'Can't see any other obvious injuries. We'll see what forensics and the post-mortem turn up. And we'll need to see if there's any history of similar cases.'

She stood and looked at her companion. 'Are you okay, Milford?'

'Yeah, yeah,' he nodded rapidly. 'Fine.'

'Good. I don't take well to people throwing up near me. Your colour had me concerned.' Michelle was often straightforward and firm with her colleagues but had chosen to be even more so with Kevin Milford. The guy was learning, and she wanted no misunderstandings, no fuck-ups and no additional frustrations. She moved from the scene and removed her protective wear. The lean thirty-two-year-old headed at a brisk walk to the car. Milford was still floundering with his shoe covers.

Chapter 28

The Group - Part 2

Everyone took their seats in the circle. Three with coffees, and Celine hoarding a few biscuits.

'One absentee today,' said Eduardo. Myles Ramsay had not arrived. This was not particularly unusual as he had missed two earlier sessions.

'It could be my fault,' said Del, raising his hand. 'I think I upset him last week. It was completely unintentional. I made a careless comment about his appearance, and he took offence and stopped talking.'

'I won't hear of it, Del,' Eduardo waved two open hands. 'No one here is to blame. Yes, we are all fragile, and if someone accidentally pushes one of our buttons, that's unfortunate, but we all know it can happen occasionally. It's a risk, sharing, socialising, passing thoughts onto others, and I'm so proud of you all for taking up the challenge to make positive changes to some areas of your life.'

The counsellor looked at his five charges. There were a couple of nods of agreement.

'You look nice today, Eduardo,' said April with a big smile.

The Angolan man wore a light blue cotton suit with the jacket open over a white t-shirt. 'Thank you, April. Very kind.' Celine's hand popped up. 'Yes, Celine.'

'The light colours make your skin look blacker,' she announced proudly.

'Thank you for sharing that thought, Celine.' He waited a moment, then continued. 'Okay, once again, I have something to reveal about myself. First, though, a little rhyming thought for the day - *A little stress will help you think, but with too much, your brain will kink.*' Del and Tom smiled. Celine tilted her head and pulled a face. Jerome wasn't paying attention.

'I like kinky,' said April.

'Thank you, April,' said Eduardo. 'Anyway, you might like to think about that later. Share it. Pass it on, you know the drill… Now, I've already told you that I did some studies to become a priest, and you will all know that I hold a degree in counselling. It may come as a surprise and seem a tad unusual, but I've also done studies in clowning!'

Celine was the first to speak. 'You mean clowning as in being a clown?'

'Yes, that is correct.'

'Why do you need to study so that you can be a stupid person?'

'I prefer the word silly to stupid. But yes, you can study clowning. It's not essential; anyone can dress up and be a clown. There are no restrictions.'

'I think Tom is like a clown without makeup,' added Celine as she crunched on a ginger nut. 'I think it's his messy hair, unshaven face and reddish-looking nose.' Tom looked at her blandly.

'I'm working on my dreadlocks… fatso,' he said in a monotone.

'Guys,' interrupted Eduardo. 'I hark back to the group rules. We agreed to be tolerant of our differences and avoid offensive language.'

'Ahh… yeah… okay, sorry, Celine,' mumbled Tom.

'I don't think calling someone a clown is wrong,' she exclaimed, spitting out some crumbs as she spoke.

'Celine, please,' said the counsellor calmly.

'Huh… I'm sorry then, Tom,' said Celine. 'But it doesn't change the fact that your hair is a mess.'

'Good Celine, let's leave it at that. I want to tell you that I went to the London Clown School for several months. I find being a clown a joyful experience. It often amuses those both old and young. And sometimes being silly and having a laugh is a good way of releasing tension.'

'Eduardo, do you still dress up as a clown?' asked Del.

'A few times a year, that's about it.'

'Well,' said Celine loudly. 'It looks like there's some makeup near your left ear. You didn't clean yourself properly.'

'Oh dear,' said Eduardo. He grabbed a bunch of tissues from the centre table and wiped away some whiteish makeup. 'Thank you, Celine. Perhaps we should see how the homework went this week.'

The five looked less than excited, but some discussion about barriers to effective communication got underway.

*   *   *

During the short break, April again chased up Del for a chat, her antics from last week far from her mind. Del had done his best to chat with Jerome, but the scarred young man wasn't the greatest talker, and April had little trouble inserting herself into the conversation.

At first, she stood close and grinned at Del, then took a deep breath and placed her hands over her heart. Her head tilted as she pursed her lips and then spoke: 'Can you read my nonverbal communications, Del? What do you think I'm saying?' She turned herself a little, so her back was now towards Jerome.

'I think you have some chest pain, and you're telling me you'd like to get Botox,' he said quickly and took a step back.

'You!' she shouted as she tightened her fists but quickly relaxed. 'Ah… you're joking with me.' She waved a finger at him. 'But being a fucking clown does not suit you, Del. So, don't be a smart arse.'

'I do think that your body language is isolating Jerome.' Del stepped around her to include him in their circle.

'Yes,' she said, throwing her head back. 'That was intentional. At least you got something right.' She strode away.

'She's got the hots for you, mate,' said Jerome.

'Yeah,' sighed Del. 'Lucky me,' he added with a roll of his eyes.

*   *   *

With the group back together, Eduardo continued.

'I would like to *focus* our last thirty minutes… and saying *focus* is very apt because I'm referring to eyes. Focusing on the eyes.' The counsellor placed a finger on either side of his face and opened his eyes wider. 'Eyes can be, as we already know, a powerful form of nonverbal communication. What can the eyes tell us? There are so many things, so if you have an idea, let the group know, and if you could physically demonstrate it, that would be useful.' A hand shot up. 'No hands required, Celine.'

'They can show you are hungry… like this…' she opened her eyes and mouth wide then licked her lips '… especially when you see pictures of yummy food.'

'They can show boredom,' said Del, exaggeratedly rolling his eyes.

'Not with me, I hope, Del,' said Eduardo.

'No, no, definitely not Eduardo… they can also… make you think that someone is…' his words petered out.

'Is what?'

'Is… like… sorry. I've just remembered something from when I was young.'

'Do you feel inclined to share this with the group, Del?'

'I could… but it's a bit unpleasant. If no one minds…' he looked around, there seemed to be no objections. The counsellor nodded. 'Okay, when I was much younger, my father, who was not well, said my and my sister's eyes were black. Like some evil possessed us.'

'Oh dear, how did this make you feel?' asked Eduardo.

'Frightened. We thought he was going to hurt us, but he didn't. Not long after, Mum took us to Aunt Theresa's place.'

'That's so awful,' said April.

'Sounds scary,' added Tom.

'Excuse me,' said Celine. 'I need a biscuit.' She left for a quick visit to the beverage table.

There was a loud knock on the door, followed by it swinging open. A policeman's head appeared. 'Counsellor!' he yelled. 'A moment, please.'

Eduardo Mendes got up immediately and moved quickly to the officer. 'This intrusion is uncalled for. We should not be interrupted.'

'Your absent client. Mister Myles Ramsay has been murdered,' said the officer bluntly. 'Some detectives are here.'

Chapter 29

Bad News

Despite his reluctance, Eduardo accepted the detectives' need to interview the group members individually. First, though, he had to inform the group of the event, make them aware of the detectives' requirements, and invite each to go to another smaller room for a recorded interview if they agreed.

The group reassembled. The two detectives and the uniformed officer stood a few metres away. There was obvious discomfort in the five attendees, with head-turning, fidgeting and soft chattering.

'Thank you all for shortening your break to reassemble. Something has happened. I must tell you all that I have some very sad news. Whatever I tell you, and however it affects you, you must all stay here with me, with each other, so that we can look after one another.' Eduardo spoke with his usual sing-song-type voice, using a higher melodic tone on some keywords. With a brief pause, he checked out his flock. They were already rattled, with Jerome, April, and Del even more so.

He decided to deliver the news clearly and succinctly, then manage the fallout as best he could. 'I'm shattered to my core to tell you all that our good friend Myles has been murdered.'

April squealed and dropped to the floor, lying face down and bawling loudly. Del had his head in his hands and was over-breathing. Celine darted over and grabbed more biscuits. Jerome looked calm but started dragging his fingernails over his forearms. Tom disregarded a group rule, switched on his phone and began scrolling through social media.

First things first, the counsellor sat on the floor with April. Her noises had quickly diminished into sobs and stilted gasps for air. 'We are all here for you, April.' He stroked her hair. 'When you feel ready, take your seat.'

She rolled onto her back and looked at Mendes. 'I... I always liked Myles... he was... truly... my second favourite after Del...,' she panted. 'I think he liked me... he was timid... his non-verbal behaviour was always a bit negative though...'

'Hmmm...,' nodded Eduardo. He helped her up and got her to her seat. 'There you go. Thank you, April.' He returned to his chair.

'I'm so sorry for all of you. This is an unimaginable tragedy. I'll do something today that I rarely do: I'll give each of you my mobile number. I want you to feel free to call me anytime over the coming week...' he paused.

'How was he killed?' asked Celine.

'Really, Celine, I don't know or care to know.'

'Huh... I thought it was a good question. Anyway, Myles called me Biscuit Barrel once... I didn't like that much.'

'You will all have noticed our onlookers. They are police and have requested an interview with each of you. This, of course, is entirely up to you. You may chat with them on your own, with me, or maybe some other time with another support person.'

The three police turned to one another and mumbled. The red-haired Detective Milford shook his head as if he disapproved of the comment.

'Naturally,' continued the counsellor. 'You are welcome to seek legal representation if you so choose.' Celine's hand shot straight up in the air. Mendes took a moment, checking out the others first, hoping someone else might have something to say. The nineteen-year-old continued thrusting her arm upwards and began making a soft grunting sound with each thrust.

'Celine?' said Eduardo, reluctantly inviting her next question.

'Do they think one of us murdered Myles?'

'Definitely not, Celine…,' replied the counsellor, conscious he had raised his voice louder than necessary. He took a breath. 'Please note that these interviews are all part of routine police enquiries. We all knew Myles, and it stands to reason that, whether we are aware of it or not, we may know something that can help the police with this matter. We do this for our loved friend, so we get justice for Myles.' Jerome, Tom and Del all nodded. Celine shrugged. April blew her nose.

'The plan now is to take your time,' continued the counsellor. 'If you feel ready to chat with the police, let me know. It would be best to leave the premises and not return here to see your friends when the interview is over. Remember, you will have my number. We will gather again next week as usual.'

Chapter 30

The Interviews

Tom was the first to go. He seemed to be the least fazed by the news. He had seen death firsthand several times, losing four friends over the years to drug overdoses, both accidental and otherwise.

Gardiner and Milford asked the questions with the uniformed officer standing a few metres from the door. For the most part, the questions were the same for all - asking details about their relationship with the deceased, checking if they had seen anyone loitering near the community centre, whether they were aware of anyone who may have wanted to harm Myles, how well they knew the Broadbeach area, and had they ever been to Albert Park; what were they up to last Thursday evening; a general enquiry about other group members, including Eduardo, and finally did they collect, play with or have any interest in marbles.

Celine went in with Eduardo. She wore a grimy floral top that was two sizes too small; nevertheless, she had managed to squeeze a good supply of biscuits into the side pockets. The counsellor sat a metre away from her and shifted his chair from the table.

She never really answered the first question; instead, she blurted out one of her own, causing Eduardo to cringe. 'Do you have any photos of the murder? Can I see them?'

When advised they would not be displaying any pictures, her follow-up statement was, 'My Grandad was hit by a truck when we were out for a walk. He flew through the air, and then the wheel went right over him; there was blood and guts all over the road.'

Celine's interview was the shortest of them all. She was excused. She and Eduardo stood. 'If you could remain, please Mister Mendes,' said Michelle.

'Oh, of course...' he turned to Celine. 'See you next week.'

'If they show you pictures, you must tell me.' Some crumbs flew from her mouth as she spoke. The door closed behind her.

Mendes sat back down. 'Apologies for poor Celine. She's had a few traumas in her life. Unfortunately, she's forthright, sometimes to the point of rudeness, but she is improving.'

The detectives shuffled through some folders and paperwork. Eduardo spoke first, advising that he could not discuss the clients individually without their written consent.

'That's fine, counsellor,' said Michelle. 'We want to talk more about you at this time.'

'Oh!' he replied with surprise. 'No problem.'

Eduardo had known Myles the longest, having had several individual sessions with him before he joined the group. He answered in the negative to the marble question, but he did wonder how Del might deal with it. There were no surprises in anything he had to say. 'Thank you for your time, Mister Mendes. You are free to leave now... oh, by the way, you have something...' She moved her hand to her left ear. Eduardo did likewise. 'Sorry, the other ear,' said Gardiner. The counsellor rubbed his finger below his ear and then looked at his hand. 'Ah... a bit of makeup is still there. Sorry, I thought I had removed all that. I do a bit of dress-up... as a clown. Something I've done for years. He's Pesky.'

'Pesky?' questioned Milford.

'That's my clowning name.'

'Oh… interesting,' continued the detective. 'Do you do parties?' he scoffed.

'No, not parties, unless it was a fancy dress to which I had been invited. I do Halloween sometimes. Other times, like yesterday, I wear the full outfit and chat with kids in the park…'

The detectives looked at him and then at each other.

'Nothing unsavoury, please,' he said loudly while motioning with his big arms. 'Strictly daytime amongst many other adults.'

'Okay, thank you again.' Detective Gardiner gestured with her head to the door.

*   *   *

For Del, one of the final few questions caused him to jerk his head straight and raise his eyebrows. 'Well… yes…' he said, then hesitated, knowing he'd already given himself away to some extent. 'I love marbles. That's surely not a crime, is it?' he asked unsurely as if maybe it was.

Michelle Gardiner smiled lightly and shook her head.

'Okay, guys,' continued Del. 'I've loved them since I was a small child. I have a collection of over three hundred.' His eyes lit up at the thought of having a marble-related conversation while his fingers fidgeted nervously about the context.

Michelle rolled a large marble across the table to him. Without hesitation, Del grabbed it and turned it around in front of his face. 'It's a boulder or tom-bowler… although some people call these larger ones shooters, dobbers or mashers, amongst other terms,' he announced proudly. 'A two-colour, green and yellow cat's-eye. Nice, but pretty regulation. Not special in any way.' He slowly moved it away from his face. 'Sorry… I've become a bit distracted. Oh dear…' he rolled the tom-bowler back.

The two detectives stared at him. He shifted his gaze between them. 'Apart from playing games,' Michelle eventually asked. 'What function do these things have.' She looked at the glass ball.

'Decorative mostly. Some rare or special ones can become collector's items.' said Del. 'Why are you so interested in marbles?'

'We found two of these at the murder scene,' said Gardiner without giving too much away and holding up the marble between her fingers.

'Oh… I see.' Del dragged a hand across his face and over his chin. 'I haven't killed anyone.'

'That's nice to know,' said Milford.

'Maybe the marbles just happened to be there where Myles was killed,' added Del.

'No,' said Detective Milford sharply.

'Do you think marbles have any power? Like, maybe of a spiritual nature,' asked Gardiner. She leaned back in her chair and began rolling the marble back and forth across the wooden table between her hands.

'Ah… well, some people say they have protective qualities. Studying them intensely can help with relaxation - like mindfulness.' Del rubbed a hand across his head. 'I should tell you upfront that I have an anxiety disorder.'

'Thank you, Del. We know all of you attend therapy. We are happy to go slowly at your pace,' said Michelle. She leaned back in her chair.

'I manage fairly well these days,' continued Del. '… but I've had blackouts before. So, if I go pale and fall off the chair, that's why. Just position me comfortably and make sure I'm breathing okay. It shouldn't last more than a few minutes.'

'Okay, Del. We'll do our best to avoid such an outcome.' She looked at Milford, who nodded rapidly when he caught her eye.

'Yes, that's right, Mister Johansson,' he said hurriedly.

'Mister Johansson... wow, don't get that so often,' Del smiled.

'Del, tell us more about the protective qualities of marbles,' asked Michelle. She sat forward again and let the marble roll from one hand to another. Del could barely take his eyes off it.

'It's mainly protection from harm by others or evil spirits. Poor Myles wasn't helped much by the sounds of it,' Del sighed.

'On another matter,' asked Gardiner. 'We were told that you and Myles argued last week while in your group meeting.'

'That... huh. Not an argument.' Del puffed out a quick breath. 'I made a comment about his eyes, which upset him. That's all. No big deal. He was a very sensitive guy... anxious as well, nearly all the time.'

'His eyes?' queried Milford.

'Yeah, his eyes were two different colours. I pointed that out, and he got upset. I visited him to apologise. Only stayed there five minutes.'

The conversation stalled as the two officers looked at him.

'Oh dear. Oh dear. Oh dear,' panted Del.

'It's okay, Delaney,' said Michelle quickly. 'You've been honest with us. That's all we ask. Please take a moment to breathe and relax.'

*   *   *

The detectives completed all the interviews, packed up and made their way out of the building.

'Thank you, sergeant,' said Michelle. 'We are done here for now.'

He tipped his head.

'It looks like Delaney Johansson is at the top of our list,' said Milford as the two exited the premises.

'He and April are the only ones that admitted to visiting Myles. Del went there to apologise, while April was hoping for sex. But, yes, I agree, Delaney currently sits at number one, and if he's not the perpetrator, he's our go-to expert on marbles.'

Chapter 31

But What Happened to Cassie?

It was six in the evening, after leaving her sister's home, when the taxi pulled up. Cassie paid cash and waved the driver off. Jasper stood at the open front door with his arms crossed, waiting.

'Hello, honey,' she said warmly. She stood in front of him, looking up at his unshaven jaw. 'Can we have a chat? See if we can sort things out.' She hopped up the three steps to the small landing. Her husband stood there, unmoved. Cassie placed a hand gently on one of his folded arms. Without a word, he turned to the side, and she entered the house.

The first thing she did was switch on the kettle. 'Can I get you a cuppa, sweetheart,' she called, assuming he was still at the door.

'No!' he yelled. He was right behind her. Cassie jumped with fright.

'Jasper Graham Johansson! Oh my God. You'll be the death of me.' She placed a hand over her heart.

'Hmmm.'

'Let's sit at the table where we can chat. I'll get this cuppa for myself.'

Jasper dragged out a chair at the long end of the dining table and sat, not taking his eyes off her.

Cassie bounced her tea bag up and down, then dropped it in the sink. She picked up her cup and saucer, needing two hands to hide her tremble.

'Sit at the other end,' he insisted.

'What, right down here, all this way from you?'

'Yes.'

'Okay, then. I'm sure we'll still hear one another.' She sat at the other long end of the table.

'Is the task done?'

'The children are out of the way for now. We need not involve them, sweetheart.'

'For now is not forever! What the hell have you done, Cassie?' The big man belted his fists on the table and then stood. Jasper's eyes were wide, and his face shook with rage. 'Give me your phone!'

Cassie stood. 'Take the bloody phone,' she shouted back at him, giving up the *steady as she goes* approach. She flung the phone down the table. 'Our kids are not to be harmed, Jasper. By you, by me or by anyone else. Get that point through your thick head.' Cassie tapped her forefinger into her temple as she leaned over the table.

'You don't understand.' He pointed a stabbing finger at her. 'Those two things are not our children anymore. They are part of The Torment. Sent to take us all to hell. Destroy the world.'

'You've lost your mind! You need to go to the hospital,' she said, grabbing Theresa's mobile.

'Demon!' bellowed Jasper. He charged around the table and dived into her chest, sending the mobile through the air and knocking her heavily to the floor. He rolled off her and got back on his feet while Cassie groaned and tried to catch her breath.

He grabbed the second phone and shoved it in his pocket, then spun around and instinctively snatched one of the metal skewers from the dish drainer. He clenched his fist around the skewer such that the metal loop on one end was locked in his clenched hand, and the shaft protruded between the fingers of his fist. 'I defy you!' he yelled. 'Be gone with your evil.'

Cassie looked up at her husband. 'Jasper, I love you. Please come back to me. I know you're in there somewhere. Please,' she begged as he stood over her.

'Manipulation, a tool of the devil. A tool of satosayoman. Cassie is gone!'

She swept her leg as hard as she could into his. As he staggered slightly, she sat up and grabbed his ankle with both hands, giving it everything she could as she reefed it sideways. The tall man stumbled more, then fell to the floor, breaking a dining chair and striking the table on the way down. The teacup and saucer crashed, spilled, and broke over the floor. Now Cassie was the one on her feet.

'I want my phone back,' she shouted. Jasper took both phones from his pocket and threw them backwards over his head. They hit the wall a metre behind his outstretched body.

Cassie quickly assessed the situation. She was sure she could get to at least one of the phones if she could get past him. He was on the floor, not yet attempting to get up. She ran and jumped so her legs would avoid his clutches. Her jump was compromised by slipping on the spilt tea, and she fell towards her husband.

Jasper had his arm outstretched, still holding the skewer. Cassie fell. It all happened in a second - the skewer slid over the bridge of her nose into the corner of her eye and penetrated deeply into her brain.

Jasper pushed her off him and used the table to help himself get up. Cassie was on her back. Her breathing was immediately stertorous and irregular. Some blood pooled in the corner of her left eye around the metal loop of the skewer.

*　　　*　　　*

Later that evening, Jasper drove west towards Rosemeadows and Gilead - about a seventy-five-minute trip. Sunset was half an hour away. As he headed off, he could already see the faint glow of bushfires in the distance.

Lying across the back seat, wrapped in the grey lounge room rug, was the body of his wife. On the passenger's seat lay two mobile phones. He had intentionally left his own at home.

Think, plan, act, and defy the evil Torment - these words he repeated to himself. Just to be sure, he pulled over five times before arriving at Rosemeadows; he had to know that the evil one was still in a state of vanquishment. On the fifth stop, he checked the two phones; both displayed *"SOS Only"* - this could be helpful if anyone were tracking them. Nevertheless, he switched them both off.

It was dark as he stopped slowly and turned off his headlights near his construction worksite for the new shopping centre. He needed a few minutes, then back on the road. The site was surrounded by temporary fencing with Keep-Out signs every few metres. He knew some of the fences were not secured to each other at the base. He lifted one from the hole in the concrete support, partly opened it like a gate and then hurried back to the car.

With Cassie's wrapped-up body in his arms, he returned and laid her down near some concrete wire reinforcing. He held back some of the carpet and looked at her face. He grabbed the skewer and pulled it free. 'The demon is subdued,' he said with a satisfied nod.

Jasper secured the fencing and then drove back to the main road, where he turned the phones back on and proceeded towards Gilead, only two kilometres further. The bushfire glow ahead was now prominent, and he was unsure how far he could go without being stopped by road barriers, police or fire service workers.

Three kilometres after driving through Gilead, as expected, he saw the flashing lights two hundred metres ahead through a thickening smoke haze. He turned the vehicle around and headed slowly back, checking both sides of the road. After five hundred metres, he pulled over to a small clearing on the side of the road. Carrying a torch, he crossed over and checked the other side. Beyond the first section of overgrowth, there was a disused track.

At this point, Jasper smiled and looked skyward. 'If you're listening, I'm thankful. Thank you for positioning the skewer, spilling the tea, revealing this old bush track, and helping me think, plan, and act.'

It was a bumpy trip for several minutes, knocking over saplings and small shrubs before he had to stop. The fires were all around, and he could go no further. Embers flew overhead, and the smoke was dense. Jasper tied his t-shirt around his nose and mouth, left the vehicle and ran back from where he had come. Behind him, the car quickly became engulfed in flames. He coughed and ran, stumbling and nearly falling many times. The torch was next to useless. Around him, the fire seemed to be closing in from all sides. The ground at his feet smouldered, and burnt twigs and grass cracked into sparks beneath his feet. The heat was penetrating his shoes.

Coughing and nearly at the point of collapse, he burst from the bush and onto the bitumen, running straight across the road to the opposite side where the fire had not yet taken hold. Jasper rolled over and over on the patch of bare ground to extinguish embers on his clothes. He threw off his smouldering shoes and then lay panting, coughing and looking up at a grey smoke cloud that flickered with an orange glow. 'Thank you…' he panted, '… for testing me… I am stronger, thanks to your guidance.'

After taking a moment, he stood. The pain from burns to the soles of his feet made him cringe and gasp. 'Your feet are still functional. The pain is temporary. Evil will not prevail.'

Looking back toward Gilead, he realised the roadblock had moved, and he was now between the advancing fire and the fire service personnel. There were plenty of flashing lights and fire vehicles. People were shouting instructions. He would have to skirt around them through the bush, attempt to emerge further up the road, and remain out of sight.

*   *   *

An hour later, with his t-shirt torn in half and tied around his feet, he was back at the Rosemeadow building site.

A large area had been prepared for concrete pouring. This was planned for Monday, and with no rain in the coming days, it should go ahead.

It was hard work lifting part of the reinforcing wire, hauling out the greyish rocks by hand, and then dragging and pushing the rug-wrapped body underneath. After pushing some of the stones back and finally lowering the wire, his hands were cut and bleeding, but the body was concealed, and most of the grey rug was out of view. He was satisfied with his work.

Jasper was a mess. He had burnt feet, cut and bruised hands, no shirt, dirt, ash, and charcoal smudges over most of his body, and some burn holes in his filthy jeans. He arrived at the Menangle Park train station, which serviced the Gilead area, with only five minutes to spare and caught the last train of the evening back to Claymore.

On Monday, he would ensure he was holding the concrete hose and filling a particular section of the slab. He had arranged for his boss to pick him up as *his wife had run off and taken the car*. This would be his last day of work.

Chapter 32

Finally

Delaney Johansson lived alone in a one-bedroom flat in Ashmore, only a few minutes from the Broadbeach Community Centre. This had been his home since he left Hal and Fiona's at Mermaid Beach when he turned eighteen.

Del had no driver's licence and felt he had no use for one as he was a competent electric scooter rider. For now, this served his purposes well - getting to and from his part-time work at the carwash, visiting Hal and Fiona every few days for food, laundry and a quick hello, getting to the beach on the warm days and attending the community centre for his group meetings. For now, it was a good lifestyle with minimal contact with people. His interest in marbles had not waned, and while he had little opportunity to play, he actively sought out other collectors online. Hal had been a great help in teaching him the skills necessary to navigate the web.

Del arrived home at ten-fifteen in the evening after finishing a four-hour shift. He swerved his scooter into the driveway across the front lawn and skidded up to the two concrete steps at the front of the block of flats. A dull motion sensor light illuminated the grassed area. He lifted the machine up the steps to the narrow, covered verandah running past the front of all three ground-floor units. There was movement in the dark near his front door.

'Oh! Hey! Who's that?' He placed a hand on his chest.

'Relax, Del. It's me,' came a soft female voice. The person moved out of the shadows into the dim lighting. They were dressed in black.

He first saw the outline of shoulder-length, curly hair. Then he saw the smiling face. He let the scooter fall and jumped forward.

'Oh my God!' he squealed. 'Faith, is it you?' He stared wide-eyed and slightly stunned, then threw his arms around her and squeezed tightly. He buried his head against her hair and neck and sobbed. 'I've dreamt of this day… for so long. But I never doubted it would happen. Never for a second.' He lifted his head but continued holding her as he talked through gasps and sobs. 'Your hair… it still smells the same… I've missed that. Your big brown eyes.' He scanned her face.

'I've missed you, Del, my lovely brother.' She looked him up and down. 'You've got taller. Come on… Let's go inside. There's so much to talk about.'

'Faith. Look at you. This is a dream come true. How did you find me?'

'Inside, please, Del.' She looked out towards the road. Instinctively, he did the same.

'Sure, sure… is everything okay?'

'I think so.'

Del fumbled for his keys, then opened the door.

'Your scooter,' said Faith.

'Oh, yeah. Of course.' Del picked it up and pushed it inside. Faith grabbed a small overnight bag and followed him.

*   *   *

The one-bedroom flat was neat, tidy and uncluttered. The pair hugged some more. Del poured two large tumblers of orange juice, and the siblings sat on the sofa and chatted.

'Oh, this is amazing,' he said excitedly. 'So, how did you find me? Where have you been? What's been happening?'

Faith smiled, reached out and touched his face softly. 'We have so much to talk about. So much lost time. With the help of my foster father, Ted, who I'll tell you about shortly, I've become a bit of an amateur detective. He is a bit of a whiz with IT, data management and online security systems. I was able to find where you went to school and get your address from the school records. I dropped in earlier today and visited Hal and Fiona Bradshaw.'

'You visited my foster parents?'

'Yeah.'

'They're good people. They've been very supportive and protective of me. Surprised they would disclose anything at all.'

'They are lovely, and yes, they were a bit hesitant at first, but after I went through some family history and asked them if you were still into marbles, they knew I was your sister. They gave me your address. I think I saw you leave on your scooter as I arrived. I did a little window shopping, then came back and waited.'

'Wow. I feel a bit jittery.' He held his own hands and squeezed at his fingers.

'It's okay, Del. I'm not going away again… ever.'

*   *   *

There was plenty to catch up on as they both related events of the past few years and laughed at what they had gotten up to at school and several past foster homes. They were both very open and honest with each other, revealing the emotional difficulties and personal challenges they had and continue to face. Nearly an hour later, the conversation slowed, and Faith walked to the window and shifted the curtains aside.

'What is it?' asked Delaney.

'For a while, someone or something has been following me.'

'Something? Like what?' He moved alongside her, and both looked out. There was the road, reasonably well-lit by streetlights; another six-pack of flats across from theirs and several low-set houses; two cars drove slowly by. 'I don't see anyone,' said Del.

'No. Me neither. And I don't get any sense of a presence, which is good.'

Del looked at her. 'What presence?'

'Not sure, exactly. Something unpleasant… possibly evil.'

'You said you were seeing a psychiatrist.'

'Lulu Huang, yes. She's lovely.' Faith let the curtain fall back in place.

'Huang? Are you kidding me? I saw her… just once at the mental health outpatients.'

'I saw her privately.'

'Well, of course, you did,' he scoffed. 'Did you chat with her about this *presence?*'

Faith smiled and chuckled. 'Fuck no! She'd think I was crazy.'

'Huh… that's funny.' Del grinned.

'Well, it's true, Del.'

'Oh yeah… I know that. That's not the funny thing. You know, I don't think I've ever heard you use the word *fuck* before.'

They headed back to the sofa. 'I started using it shortly after moving in with the Scriver-Bunts.' They sat. 'This might sound like the biggest coincidence of all time,' continued Faith. 'You said before you were doing group therapy at the Broadbeach Community Centre.'

'Yeah. Every week.'

'I'm going to be attending group therapy too. With you.'

'What! With Eduardo Mendes?'

'Yep. I start next week.'

'We saw the same psychiatrist, and now we're going to the same group. That's more than a coincidence, Faith.'

'Everything is meant to be. I think we both know there are no coincidences. Doctor Huang sends many referrals to the Mendes group.' She shrugged off the comment. 'So, no big surprise there.'

'Really though, I don't know if that's good. Brother and sister. It's not family therapy, sis.'

'No, I know that. We have different surnames now. No one needs to know. It'll be fun.'

Del started rubbing his hands over his knees. His breathing rate increased. 'It's not meant to be fun. The word they use is therapeutic,' he said.

'You said yourself there was a vacancy since that guy left…'

'He didn't leave, Faith. He was murdered.'

'Whatever. Can't you see this was meant to be?' She leaned closer to her brother. 'We were meant to be together. It's the world getting back in proper alignment.'

Del threw himself back against the sofa, closed his eyes and panted.

'Are you still having those turns?'

'Quiet…' he breathed. 'Give me… a moment.'

'Sure.' Faith stood and wandered around the flat, checking the cupboards, the fridge, the bathroom, and the bedroom. She noticed a row of marbles stuck with Blue Tac on the bedroom windowsill. She returned to the lounge and took another quick peek out the window before returning to her brother's side. Del opened his eyes and sat forward.

'I still get them,' he said. 'Those turns. Mostly, though, I can control them. Eduardo and the group have helped with that.'

'I'm sorry if what I said caused you stress,' she touched his shoulder. We can revisit the group thing in the morning. Is it okay if I spend the night on the sofa?'

'Sure. Of course. But I'd like it better if you have the bed and I have the sofa. I'm used to it. Slept here enough times already.'

'That's nice of you, but let me settle out here. I can watch some of the late news after you go to bed.'

'You still doing that? Late-night TV and news stories. Not many hours of proper rest.'

'Yeah. I seem to need very little sleep. And I like to know what's going on here and elsewhere. I feel I function better if I'm fully informed. There's so much wickedness out there, and I feel I have some responsibility to handle it, particularly when it's close to home.'

'I'd prefer not to know.'

'I realise that. That's you. This is me.' She placed a hand on her heart. 'We're different but the same, too, in other ways. You know you look more like Dad now than when you were younger. You have the squarer jaw and thick eyebrows.' She smiled at her brother.

'You talk a bit like him,' said Del. 'He said stuff like you've been saying.'

'Does that make him crazy or just better informed?'

'I think I was too young then to understand the difference. He did scare me sometimes,' sighed Del.

'Being scared is okay. It helps motivate you to be prepared. It helps with thinking, planning and decisive action. There's still so much we've got to talk about. Our futures. Our destinies. Mum and Dad.'

'Let me freshen up a little,' said Del, getting to his feet. 'I'm still a bit too hyped up to sleep.'

Chapter 33

The Disturbing Truth

'Tell me about our parents,' asked Delaney as he returned to the lounge following a quick shower and change into a loose tracksuit. He shook some droplets from his collar-length brown hair and sat beside his sister. Even though it was after midnight, Faith had made two coffees.

'Dad was an inpatient in the psych ward for nearly a year. This happened sometime after you and I were separated and were sent to different foster homes.' She passed him a mug.

'Thanks. A year. Wow! That's a long time to be crazy.'

'Yeah, but I'm not sure he was mad the whole time or even any of the time.'

'What? You think he planned to stay there that long?'

'I believe he was thinking and planning. Waiting for the right time to act. I have a copy of his discharge summary.'

'Huh?' Del's brow furrowed as he looked at Faith. 'You've turned into a super sleuth.'

'Ted helped me a lot. He was, and I guess still is, to a degree, despite being blind, an expert in data management and website security...'

'This is the guy who you threw the acid at?'

'Sure,' said Faith nonchalantly. 'I own that family now.'

'Okay.' Del exhaled through pursed lips. 'Wow.'

'Anyway, he has contacts in many areas, including health. Someone took a photo of the discharge letter and sent it through.' Faith pulled her phone from her pocket. 'Let me read it to you.'

'Go for it.' Del let himself drop back against the sofa.

Jasper Graham Johansson was discharged home after a protracted eleven-month and five-day admission. Follow-up has been organised through his GP, Dr Goldsmith.

On admission, he was floridly psychotic with paranoid delusions, hallucinations, confabulation, word salad and tangential thinking...'

'What's that all mean?' interrupted Del.

'Basically, he was yelling out a lot of nonsense that no one could understand. He allegedly saw non-existent things and was out of touch with reality.'

'Ah ha,' nodded Del. 'Sounds a bit familiar.'

'Yes, from around when Mum took us to Aunt Theresa's place,' added Faith.

She continued reading from her phone... *His psychoses mainly focused on thoughts of an evil entity he referred to as "The Torment" that was taking over people's minds. He could see darkness in some people's eyes and would say he could even smell death and decay on their breath.*

His drug screen was positive for amphetamines. It was clear that his self-care had declined substantially, and he was malodourous and malnourished.

'Geez. Poor Dad,' muttered Del. 'But that's how he saw us, Faith. Our eyes were different. I remember he said that.'

'I know. I remember, too. But do you think if someone were about to be taken over by some mysterious evil force, they would know it was happening?'

'You would feel something. It would have to be weird in some way.'

'But... total awareness?'

'Huh... probably not,' conceded Del. 'Not totally, I guess. Are you suggesting that we might have been possessed or something?'

'I really don't know... just posing the question, that's all.'

Faith looked back at her phone. *He was admitted as a voluntary patient in the company of police, who had escorted him to the ED at his request. He remained voluntary throughout his admission despite several relapses. He never pursued premature discharge and was always compliant with treatment.*

While Mr Johansson has had a diagnosis of schizophrenia in the past, it was felt a more accurate diagnosis now is schizoaffective disorder exacerbated by illicit drug use.

It is hoped that he will remain on his current medication regime for the long term. After a social worker review and assessment in the coming months, he could be assisted in establishing contact with his children via the Department of Family Services...

Faith paused. 'Obviously, that never happened. But I believe that option remains open for us. I'll explain that a bit later.'

'Okay, Faith. Carry on.'

'Now, this next part has some information about Mum. I don't believe it for a moment. Please, Del, don't be alarmed. Stay relaxed for me.'

'Okay, I'll do my best,' he shrugged.

Faith started up once more... *Unfortunately, his wife, Cassandra Johansson, has been the subject of a coroner's investigation. As of the time of Mr Johansson's discharge, the coroner's findings were death by misadventure, most likely in the bushfires in or around the town of Gilead, NSW.*

She looked at her brother. He seemed okay. 'I have a police report on this. But I'll finish this first.'

'Really? A police report? There must be a plethora of business opportunities waiting for you.'

'I don't need a job. I like to stay informed.'

'You and Mister Ted seem to be a formidable team!'

'It's my persistence that pays off,' she smiled.

'Or annoyance. I do remember that too,' chuckled Del.

'Mister Ted might think he knows me, but honestly, he has no fucking idea.' Faith grinned. 'I'll continue, shall I?'

'Oh, please.'

The family traumas Mr Johansson experienced are the most significant contributor to his multiple inpatient relapses. He was managed in the acute phases with Diazepam and Haloperidol with good effect. On two occasions of relapse, he required restraint and seclusion. His long-term management now includes Paliperidone Depot injection (Trevicta) 350 mgs (three monthly) and Lithium Carbonate 600 mgs twice daily.

He has progressed well with the above treatments, and we trust he will remain so with continuing abstinence from illicit substances and alcohol, together with regular monitoring of Lithium levels and administration of his depot injection via his GP.

'He was supposedly discharged home to nine Gould Road at Claymore in Sydney,' added Faith. 'But number nine, Gould Road, is the Community Centre, and I'm sure he hasn't set himself up there.'

'That was years back.'

'Yes, it has been ten years since we last saw him,' nodded Faith. 'Eight and a half since he left the hospital.'

'He could be anywhere now.'

'Here's the thing,' continued Faith. 'Under normal circumstances, Dad would never ask the police or anyone else to take him to the hospital. He would never agree to have that injection. He hated the thought of a needle every two weeks. No way he would have a three-monthly dose.'

'But he did. It says so in the letter.'

'Exceptional circumstances. He had lost weight and was barely able to look after himself. He spent money on drugs - amphetamines.

He would've been broke. Eleven months in the hospital gives you plenty of time to build up your resources and save money.'

'So, you think he planned this admission? And the relapses as well.'

'I do. One thing we know about Dad is that he is a very patient and thoughtful man.'

'Where is he now?'

'He purchased a one-way plane ticket two years ago. Sydney to the Gold Coast.'

Chapter 34

Death & Other Concerns

'The cause of death was a cerebral haemorrhage caused by a severing of the left posterior cerebral artery,' said Detective Milford as he walked to Michelle Gardiner's desk with a document in hand. 'A sharp, narrow instrument was forced through the left eye socket. Both eyes were excised post-mortem with a sharp round scooping tool. Holy fuck!'

'Yes. Death was quick,' added Michelle. She was online, sifting through some New South Wales police reports going back over the past five years.

The two detectives were on the fifth floor of the Surfer's Paradise Police Headquarters with several other officers. They were all in civilian dress, working through an expanding collection of statements, CCTV footage, and forensic evidence.

'The indexing of these past cases is less than perfect. There are some lazy bastards out there,' scowled Gardiner. 'I know there's a cold case somewhere with some similarities.' She looked up at Milford's double chin. 'Any luck on that old guy with the shopping trolley we saw on the CCTV footage?'

'We've been doing some door-to-door. Spoke with some of the regulars in Albert Park. So far, nothing.' He moved closer to her and peered at the screen over her shoulder.

'How about you visit a few homeless hangouts then? Take Perkins with you. And don't breathe in my ear!' She moved her chair.

'Good idea!' he replied brightly, still checking her computer screen. Michelle turned and glared up at him. 'What?' he exclaimed. 'What's the matter? It is a good idea. Right?' He stood upright.

'Of course, it's a good fucking idea, Milford!' she roared, then looked back at her monitor and flicked through a couple more reports. 'And one that is common fucking sense,' she continued without looking back. 'You shouldn't need me to tell you this basic shit.'

'Ah… apologies. I'll go then… take Perkins.'

'Ah! Got it!' she yelled proudly.

'What?'

'Never mind. Yes, fuck off.' She waved him away. 'Take Perkins. Get out of here. And come back with something useful.' Detective Milford backed away cautiously, then shrugged and headed to the chaotic desk of a gangly, thin-faced Detective Lucas Perkins.

Gardiner double-clicked a file, which opened to show text and images.

An image of a partially skeletonised body lying half immersed in a stormwater drain showed two large marbles in the bony eye sockets.

After two years, the male body remained unidentified and was believed to be that of a vagrant. The corpse was discovered by three young boys who were playing and smoking in the drain. The cause of death was blunt force trauma to the back of the head, consistent with striking the edge of the concrete drain. Drug use was a contributing factor. There were coarse scrape marks on the bone where the eyes had been forcibly removed. Traces of heroin were detected in some of the clothing, and toxicology reported that morphine and diazepam were present in the decayed body. The coroner had recorded an open verdict with a conclusion that the body had been tampered with after death.

Chapter 35

Breakfast at Delaney's

At two in the morning, Delaney Johansson asked his sister to stop. It seemed the sibling's father was, likely, somewhere on the Gold Coast; his mother was presumed dead by the coroner but not by Faith. His sister was attending his therapy group in a few days, and she was possibly being stalked by something intent on harm. Del was overwhelmed with all this new and concerning information and needed time out to relax and hopefully sleep. As delighted as he was to see her after all this time, anything further would have to wait until he was ready to continue processing. He went to bed. Faith switched on the TV and found a station broadcasting world news.

* * *

In the privacy of his bedroom, Delaney lit a candle on his bedside table and then turned out the light. He picked up Jupiter from the line of marbles on his windowsill and polished it on his track pants.

While sitting on the side of the bed and holding the larger marble near one eye with the other closed, he slowly leaned forward towards the candle flame. Inside Jupiter, the colours swirled, becoming brighter as he neared the candle. The leaves inside the large cat's-eye marble seemed to reshape into four hills of different colours. He moved still closer to the flame. The hills narrowed and morphed into the outlines of four people.

'My family,' breathed Delaney quietly. 'Wow!' He did his best to hold the marble steady. 'There's Dad and Mum... then me and Faith. The colours... what does it mean?'

As he looked intensely, he saw his father was the darkest. The image he believed to be his mother was a transparent white; his colour was orange and brown; Faith was a bright red which glowed and pulsated as the flame flickered. He moved too close to the candle, and the flame flicked over his finger. He dropped Jupiter. 'Ouch!'

Del blew out the candle and let himself fall back to the bed, leaving his favourite marble on the floor for now.

'Everything means something, Dad. You knew that,' he said, looking at the ceiling and panting. 'Jupiter is trying to tell me something. And something is not good. All is not as it should be,' he murmured, continuing to over-breathe.

'I need to chill. Relax, Del.' He closed his eyes and thought back to his trip to Sydney with Hal and Fiona - the museum, the naval shipyard; he thought back to his school days and his friend, Angus - laughing and playing marbles; he thought back even further - finding his first glass balls in the street - finding Jupiter. He fell asleep.

*　　　*　　　*

Del surfaced at ten. He staggered to the kitchen and stuck his head around the corner.

'Good morning,' said Faith brightly. She was making toast and coffee. 'Some for you?'

'Sure,' he grumbled.

'How did you sleep?'

'I've done better. I'm going for a shower.' He wandered off.

*　　　*　　　*

Faith had changed from black to different black clothes, added a thick studded leather bracelet to each wrist, and had a dangling wooden crucifix around her neck.

Del returned wearing cargo shorts and a long-sleeved fishing shirt with many pockets. His sister was sitting at the small table with the coffee and a dinner plate full of toast.

'I made an assortment. Vegemite, honey, jam and anchovy paste.'

'You found my secret anchovy paste stash?'

'Behind the cream cheese spread.'

Del sat across from her. 'Have you become religious now?' He gestured at her crucifix, then shifted a couple of pieces of toast to access an anchovy piece.

'Not really. I'm not a disbeliever. If there's evil, there must also be goodness. Be that God or some other divine being.'

'Huh. Maybe.'

'You don't agree?'

'It's too early, Faith. My brain works a bit slower than yours. Wait till I've had two coffees.' Del lifted his mug, smiled and sipped. 'How many hours did you sleep anyway?'

'About three. Went for a walk at seven.'

'Did you feel any *presence* out there?' He used his fingers to represent quotation marks.

'No, I didn't. Do you doubt me?'

'Hey, no. Not at all. I believe and trust you, even though you escalate my anxiety. And I'm overjoyed you are here. So happy you found me.'

Faith bounced up, darted around the table, and hugged him from behind. 'Me too.' She kissed his cheek and then returned to her seat. 'I see you're still into the marbles, then. I saw a row of them in your room.'

'Oh yeah. Collecting, not playing. It might seem odd, but they help me relax.'

'By scrying?'

'Well… yeah. You know about scrying?'

'Sure, I tried it a few times, but it doesn't work for me. You have a gift, Del. Keep scrying. You never know what it might reveal.' She got up and went to the kitchen.

'Yeah, you never know.'

'I'm getting you a second coffee. I want to talk about Mum.'

Chapter 36

Warm up the Cold Case

Michelle's mood didn't improve after she was left on hold for twenty minutes while someone chased up Detective Harry Truman, the lead investigator on the cold case of interest.

'Truman,' he eventually answered.

'Gardiner. Gold Coast. The vagrant death in the stormwater drain two years back - that was your case?'

'Yeah... ah... good morning, Gardiner.'

'It's not. We're looking at something similar up here.'

'Sorry to keep you waiting.'

'Let's get on with it, shall we,' she snapped.

'Someone's given you the shits. I get that. But it wasn't me, and I'm pretty busy right now.'

Michelle took a deep breath. 'Apologies. Inexperienced buffoons surround me.'

'I understand the frustration.'

'And the poor indexing of the cases down there hasn't helped.'

'Well... yeah... inexperience is not exclusive to Queensland. What do you want to know?'

'Whatever's not in the case notes.'

'I think the notes spell it out pretty clearly.'

'How do you think the marbles ended up on the body?'

'I'd just be speculating.'

'Do me a favour, Truman. Speculate away.'

'My strongest hunch is that the kids that found the body put them there, despite their denials. They were a bunch of stupid teenagers.

They'd done some dope and seemed to think the whole thing was amusing. I think it was probably them too that rifled through the suitcase that was there… you read that in the report?'

'Yeah, clothes were strewn all over the place,' said Gardiner as she referred to the details on screen. 'A ripped-up sleeping bag was nearby. One of the kids had a slingshot and some marbles.'

'See, it stands to reason why I blame them. The slingshot kid had a distinctive Zippo cigarette lighter with the initials R S on the back and an image of a skull on the front. He insisted he found it somewhere else, so I gave him the benefit of the doubt.'

'Okay, and I see there was no documentation on or near the body. It looked like he may have been travelling somewhere and possibly stopped there for the night.'

'That's it,' said Truman.

'The drain was supposed to be a restricted area. It was fenced-off and secluded.'

'Supposedly, yes,' said Truman. 'It was probably good for a temporary stop if you're running away from something or someone. Kids find their way in there from time to time. The fence maintenance is poor…'

'What about the deceased? Any *hunches* on an identity?'

'There was a guy around here called Randy, which fits in with the R on the lighter. He has no police record. And I only have a first name. I met this arsehole a few times.'

'Did he have any ID?'

'I asked, but he always had an excuse for not having it on him. At the time, I was busy enough with other shit, and chasing up this dude who, at the time and to the best of my knowledge, had not committed an offence was a waste of time.'

'Okay. What else stood out about this Randy guy?'

'My information is mostly second-hand, but I heard it often enough to reckon it's pretty much fair dinkum. He used to hang out with the homeless guys and sometimes the junkies. This guy Randy was a proper cunt. He would intimidate and manipulate them for money and other shit. He had a couple of women he pimped. Pimp to these poor suckers who had fuck all, and sometimes to drunks and other doped-up pricks. I haven't seen him since the body was found, so he's top of my list but unlikely to be ever confirmed. The case is now closed.'

'Yeah. I know. Do you have any images or maybe a solid description of this Randy guy?'

'No pics, unfortunately. About one-eighty, same as the body. Short-cropped dark hair; receding hairline, sinewy dude with some fitness level; Caucasian; lips like Mick Jagger; a big scar on the inside of his right forearm; sounded like a growling dog when he spoke.'

'And was a lot of that a match with the body?'

'Look at the pics, Gardiner. A lot of the body had rotted away.'

'Yes, of course. So, this Randy guy, he wasn't a vagrant then?'

'Could've passed for one. Let's call him a business vagrant.'

'What about the women he pimped?'

'Don't know. They're gone now. I have no clue about that. It was a bit out of scope for the case.'

'Maybe, but they could have killed him.'

'Gardiner! We don't know who the body is, and the coroner's findings indicated it was an accident.'

'Were you convinced?'

'No comment. And these women couldn't have killed anything. They were like… damaged… drugged maybe… couldn't give a shit about anything.'

'These women. You met them?'

'I met them. Not a pleasant experience. They were filthy, like, I mean, literally disgusting. And they both seemed dim… unconcerned… they didn't give a rats. Probably because of the drugs. Stunk like a fly-blown stack of dog shit.'

'Your turn of phrase is concise but disgusting, detective.'

'I'll take that as a compliment.'

'You shouldn't. But Truman, I need a favour.'

'Fuck me! Here it comes.'

'Get your sketch artist onto it. I want to see Randy's face.'

Chapter 37

Is She Alive?

'The police report submitted to the coroner showed they found the car burnt out near Gilead.' Faith scrolled through a document on the phone screen. They were still at the dining table. Del had finished his second coffee. 'There were bushfires around the time she went missing. The area was searched twice, but no body was ever found.'

'Either Mum or Dad, or both, would have to have driven there,' said Del.

'True. But Mum had friends out that way. Not that she ever arrived at their house. We know she went back that afternoon to see Dad. And we know she was scared. I think she ran off with the car and went in the opposite direction to Aunt Theresa's to throw him off our trail. She wanted to make him think she had disappeared or died in that fire.'

'No. That doesn't add up,' Del shook his head. 'If that was true, and if she is still alive, she would've found us years ago.'

'Maybe she tried, and something else happened to her.'

'Like what?'

'Not sure… a sickness… an accident… or something far fucking worse.'

'Maybe Dad found her? Did something to her,' suggested Del.

'No. I've thought about Dad killing her, but I doubt it.'

'What's the *something far worse*?'

'The presence, the thing… whatever it is, that haunts and follows me. Maybe that's it.'

'Sounds a bit far-fetched and a little bit mad… you've got to admit that, sis. And don't go saying that in the group.'

'I've learned over the years that repeating these thoughts in some circles is counter-productive.'

'Yeah, it'd get you locked up and medicated.'

'Yet I know it exists. I saw it in Ted's eyes… at least, I did when he had eyes.' Faith chuckled. 'Maybe you saw it in that kid's eyes back at school when you rigged up that clever contraption?'

'I don't know about that.'

'Well, you targeted his eyes and only his eyes. What do you make of that? I know you sense things too, Del. You too can look at others and form accurate conclusions. You do the scrying thing.'

Delaney's chair squeaked back as he stood. He walked to the kitchen and gulped down a full glass of water. 'Maybe I can sense things,' he said. 'I'm not sure. I hadn't given that aspect of the whole thing much thought.'

'But you were pleased with yourself. You defeated that wicked boy.'

'I was delighted, that is after I recovered from my blackout.'

'We are not that different. I think in many ways we take more after Dad than Mum.'

'Huh… Not sure that's such a good thing,' he chuckled.

'I tell you, Del, I know this thing exists. I know it as an absolute truth. And I honestly believe that Dad knew of it, too. I grant you that he had serious mental health issues as well, and he used drugs that compromised everything. But he sensed it and saw it affecting Mum and probably us. This torment thing drove him mad, not the other way around. I guarantee we will be of one mind when we encounter it together.'

'No, no, no. That's not something I need to experience. No way.' Del waved his open hands at her and shook his head. 'That would be a test of my relaxation skills that I might not pass.' He held out a hand. His fingers trembled. 'See! This is just from thinking about it. Fuck! This is a worry,' exclaimed Del. 'And now you've got me swearing.'

'I'm here to protect you. I'm so sorry I've missed doing that for so many years, but now my arrival is timely. Strange and nasty things are happening, and I have a plan.'

'I've been doing okay, you know.'

'Why don't you move in with me at the Scriver-Bunts? There is plenty of room. I don't need to ask their permission; I tell them. You will be safe there.'

'I'm not a big fan of people. I struggle through the group. And that's more than enough people contact. I'd be happy if ... well, more than happy; I'd be over the moon if you came here regularly. That works for me, and you can do your thing, you know... check the area, make sure everything's okay and secure for me.'

'Okay, Del. I can go with that plan for now, but the offer will always be there.'

Chapter 38

The Group Has Faith

Despite Del's reluctance, he had agreed with his sister that they should keep their distance and not seem too familiar with each other at the next group meeting, which would be Faith's first.

Eduardo Mendes greeted the recruit on her arrival and took her aside to explain the group rules and give her an overview of how the sessions would run. Faith wore her trademark black clothing and tied her long, wavy hair back with a black ribbon. She had studded leather bands on both wrists.

Mendes took his seat next to her. The other five meandered over.

Eduardo clapped his hands together loudly. 'Good morning, everyone.' He gave a big, cheery smile, displaying his very white teeth. 'I'd like you to welcome our newest member. This is Faith.' He turned partly towards her and gestured with a welcoming open hand. 'If you could all introduce yourselves, and if you like, add a simple comment and share it with Faith.'

'Hello Faith, I'm Tom. I'm a homeless ex-junkie,' he said.

'Welcome,' said Jerome with an uncharacteristic smile. 'Jerome.' He pointed to himself awkwardly. 'Ah… that's me… and I've stopped self-harming.'

'Good morning,' said April. 'My name is April. I love going to the beach, and I think Del is pretty cute.' She tossed her head side to side and giggled.

'Yes, and I'm Del.' He shook his head at April. 'I work at a carwash.'

'I'm Celine. Why are you dressed all in black?' she asked.

'Hello, everyone,' replied Faith coyly. She gave a quick wave and then looked at the floor.

'The black. Why the black?' repeated Celine sharply.

'I think we'll give Faith some time to settle in before we bombard her with questions,' responded Eduardo. 'Thank you, Celine.'

'You do have lovely hair,' said April. Faith briefly raised her head, and mouthed *Thank you*. The bleached blonde gave a big, satisfied grin. Eduardo nodded back.

'Before we get underway, I would first like to take a moment to ask if everyone is okay,' said the counsellor. 'I've brought Faith up to date with our tragic news. Two of you called me over the past week, and we were able to work through some things. That was great...'

'Faith,' said Celine loudly, interrupting Eduardo. 'You know you're sitting in a dead guy's chair, right?'

'Celine, please!' said Eduardo.

Sitting on Celine's left, Del cringed and took a couple of deep, settling breaths.

Faith looked up and made eye contact with the short, overweight nineteen-year-old as Celine crunched down on a ginger-nut biscuit. 'I imagine Myles sat in all these chairs at various times,' replied Faith. 'I'm so sorry you all lost a friend in such a horrible way.'

Celine grunted as she chewed. Eduardo raised an eyebrow and nodded.

'That's a nice thing to say, Faith,' said Jerome in a loud whisper. He gave her a warm smile.

Eduardo continued. 'If anyone has misplaced or forgotten my number, please see me later or get someone to pass it on to you. You can contact me at any time about this matter.' Mendes paused and was thankful there were no more interjections. 'A quick thought for the day if I could - *Learning patience will not happen overnight. And gaining confidence requires patience…* please share this and pass it on, as usual, guys. Now, I would like to tell you a little more about myself. I had spent some time in Sydney before coming to the lovely Gold Coast.'

'Did you do clown stuff down there?' asked Celine.

'A little, Celine. What I did most, though, was counselling very sick people before they went for major surgery. For the most part, this was for people undergoing serious cardiac or cancer-related operations.'

'Sounds very difficult,' said Del. 'This must be a walk in the park after that.'

'I understand you could think that Del, but all forms of counselling have both challenges and rewards.'

'I guess a lot of your clients died,' said Celine.

'Not a lot. But some, yes. However, many survived when they thought their lives were over. It was very uplifting.'

'Sounds the same as here to me,' scoffed Celine. 'We are the survivors.' She looked away and searched the pockets of her tight yellow dress for more food.

Eduardo sighed and briefly closed his eyes, not attempting to hide his frustration. 'Normally, we would now review last week's homework, but, as you know, due to our tragic loss, there was none. That being so, I would like to move on to *mindfulness*. No doubt you all have heard this term many times. And I'm sure you all have thoughts on what it means.'

Eduardo stood, walked a few steps back and then wheeled over a mobile whiteboard.

'Let's do some brain-storming. I'll make a list.'

The group settled into the task. All contributed to the exercise. Celine was a bit over-zealous with her hand thrusting in the air, and Tom, despite being the quietest, still managed to add a couple of thoughts to the discussion.

Following this, Eduardo summarised the notes on the board and underlined some keywords. Then, it was time for the group to divide into pairs and practice. The counsellor allowed them to self-select their partner in the first instance, noting that they would be swapped around after a time. Jerome made a beeline for Faith, while April did the same for Del. Tom was lumbered with Celine.

*   *   *

During the short break, April once again sought out Del's company. Delaney had attempted to engage with Tom and had his back to her, but she pushed in against his shoulder and started chatting anyway. Jerome watched Faith as she moved away from the others. She stood at a window that looked out onto the community centre courtyard. The area was lush, with many varieties of plants and grasses in attractive gardens. So far, she had spotted six bearded dragons sunning themselves near a cement path.

'Do you like the lizards?' said Jerome in a flat, monotone voice as he moved alongside her.

'To look at only. Some of these are pretty big,' replied Faith as she glanced at him, then back at the garden.

'They are used to people being around. You can sit out there, and they move around near you. They are better company than a lot of people.'

'Oh dear, Jerome,' chuckled Faith. She looked at him. He remained focused on the lizards and didn't turn his head. 'I hope I'm not included in that.'

'No. You seem nice.'

'Thank you. As do you. Troubled, but nice too.'

'I guess my arms give me away.'

'True. But you sound a trifle mournful when you speak.'

'Eduardo told me that too.'

'Jerome, do you get any enjoyment out of life?'

'I think life's overrated.' He finally turned to look at her. 'What about you?'

'I get pleasure from small things, like looking at this garden or talking to you, Jerome.'

'Really? That's the nicest thing anyone's said to me in a good while,' he replied with a slight change in his tone. 'I don't know why you're even here. You seem fairly normal compared to the rest of us.'

'And that might be the nicest thing anyone's said to me in a while, too, Jerome.' Faith smiled warmly at him.

Chapter 39

Randy

When the image arrived in her email, Detective Michelle Gardiner clicked the print button for a dozen copies. She studied it on the monitor. It was an elongated face with pouty lips and narrow eyes, and apart from the receding hairline and cropped hairstyle, it was not unlike a middle-aged Mick Jagger. At the bottom of the sketch were a few lines - *RANDY - Last Known Location: Central Station - Sydney; Last Seen: mid-January 2022; Age: approx' 40; Height: 179-183 cms; Weight: 75-78 kgs: Hair: dark; Eyes: Brown; Build: sinewy/athletic; Complexion: ruddy; Features: a large scar on R forearm.*

Gardiner nodded. 'Nice work, Truman,' she said to herself.

*   *   *

Michelle distributed copies to her entire team.

'There might be some doubling up, but I want you all to revisit almost every person you have spoken to. Those persons who knew Myles Ramsay, those we've picked out from the CCTV, those other evening joggers near Albert Park and the homeless in the Broadbeach area. Firstly, see if any of them were in Sydney around January 2022, then see if they recognise this face.' She held up the sketch. 'Look for a reaction.'

'Seems like a bit of a long shot, boss,' said Perkins.

At first, it was a stare, then her hands took a moment to massage her temples before she spoke. 'Please, Perkins, share your insights. Tell us what we should be doing next in this case.'

'Maybe a more thorough search for the murder weapon… just saying.' Perkins nodded and glanced about for support. There was none.

'You know we've had divers in the channels, right?'

'Sure, but…'

'And we've scoured a lot of the park and used metal detectors, right? We've even checked all the garbage bins.'

'Oh… .I wasn't aware …'

'That happened on your RDO Perkins, which, by the way, I didn't approve. If you made yourself more familiar with the case notes, you'd be up to date and wouldn't look like such a dick in front of everyone.' A rumble of murmurs and snickers filtered through the room.

'I agree with Perkins on one thing,' continued Michelle. 'This is a long shot. However, two cases that are so similar, despite the geographical distance and the two-year time frame, can't be ignored. If they are connected, it suggests there could be more victims.' Gardiner gestured to a nearby photo display. 'We need to be ahead of this.'

Nearby, a large whiteboard was divided in half with a thick black line. One side was titled *Myles Ramsay*, the other *Randy ???*. Both had notes of places, dates and names, and gruesome images of corpses with marble eyes.

Chapter 40

The Intruder

The caretaker of the Mermaid Beach Ocean Breeze Apartments spent four hours at lawn bowls every Thursday morning. Thus far, he had only been interrupted on one occasion when a resident became stuck in an elevator that came to a halt between floors. Even then, he managed a couple of phone calls to sort out the issue, only missing one end of the mixed-fours game.

As Caretaker Wally Goodall sent off the first bowl of the morning, a person dressed in bowling whites, including a broad-brimmed hat, casually entered the men's change room, opened Wally's unsecured locker, and helped themselves to a large set of keys from a zipped, leather overnight bag.

Twenty minutes later, on level three of the Ocean Breeze Apartment building, a master key turned in apartment twenty-three.

The intruder, now attired in board shorts, a t-shirt and thongs and carrying a shopping bag, was quiet and efficient.

The apartment was spacious, with two bedrooms, a kitchen opening onto the dining and living areas and a medium-sized balcony with filtered sea views.

The intruder stood and checked the place out before closing several blinds.

In the main bedroom, the built-in wardrobe was examined. A few hanging clothes were pushed aside and then straightened. The intruder checked the shelf above. There were two old-looking shoe boxes and two silver urns, one inscribed with FRANCISCO - 13th October 1914 to 1st June 2015, and the other, DELFINA - 5th July 1927 to 7th

November 2012. The shoe boxes were lifted down and examined. Both were full of old photographs. Behind them, on the shelf, were three porn magazines and two porn DVDs. All items were returned to their original spot.

The visitor checked the bathroom, opened all the drawers, and noted their contents before heading to the kitchen.

The fridge door was opened, and a gloved hand checked the items in the door before moving onto the shelves and pushing some items around as if looking for something specific. A half-empty jar of pickled gherkins was ultimately selected and placed in the empty shopping bag.

In the pantry, the gloved hand repeated the same procedure, selecting a glass jar of peanut butter and another of raspberry jam. Both items were carefully placed in the shopping bag.

The blinds were opened, and the intruder departed.

*   *   *

Thirty minutes later, at a locksmith kiosk in a shopping centre, an aged-looking man with a grey beard, glasses and a tweed flat cap shuffled to the counter and held out a key.

'Need a copy, young fella,' he said softly, with a deep gurgle, then coughed into a handkerchief.

'It's a registered *do not copy*. I need to check.'

'Sure,' breathed the old man. 'It's fifteen years old.'

The locksmith returned after a minute. 'No worries. Copy restrictions expired five years ago.'

'Thank you, kindly.'

The man waited patiently, took the copy, paid cash and tottered away.

*   *   *

It was nearly two hours after first entering the bowls club that the intruder, once again back in full whites, returned the key set to the leather bag in Wally's locker and then left the premises.

Chapter 41

Group Conflicts

It was Faith's third week in group therapy. For April and Tom, this was their last day. Jerome and Del had one remaining and Celine two. The brother and sister duo had been successful in concealing their relationship.

The past two meetings had some tense moments. Out of nowhere, in the middle of a discussion on positive emotional triggers, April had blurted out…

…'Faith is always making eyes at Del.' This was despite the siblings deliberately avoiding each other as much as possible. April continued with, 'It's very fucking obvious to everyone.'

'It's not to me,' interrupted Jerome.

'Fuck off, Jerome. You don't know shit,' barked April. 'She is deliberately trying to upset me. She wears black because she has a black heart.' She pointed angrily at Faith and raised herself out of her chair as she ranted. Faith said nothing. She held eye contact, smiled and tipped her head slightly from one side to the other. At first, Eduardo spoke directly to April about her choice of the words, "always", "obvious to everyone" and "black heart", as he harkened back to a previous session on generalisations and over-inclusive language. April responded with, 'The stupid, black-clothed bitch should leave the fucking group.' The session ground to a halt. Eduardo called a break and took Faith and April to his office to de-escalate the hostility…

*   *   *

Today, the six participants helped themselves to beverages and gravitated into two groups while waiting for Eduardo to enter. Jerome and Faith sat next to each other in the circle of chairs.

'Have you met him yet?' Faith asked Jerome.

'Yes, only once so far. He was just like you said - caring, honest, thoughtful.'

'He sees things differently. He has a higher level of understanding.'

'Yes, I could tell that,' said Jerome. 'Thank you for setting up the meeting. We'll be seeing more of each other. He's going to help me, and he's got a plan that will add value to my existence.'

Faith smiled warmly and gently touched Jerome's shoulder.

The other four group members sipped their drinks a few metres from the coffee-making area.

'I saw you at the carwash, Del,' said April. 'I wanted my housemate to drive in, but she said it was too busy and she'd wash her car some other time. I could see you were helping others. You'd be good at that.'

'Thank you, April. Why were you there? Were you stalking me?' asked Del with a half-smile.

'I reckon she was,' said Tom. He blew over the top of his hot coffee.

'Does anyone like the Monte-Carlo biscuits? I think I'll grab the last two,' announced Celine.

'No, I wasn't stalking you, Del,' continued April. No one gave Celine any attention. 'Although I had been thinking a lot about you.'

'Thinking a lot about sex, more likely,' scoffed Tom.

'What about the Shortbread Creams?' said Celine. She glanced at the others who were not listening to her.

'Tom, I've never heard you be that cheeky before.' April pushed him lightly on the arm.

'It's my last day. Maybe the therapy is helping.'

'That's good, Tom,' added Del.

'And it looks like I've found a decent place to live. Away from users and dealers.'

'Now that's real progress,' said Del. 'We could catch up sometime if you like.'

'Sure.'

'You can give me the address later,' said Del.

'Can you give me yours, Del?' April asked. 'Maybe we could catch up, too. We could go to my favourite beach at Miami. You could see my new swimsuit.' Delaney's vision clouded as she looked into his eyes, and he became unsteady. The colour drained from his face. Tom took his arm.

'Steady there, mate.' Tom guided him to a chair. 'Park it there.' Del sat and let his head go forward between his knees.

Not far away, Jerome had inched his chair as close as he could to Faith, and the two had been talking quietly. She turned her head and saw Del as he sat with Tom guiding him and April looking on with a scowl and crossed arms.

'Jerome, excuse me. It looks like Del is having a problem.' Faith stood and looked at her brother, then quickly turned back to Jerome. 'We will pick up this conversation later. I hope that's okay.' She gave him a wink and a smile. He nodded back. Faith went over to Tom and Del.

'Delaney, are you okay?' she asked. She squatted near him. April moved closer. 'What happened, Tom?'

'He was fine. Then suddenly went all pale and got wobbly.'

'It's nothing,' interjected April. 'He's simply avoiding me and not telling me his address. And you have no reason to be fussing over him, Faith. So off you go.' She waved as if shooing away a fly.

At first, Faith remained squatted beside her brother and glared up at April. 'You are poison! Be gone.' Then she slowly stood and eyeballed the taller twenty-five-year-old. 'Leave this place. Take your wickedness elsewhere.'

April charged at Faith with her fingers raised like claws to tear her face. 'You bitch!' she shouted. Faith ducked, rose quickly with her shoulder and sent April backwards to the floor. Jerome moved quicker than he had in a decade and jumped to his feet, but it happened so quickly that he only managed two steps before seeing he was not needed. Eduardo entered and ran over.

Del raised his head, now having some pink in his cheeks. 'What the hell is going on?'

April hauled herself to her feet, screamed and was ready to run at Faith again, but Eduardo wrapped his big arms around her from behind, pulling her arms down simultaneously.

Celine watched for a moment, then returned to the biscuit tin.

'No more, April! Stop!' said Eduardo loudly.

She squirmed. 'Let me go. Let me go. She started it. That rotten bitch started this.'

Eduardo tightened his grip, lifted her off the floor, and held her upright as he walked to the door, with April swearing at Faith the whole way.

'I've dealt with some situations before, but I've never had to kick someone out. Sorry, April, but that's a wrap for you. It's a good thing this is your last day. It would be best if you went now; otherwise, I'll contact security, and the police may be involved. I hope you find your peace. Goodbye.' The counsellor bundled her out the door, then closed and locked it. April banged and shouted for a further thirty seconds, then left.

Eduardo Mendes directed everyone to take a rolled-up floor mat. He put on some tranquil music, and the group started with a voice-directed relaxation and meditation exercise.

Jerome lay next to Faith. His hand went out and touched hers. 'Are you okay?' he whispered.

Chapter 42

A Hesitant Visit

'I'm not so keen on this, Faith,' sighed Delaney.

'I know. It will be fine. No one will be in your face, and there'll be plenty of time to step aside and chill out if needed.'

Faith had picked up Delaney, and they were driving Ted's metallic blue Audi Q7 SUV to the Isle of Capri and the Scriver-Bunt's canal-front mansion.

'Maybe… but let's be clear, there is no way I'm moving in with them.'

'The choices are all yours. There is no pressure at all. Anyway, besides a brief meeting with the family, the main purpose of your visit today is to sit with Ted and me and look at a couple of online sites.'

'That's fine,' said Del. 'You be the detective, and I'll be the student.' Faith smiled. 'So, is this your car now? It's a bit flash.'

'Mostly. I drive it, and Ted pays for everything. I drive him, and sometimes Gayle and Nadine around as part of the deal.'

'Perfect… I will like this guy, won't I? The fact that he once attempted to rape you puts me on edge.'

'He's a sleazy arsehole turned tame pussycat. It's all good, Del.'

The vehicle pulled up at traffic lights in the heart of Surfers Paradise. It was mid-morning on Friday, and the retail outlets were already busy. There were businesspeople in suits, women and men in skimpy swimwear, plenty of casually dressed tourists, young people on various forms of battery-operated transport, and smartly dressed people filling the coffee shops. In a bus shelter, a homeless woman lay across the seat. Next to her was a shopping trolley overloaded with her possessions, which, unfortunately, looked more like a pile of filthy, worthless rubbish.

'Plenty of homeless around here,' said Del.

'Yeah, not as bad as Sydney. Particularly Martin Place and the railway stations.'

'When were you last there?'

'A couple of years back,' replied Faith. 'I went down to catch up with a friend. What about you?'

'Gee, we were probably there around the same time. I went on a trip with Hal and Fiona. We kept away from the crowds pretty much. We did the museums, the naval shipyard, and a couple of picnics under the Harbour Bridge.'

'Nice.'

The Audi moved along Surfers Paradise Boulevard, looped around into Remembrance Drive, and left over the bridge to the Isle of Capri.

'Are you still okay about yesterday?' asked Del.

'April?'

'Ah ha,' he nodded.

'I'm completely fine,' said Faith. 'I was more worried about you.'

'That was nothing. It only lasted five minutes.'

'She did that to you.'

'You think? Not sure how.'

'She's a nasty piece of work. Did you see her eyes?'

'Well… briefly, then everything started to blur and darken.'

'Exactly.' Faith waved a finger at her brother. 'That's the darkness. She has it. I saw it.'

'Right… I guess,' he replied unsurely. 'She was a right pain in the arse though.'

They pulled up outside a two-storey, Spanish-style home. A long metal gate slid slowly open as Faith drove into the driveway.

Chapter 43

Super Sleuths

Ted's office had a built-in desk across one wall facing the canal. The plantation shutters were open, and the waterway looked like glass, reflecting the images of several motor yachts moored at other prestigious homes. At the rear of the Scriver-Bunt's house was the pool and a spacious pontoon but no yacht. Beyond the canals, the high-rises from Surfers Paradise stood proudly silhouetted against a blue sky.

'This is pretty neat,' nodded Del as he took in the view.

Moments earlier, he briefly said hello to Gayle and Nadine and was offered a lemonade and a chat on the pool deck. But Faith quickly ushered him to Ted's office, saying, *we have some critical work underway; sorry guys, maybe later.* She hadn't missed Nadine's eyes lighting up when she spotted her brother.

'I remember this view being so perfect, day after day,' sighed Ted. 'I still see it in my mind - my boat, out there waiting for me. All set for the next cruise.'

Ted was sitting. From his standing position, Del could see down the sides of Ted's sunglasses and noticed his eyes were narrow and completely white. He had no eyebrows. Coarse scar tissue and skin that looked like patchwork extended across his forehead and over both cheeks beyond the coverage of the dark glasses.

'Are you checking out my arse, son?' asked Ted.

'Oh no, sir. Definitely not. I wouldn't do such a thing.'

'I think you might be. My face has skin grafts from my arse… so, yes, I think you are,' laughed Ted. Faith chuckled, too.

'It's okay, Del,' she said. 'He trots out that old favourite whenever there's someone new around.'

'Are you on that site yet?' Ted turned to Faith, who was sitting in front of the keyboard.

'Okay, Ted. Yep, I've just logged in and created an account,' announced Faith.

'Good, my love,' he smiled. Del cringed. 'This shouldn't be a difficult hack. Open my program, Hackologist 0.14. Put in the site URL and use your new account details when prompted.'

'What site is this?' asked Delaney. He took a step closer to his sister and watched her at work.

'It's the Angolan seminary of the Catholic Church,' replied Ted.

'Faith, that's where Eduardo Mendes did some training.'

'Yes, I know,' said Faith as she typed.

'We were aware of some rumours about what happened there,' added Ted. 'Stuff I saw... well, had read out to me from the dark web. Now we seek the truth.'

'Don't you need permission...' Del paused. 'Sorry, that's a stupid question; it's a hack, so I guess not. What about the password and the site security?'

'Faith's created a new user profile. My program will change her status from being a casual visitor to being a *Super-User*. Then she... or I should say we, can access whatever we want.'

'I'm in the archives,' said Faith. 'Searching Mendes.'

'Your sister has been an absolute blessing for me, son,' said Ted, turning in Del's direction. 'Thanks to her, I've learned how to type and use more voice control commands, getting close to one hundred percent accuracy. I even have a little casual employment from time to time with some old colleagues.'

'Ted has a lot of useful contacts from when he was fully employed,' added Faith.

'They say it's often who you know, not what you know, but in my case, it's both,' chuckled the blind man.

'Here it is,' announced Faith. 'A report on the Mendes separation from the seminary. Copying now. It's written in Angolan Portuguese. I'll open Google Translate.'

'See, Del, the apprentice, becomes the master.'

'She's amazing, that's for sure.' Delaney took a deep breath and placed an open hand on his chest.

'I was in the depths of a major depressive illness,' said Ted. 'I was suicidal. Faith literally saved my life. I threw out my antidepressants, and I've never looked back... so to speak.'

'Ah... I see they keep two files of all their documents,' interjected Faith. One is in Angolan Portuguese, and another is in Latin.'

'She has rescued me often enough from tricky situations,' said Del.

'If you two are finished trying to butter me up, I'll have this ready to read in a few seconds.'

'Fire away, love,' said Ted.

'Sure, Faith, when you're ready,' said Del.

'To keep it simple. I'll read the English translation,' she giggled.

Eduardo Mendes commenced his studies on April 5, 2011. It was in October of that year when a ten-year-old male visitor (and brother of trainee Carlos Paulo) reported to his parents that the trainee, Mendes, had inappropriately touched him.

It was alleged that Mendes took the child aside to a private confessional booth with the suggestion of playing a game, where he blindfolded the boy, then proceeded to rub his groin and attempted to kiss him on the mouth. The child yelled out, struggled and was released.

Mendes vehemently denied this allegation, and there was no corroborating evidence to substantiate the claim other than the child's word. At the time, it was noted that the young boy did not appear overly distressed by the matter despite the serious allegation. His parents were quite the opposite. Security was required to escort the family (particularly the father) off the grounds.

Mendes was provided three counselling sessions and required to report to senior staff weekly for three months. He would go through his diary, respond to questions and provide updates on his training. He complied fully with this process, which ultimately ceased, and the case was closed in February 2012.

'That is the first of three reports,' said Faith as she opened another file and read the second document.

Del rolled out an office chair. 'This is unbelievable,' he shook his head as he sat, closed his eyes, and took some long, slow breaths.

As it panned out, Mendes had been accused of similar behaviour on two other occasions, with a nine-year-old girl and an eleven-year-old boy. Both times, he was using a cloth blindfold. After the second alleged offence, he was offered a transfer to the St Charles Seminary in Namibia but refused. After the third, he was dismissed. There were no ongoing investigations, and no charges were ever filed.

'This is much the same as the dark web information,' added Ted after Faith's reading. 'I remember also hearing that he was given a positive reference on his departure. Appalling, really.'

'Oh my God,' said Del. 'I'm feeling violated myself, in a weird sort of way. Of course, not that he ever tried anything with me or anyone else in the group, as far as I know. This is so shocking. He seems such a genuinely caring and honest man.'

'Sorry, Del,' said Faith, '… but it gets worse. We have details of him going to England, but we can't trace his movements or work history there. We do know he went to a clowning school in London.

He attended at least seven workshops. He left the UK and came to Sydney, where he did telephone counselling before landing a job with Central City Counsellors and Therapists. This was when he provided pre-operative consultations to those having major surgery. He got sacked from this job, too. This time, he assaulted the father of a patient. To his credit, though, it seems this was provoked, as he was racially abused by the man who also pushed and struck him. Mendes broke his nose and cheekbone.'

Del gasped. 'Oh, dear. What does all this mean, then? I felt better when I didn't know this shit. Why are you even doing this covert stuff?' He stood, sending his chair rolling back on its castors.

'I was looking out for you, Del. I had the dark web info. I landed the referral to the group from my psychiatrist. That was partly my doing, I admit.'

'How long have you two known this?' said Del a little louder as he looked back and forth at Ted and Faith. 'You…' he pointed to his sister. '… have been at the group for three weeks. Keeping this secret from me.'

'I couldn't tell you until we were sure… now we are. Being in the group was part of a twofold plan: I wanted to find out what I could about Mendes and ensure you weren't in danger. It took longer than we expected for Ted and me to get the hack program up to speed. I only finished it yesterday.'

'We do this too, son, to keep others safe. This is not the first time we've blown the whistle,' said Ted. 'It's both a community service and a hobby of sorts. I'm happy with our results.'

Del paced around the room. He looked at Ted. Here is a guy exposing people that are just like him, abusers and rapists. Had his sister not thrown acid in his face, he would be doing something similar.

'Do you need a moment?' asked Faith.

'I think so.'

'Maybe now would be a good time to enjoy a lemonade by the pool,' she said.

* * *

Del sat back in a deck chair with his drink and took in the view across the pool. Nadine wasted no time in dragging her chair next to his.

'Hello Delaney,' she said. 'Nice to finally meet you. I'm Nadine.' She sat sideways on the chair and held out her hand. Del gave it a soft shake and returned the smile.

'I think Del's hoping for a bit of time out, Nadine,' called Faith from the side of the pool where she sat dangling her legs.

'It's okay, sis,' he called back. 'I'm fine here, thanks.'

Chapter 44

Eyes on the Investigation

Finding a dead body on the beach was an unusual enough event in itself, but finding one sitting in a collapsible chair under a collapsible beach tent was unheard of.

The area was at the southern end of Miami Beach, a hundred metres from a rocky outcrop and away from the main beach area, popular with tourists and locals.

It was a Saturday morning, and a large section of the beach was now surrounded by yellow police tape. Several officers were on site to keep away curious onlookers. There was little need to erect a privacy/courtesy tent over the body as the beach tent, with its three sides and roof, seemed adequate for this purpose.

A police photographer snapped away pictures of April Armstrong as she sat looking out to sea through her marble eyes. There was a coagulated trickle of blood from the inside of both her eye sockets, running down her cheeks and past the corners of her mouth.

Preliminary estimates had the time of death at approximately nine o'clock on Friday night and suggested she was most likely murdered elsewhere and then taken to the beach. It was also suggested, due to the relatively small amount of blood loss, that her eyes were removed after she was killed.

*   *   *

Detective Gardiner and her team had all been to the Miami Beach murder scene. Once again, they awaited results from forensics and the post-mortem. Some repeat interviews were still to be completed, but now there were more questions.

Similarities between the murder of Myles Ramsay and April Armstrong had been noted. Apart from the obvious removal of the eyes and replacing them with marbles, there was more CCTV footage showing what appeared to be the same dishevelled, grey-haired elderly man in the vicinity around the time of April's murder, and the closest CCTV camera and streetlight had both been smashed.

Gardiner had set Perkins the task of researching Eduardo Mendes, who, so far, was the only one they knew for sure was in Sydney when the first marble-eyed corpse, now referred to as "Randy Maybe", was found in the drain.

Michelle Gardiner had planned to visit the therapy group early next week, hoping to catch them all together. Now, the priority had changed, so she and Milford would make the rounds and reinterview everyone from the Mendes counselling group, catching up with them at their home address.

Firstly, Michelle gave herself the difficult task of visiting April Armstrong's father to break the sad news. After this, she would visit April's share house and talk with her two housemates.

As it turned out, the visit to Nathan Armstrong differed from how she had imagined. He had not seen or heard from his daughter for several months and thought he had probably seen her twice in the past seven years since her mother died from meningitis. Both times, she came asking for money, which he didn't provide. April had blamed him for her mother's death. In addition, she had accused him of sexually abusing her when she was just a toddler. Nathan shed one solitary tear, excused himself and closed the door.

Michelle's sadness deepened after talking with April's two female housemates, neither of whom liked or spent any meaningful time with her. Their main concern was finding someone else to pay that third of the rent. While they knew she regularly went to Miami beach in her old-fashioned one-piece swimsuit with her beach tent to find men, they had no idea what she was up to last night as they were both elsewhere partying and were still recovering. Detective Gardiner checked April's room. It was spotless, and there were no signs of any disturbance. Pictures of semi-clad attractive male superheroes, including Chris Evans, Chris Hemsworth, and Henry Cavill, decorated the walls and mirror. April's diary was on her bedside table. Gardiner found references to Myles Ramsay and Delaney Johansson. Next to each of these two names was a vivid description of a fantasised sexual experience with each.

*   *   *

Celine Woods was Gardiner and Milford's first stop. She wasn't on their suspect radar, but her address was the closest. The round nineteen-year-old greeted them at the front door. She stood holding a plate and spoke through a mouthful of cheesecake. She wore snug active-wear tights and a short crop top displaying a substantial midriff.

After identifying themselves, the detectives went through the motions of showing her the sketch and asking her whereabouts in early 2022.

'If it was January, I would've been in Sydney,' she grunted through the cake. 'I've been to Sydney every year for the past four years. That's when they have the Sydney Cakebake and Sweet Show. My Gran takes me.'

'And this man?' Gardiner held up the sketch again.

'Looks cute, but I don't know him.'

'Can we come in for a few minutes?'

Celine said nothing, then turned and walked down a short hallway and into the lounge. Gardiner looked at Milford, who shrugged. She gestured with her head, and the pair entered the home.

'It's my Gran's place,' said Celine. 'That's why there's all this old crap around the place.' She licked her fingers and set the plate down. The detectives sat opposite her.

'I have some more bad news, Celine,' said Gardiner, pausing to gauge the girl for a reaction of which there was none. 'April from your group has died.'

'Huh.' Celine ran her finger over her plate and then sucked it clean. 'Died like hit by a bus, murdered or just dropped dead?'

'She was murdered.'

'What did it look like? Was there much blood?'

'We are not at liberty to disclose details, Celine,' said Michelle politely. Kevin Milford lowered his head. 'What were you up to yesterday evening?'

'Watching telly here with Gran. She's out in the back garden.'

'We will chat with her before we leave.'

'She had a fight, you know. April was in a fight at the last group,' continued Celine. She had the detective's attention.

The teenager described how Del became dizzy, the fight with Faith, and Eduardo's marching April out of the building.

'Do you know Faith's last name?'

'Don't know anyone's last name apart from my own. She is beautiful. Has lovely hair. A bit skinny.'

'And she's new to the group?' asked Gardiner.

'Been there three times, I think. She seems kinda nice.'

Chapter 45

Suspects

'It's not even as if she has a real face,' retorted Faith. She glanced at her brother and then back at the road.

'What's that supposed to mean?'

'She's full of Botox and chemicals. Her hair is bleached. The makeup is caked on.'

'Maybe that's true, but it's nice to have someone who shows some interest in me. It doesn't happen very often.'

'I'm interested in you. I care for you. I love you, Del.'

'Yes, but you're my sister. You're supposed to. It goes with the territory.'

'Nadine is a very shallow person. I'm not sure why you like her. I never have.'

Del watched Faith as she drove. He smiled, stopped talking and peered out the window as they cruised slowly along the Esplanade with the surf beach and ocean on their right. They stopped at lights and a crowd of families, couples and individuals, most in swimsuits with beach bags, crossed in front of them.

'It's a great day for it. Maybe I can get my gear, and we can come back here for a couple of hours,' said Del.

'I'm taking Ted to a function. Maybe you should've asked Nadine,' scoffed Faith.

'Maybe,' he looked at her with a grin. 'She made me feel relaxed. I needed that after all the Eduardo stuff. That was nice.'

'I noticed that,' she smiled back at him. A little anxiety and paranoia are useful assets, Del. They'll keep you alert, and being alert keeps you safe.

'Well, thank you for pushing my buttons again.'

'Apologies, but there is something else I need to ask you.'

'Oh, dear!'

'I don't want you to disclose to anyone that we're related, under any circumstances, no matter who they are.'

'What the hell. I've said nothing to anyone, but I want to tell the world because this is the best thing that's happened to me for so long.'

'For now, you must promise me. Please. Del, this may be a matter of life and death.'

'Oh, dear. Oh, dear. Oh, dear,' he panted. 'This is the evil thing. You're so terrified of this.'

'Promise me. Tell no one.'

'Okay, I promise.'

*   *   *

Faith had dropped her brother home and returned to the Scriver-Bunts. She had finished parking the Audi, and as the garage door rolled down, she noticed a deep-blue, sporty-looking BMW pull up outside. Faith moved to the property entrance and a high wrought-iron gate. Outside was an intercom to speak to the householders and gain entry. Faith waited as an overweight man, looking like a religious door-knocker and a suited woman holding a zipped leather portfolio headed her way.

'Hello,' she said as they arrived at the gate.

'Hello. Detectives Gardiner...' Michelle indicated to herself. '... and Milford from Southport.' She held up her ID. 'Would you be Faith Scriver-Bunt?'

'Yes. How can I help?' She opened the gate before they could ask. 'You could come inside or sit in the front garden.' She gestured with her hand to the garden setting.

'I think inside would be best if you don't mind. I'm sorry, but we have some bad news,' said Gardiner.

'Oh,' gasped Faith. 'Let's go in then.'

*   *   *

The living area was extensive, with an open plan style and huge panoramic triple sliding windows opening onto the deck and pool area. The home looked more like a display house than a lived-in home. There was no clutter, and nothing seemed out of place.

'This is a beautiful home,' said Michelle.

'Outstanding,' nodded Kevin.

'Thank you. If you sit in the lounge, I can bring you a glass of cold water.'

'Sure,' agreed Gardiner.

Faith delivered the cold drinks and moved a single lounge chair closer to the detectives, who sat on the long leather sofa. 'What has happened?' she asked.

'Can I check, Faith? Is anybody else home with you?' asked Gardiner.

'My mother and sister are shopping. My father is upstairs resting. I'm his carer.'

'If you don't mind me asking, why does your father require care?'

'He's blind. He has been for many years. I drive him to appointments, outings and that sort of thing. I do most of the cooking and the housework. What has happened?'

'April, an attendee at your therapy group has been murdered,' said Gardiner. Both detectives watched her reaction.

Faith gasped and, for a moment, struggled to catch her next breath. She leaned forward in her chair and placed a hand on her neck. 'Oh my God,' she eventually uttered. Her eyes watered. She took another deep breath and then spoke. 'I knocked her to the floor at this week's group meeting.'

'Really!' said Gardiner, trying to sound surprised.

'I feel so bad about that. She attacked me in the first place, though.' Faith raised her head. 'I just reacted. But I never saw her after that day.' She looked at the officers.

'Why would she do that?' asked Milford. He sipped his water.

'Not exactly sure. She seemed to have it in for me from my first day. It may have been jealousy. She was keen on Delaney...' Faith paused, blotted her eyes and sniffed. 'I can't believe this has happened. This is the second one, right? Are the rest of us in danger? I can't go back there again... I just can't.'

'The group is over. That much is clear,' said Gardiner. 'I would recommend being diligent. Don't go anywhere on your own for now. Stay around people you know. Call us if you have the slightest suspicion.' Gardiner leaned forward and placed a card on the coffee table.

Faith nodded. 'I will. Thank you.'

'You were saying something about April,' said Michelle, inviting Faith to continue.

'Yes, she thought I was keen on him… Delaney, but that was completely wrong. I did nothing to make her even think that.'

'Do you have any idea of anyone who may want to harm her?'

'Oh, no. The others probably know her better than me. I thought Mister Mendes was rough with her that day, though.'

'How so?'

'The way he manhandled her out of the building. Squeezed her so hard and lifted her off the ground. Pushed her out the door. I was shocked because he seemed to be such a kind and gentle man.'

'Where were you last night?' asked Gardiner.

'Out for dinner with my parents. Nadine stayed here. We went to the Italian place, La Porchetta Restaurant at Broadbeach.'

'What time did you get home?'

'Ten fifteen, maybe ten-thirty.'

'If you don't mind, we'd need to verify that with one of your parents before we leave.'

'Of course. I understand.'

The interview continued with more questions about Mendes and the other group participants. A garage door rumble indicated that Gayle and Nadine had arrived home.

Gayle hurried in, wearing a pale green, long-sleeved wrap-style mini dress and high heels and displaying ample cleavage. She stopped when she noticed Faith chatting with two official-looking people. 'Oh, dear.' She hurriedly set her fashion shopping bags down on the dining table. 'What's going on, Faith?'

'These detectives are looking into the death of a young girl in my therapy group.'

'Oh my God!'

Michelle walked forward and extended her hand. 'Detective Gardiner, and my colleague is Detective Milford. Yes, we are looking into the death of a young lady. We are interviewing everyone associated with the therapy group. Can you verify Faith's whereabouts from yesterday evening, Mrs Scriver-Bunt?'

'Oh, Gayle, please,' she chuckled nervously. 'La Porchetta for dinner.'

'And you got home when?'

'Oh... not sure exactly. After ten. Yes, it was definitely after ten.'

'Thank you so much,' smiled the detective.

Nadine entered, also carrying fashion shopping, and stood beside her mother. 'What the hell is all this?' she exclaimed.

Gardiner returned to the lounge, turning at the last moment to Gayle. 'If you could both give us a few more moments. We're nearly done here.'

'Sure, sure.' Gayle turned to her daughter. 'Nadine, you go upstairs for the time being.'

'Mum!' she protested. 'Are you okay, Faith,' she called to her sister.

Faith raised a hand and waved. 'I'm fine, sis,' she replied. 'Thanks.'

'Go on now, off you go,' continued Gayle.

Nadine scowled at her mother and headed for her room.

'Is it too early for a chardonnay?' asked Gayle, not waiting for a reply. She looked at the trio and giggled. 'Ah... no... I think not.' She dashed around the island bench to the fridge.

Faith and the detectives watched as she quickly poured herself a glass, grabbed her purse and scampered off to the outside deck.

'I'm sorry for my mother,' said Faith. She's a bit too fond of her chardonnay.'

'She's certainly very different to you, Faith,' said Milford as he watched the busty forty-three-year-old settle into a deck chair.

'Thank God!' smiled Faith.

Michelle Gardiner unzipped her portfolio, took out a sketch and handed it to Faith. 'Do you recognise this man?'

Faith felt her eyes widen slightly. She tilted her head. 'Um… ah… not really… but…'

'But what?'

Faith looked at the sketch. She knew this face after seeing him in a parked car near a playground in Sydney. This was a face of torture and wickedness. She knew he was dead. It was time for a plausible lie. 'Well, I don't know this person, but there is something familiar about him. Is this the killer?' she asked evenly, tipping the picture left and right as if trying to make out who it was.

'No. He's not the killer,' replied Michelle. 'But he may be connected to the person that is.'

'He looks a bit like some celebrity. Like he's been on TV or in the movies, that's why he seems familiar.'

'A partially bald Mick Jagger, maybe?' quipped Milford. He got a raise of eyes from Gardiner.

'Could be,' said Faith. She handed the sketch back.

'Have you been to Sydney?' asked Michelle.

'Oh, yes. Grew up there. Been back a couple of times.'

'When were you last there?'

'Early 2022. February, I think. My Uncle Abner was having major cardiac surgery. Well, he's not an uncle in the true sense. Sort of an adopted uncle. I spent so much time with him when I was very young. I went down to help him recover. Stayed for a month.'

'Just for the record. What was Uncle Abner's full name?'

'I called him Uncle Abner. But Abner was his surname. His Christian name was Angel.'

Chapter 46

The Marble Expert

'Hello Delaney,' announced Detective Gardiner as the door opened. 'I think you know Detective Milford as well.' She turned to her partner.

'Good afternoon,' said Milford, tipping his head.

'Have you found out something about Myles?'

'Unfortunately not. Could we come inside for a few minutes?'

'Well… yes… that's okay. I do have to leave for work in an hour.'

'No problem, and thank you.' The two plain-clothes detectives entered. Del showed them to the dining table, where they all sat. Michelle placed the portfolio on the table. Del slid the salt and pepper to one side, then brushed away a few crumbs. There was a moment of silence where everyone smiled unsurely at each other.

'What's going on?' Del shifted his attention between the pair. 'You guys are already making me nervous. I suffer from anxiety, quite bad at times.'

'Yes, we know your condition from our last chat,' said Gardiner. 'Del, have you had any contact with April Armstrong outside of the group therapy?'

'Hell no!' Del leaned back a little and chuckled. 'She would've loved that. She wanted my address. April is very forward. Tom said she was chasing me for sex. Whatever it was, I wanted no part of it.' He shook his head. 'No way. And I think she's done with the group now. Eduardo kicked her out, but it was her last session anyway.'

When asked further, Del provided a similar account of the incident with Faith and April as did Celine but added that he had a dizzy spell, so he didn't see the whole thing.

'How do you get on with Counsellor Mendes?' asked Gardiner.

'Fine. He's always been nice to me and helped me. Has he done something wrong?'

'Have you noticed any hostile, unusual or inappropriate behaviours from him?'

'I have not,' said Del emphatically. The reports that Faith had read out were right there in the front of his mind, but that information was for her to deal with. There was no way he could disclose anything about an illegal hack, and he was under a promise not to reveal that Faith was his sister. It was best to be honest about everything he had personally witnessed. 'I didn't see him remove April. As I said, I was recovering from a dizzy spell and had to sit and lower my head.'

Detective Gardiner steered away from the topic of April for a moment, showed Del the sketch, and asked him about being in Sydney.

'Never seen that man. Did he know Myles?'

'Not as far as we know. What about Sydney?'

'I grew up there, at Claymore,' replied Del. 'Been on the Gold Coast for a long time now.'

'Have you been back?'

'Not to Claymore, but I've been back to Sydney once with my foster parents, Hal and Fiona.'

'When was that?'

'It was after New Year's Day in 2022. I visited the museums and the naval shipyard. I stayed at Darling Harbour. Hal has a brother down there, too.'

Michelle took a breath and stood. 'Sorry to put a brief hold on things, but do you mind if I use the bathroom?'

'No worries. Just down the short hallway there.'

As she left, she looked at Milford, tilted her head downward and gave him a patting motion with one hand, indicating to him to go easy.

'Have you been at the carwash long?' asked Kevin Milford.

'It's been a few months now. I don't mind it. I only have brief contact with others, which works for me.'

'Right...' the detective nodded. 'I see you ride a scooter.'

'You noticed!' The scooter was just two metres away, standing near the lounge. 'Nothing gets by you guys,' he laughed.

Milford pushed out an insincere smile and gave a slight nod. 'Where were you yesterday evening?' he asked.

'Why?'

'It's a simple question. Are you hiding something, Johansson?' The detective leaned forward.

'What's happened? Has something happened to April?'

'Johansson! Yesterday evening,' repeated the detective loudly.

'Oh dear. Oh dear. Oh dear.' Del began hyperventilating.

'Where were you?' shouted the detective. 'Did you go to the beach? Did you kill April?'

The colour fell from Delaney's face, and he toppled from his chair to the floor just as Michelle returned. 'Oh, fuck!' she shouted. 'What have you done, Milford?' She went straight to Del and turned him onto his side.

'He was being a smartarse. I just asked him to account for his whereabouts, and then he went all stupid like...'

'Get a fucking pillow, you goose.'

*   *   *

'It's a good thing you gave us the heads-up last time we saw you, Del,' said Gardiner. 'If not, we would've called an ambulance.' She and Milford helped him to his feet. 'Maybe if we sit in the lounge instead.'

'Sure,' said Del. 'I'll be okay now. How long was I out for?'

'You were groggy for about ten minutes.'

'Hmmm… it's rare for me to get more than one in a day,' added Del. Michelle sat beside him on the sofa. Kevin dragged over a dining chair.

'I'm sorry,' said Milford. 'I get a bit over-enthusiastic at times. Sometimes, a steadier approach could be better.'

He got a look from Gardiner. 'Thank you, detective,' she nodded.

'It's okay. No damage done,' added Delaney.

'I need to confirm, though, where you were last night, Del,' said Michelle.

'Working at the carwash until after ten. Got home around ten-fifteen. What's happened to poor April?'

'The same outcome as Myles. I'm so sorry. Her body was found at Miami Beach. Not far from where she lived.'

Del took a moment and dropped his head. Michelle placed a hand on his shoulder. 'Are you okay? I know this is the worst news ever.'

When he looked up, quiet tears ran down his face. He rubbed them away with the back of his hand. 'Fuck!'

'Like last time, Del, we found marbles at the scene. Cat's-eyes.'

'What do you mean? Where they? In the sand? In her clothes?'

The detectives looked at each other. 'I'm happy to give Del the details, Detective Milford. It may help us understand what's going on. What do you think?

'You're the boss. I'll get ready to call the ambos.'

'I won't need the ambulance,' said Del. 'I might get upset, but passing out again is unlikely.'

'Someone with some skill had removed her eyes. The large cat's-eyes were in her eye-sockets. She was sitting up as if looking out to see.'

'Fuck that!' exclaimed Del. 'Sorry for swearing. I don't usually use that word.

'I think, fuck, fits the bill here,' nodded Michelle. 'Do you have any thoughts on what that could mean?'

'Was Myles the same?'

'Yes, except he was lying on his back.'

'Looking at the stars,' said Del. 'Do you have the marbles with you?'

'I have some marbles, but the actual ones used are safely stored away as evidence.'

'Okay. Hang on a moment. I'm going to get Jupiter.' With that, Del was up and off to his bedroom.

'Was that a good idea?' asked Milford.

'A better fucking idea than confronting and standing over him. Sending him into meltdown,' snapped Gardiner.

'Hey, I was sitting down,' pleaded Milford.

Del bounded back in and parked himself next to Michelle.

'This is Jupiter,' he held up his favourite marble. 'I use him for scrying. As odd as it may sound, I get insights and tranquillity from this.'

'Do whatever you need to do, Del,' said Gardiner. Milford rolled his eyes.

Del began moving Jupiter between his fingers, then placed the tom-bowler between his palms and rolled it around. Finally, he made a fist, sat the marble on the top near his thumb, and moved it to his face.

'Sounds to me like whoever did this was trying to protect the person,' said Del as he pondered further. He angled his head and studied Jupiter. The detectives remained quiet as the young man thought it through. 'I know that sounds stupid,' he continued. '... because they're both dead, but maybe this killer excised the evil that was there in the eyes... be it real or imagined.' Del paused and remembered back to the day when his father believed that he and Faith had dead black eyes. He nodded more to himself than anyone else. 'Yes, and then used the marbles to save the soul... give the soul freedom so it could rest in peace... or go to a better place... or something like that. Also, the marbles could prevent whatever wickedness there was from returning.'

Del finally looked at his two visitors. They both seemed a bit shell-shocked. His thoughts moved to Faith and her concerns about some evil presence following her. He remembered her glowing red when he was last scrying with Jupiter. Was that a warning?

Chapter 47

Debrief

The eight detectives had all dragged or wheeled their chairs towards the front of the open office. Before them, two whiteboards displayed the many case photographs and scribbled notes in black and red.

Three events triggered the activity on this Tuesday morning. Firstly, the autopsy and most of the forensic results were now completed on April Armstrong's body and the crime scene.

Secondly, more details on the therapy group's participants revealed that the psychiatrist, Dr Lulu Huang, referred all of them to Eduardo's group.

Thirdly, and most importantly, an article appeared in the local newspaper and online with the headline - *Counsellor of Murder Victims Shocking Past.* It quoted snippets from a report from the Catholic Seminary in Angola. The story went on to detail the assault in Sydney. The only response from Eduardo Mendes was, *That is complete nonsense;* these words were highlighted below a picture of him in the newspaper showing him hurrying into the community centre.

'We are playing catch up here, you lot,' she yelled, bringing the room to attention. Her mouth tightened as her gaze settled on the lanky detective. 'Perkins!'

'Yeah, I'm here,' he replied.

'Yes, you are at least here in body. I think we all can see that. Why are we all finding out about Mendes from the news? This was your task.'

'I knew about the assault in Sydney.'

'The man is Angolan, obviously from Angola!' said Gardiner firmly, raising a few snickers around the room. 'Some background checking over there would seem to have been appropriate...' She let him stew for a moment, then continued. 'The most significant aspect of this Mendes report, if we are to believe it, is that the victims were allegedly blindfolded. This shows a connection and a preoccupation with the eyes, which is concerning. And, as a result, we now have a warrant...' she tapped on a document on the desk near her, '... which we will execute after this friendly gathering.'

Detective Gardiner paused and looked around the room. She took a deep breath and continued. 'We are supposed to work together, supporting and helping each other. That's what is commonly referred to as teamwork, guys. Let's embrace the concept.'

Michelle removed her jacket and placed it on the back of a chair. The slender detective, wearing a plain white t-shirt and black trousers, moved to the whiteboards. She pointed to an image of April sitting in the beach chair. 'This poor girl was glued by her hair to the back of the chair so she would remain sitting up. Her arms were glued to the armrests. Interestingly, some fine ash particles were found in both eye sockets and on the marbles; this was not so with the Ramsay murder. Unlike Myles Ramsay, there was no Rohypnol in her system. The time of Armstrong's death is confirmed as being close to nine in the evening. The murder weapon, a narrow spike of some sort, is consistent in both cases. This penetrated the brain, causing death by cerebral haemorrhage.'

'We seem to have acquired more suspects,' said Milford, raising his hand.

'We have,' said Michelle. 'This is predominantly the therapy group crowd, but why don't you list them for everyone.'

'Sure…' Kevin Milford removed a small notepad from his pocket. 'Oddly, so many of these people were in Sydney at the same time in early 2022,' he said as he flicked through his pad until he settled on the right page. 'As you said, boss, the group members are all suspects: Celine Woods, Delaney Johansson, Faith Scriver-Bunt, Tom Maddison, Jerome Gillard and Eduardo Mendes. At this point, Jerome Gillard can't be located. And oddly, all those that we've re-interviewed were in Sydney at the same time when this guy, we believe to be Randy, died.'

'It is also highly likely that the killer is none of these people, so we need to keep an open mind,' added Gardiner. 'You have all been allocated a group member to research. Speak with them again. Speak with their friends, family, and work contacts if they're employed. Find out where they grew up and went to school… no shortcuts.'

She looked around at her team. There were some nods and a few whispers. A couple were jotting down notes.

Milford partly raised a hand. 'Out of those we know, we'd have to think that Mendes was the most likely?'

'Yes, but…'

'Yeah, I know. Keep an open mind,' said Milford, finishing her sentence.

'Thank you, detective,' she said. 'Of that group, I see Mendes as number one…' she held up her fingers as she spoke. '… Johansson, number two, with a question mark because he was at work on Friday until ten in the evening, but supervision there is low, and he could have skipped out. Gillard, I have at number three because of his absence, which could mean he's done a runner. Tom Maddison seems too weak and ineffectual to be likely. He has a reasonable alibi, although we do note that known drug users and alleged dealers provided this, so I put him as our fourth suspect. Celine Woods seems incapable of any such act and has a solid alibi. Scriver-Bunt was not a member of the group when Ramsay was murdered; she also has a solid alibi for Friday evening. Mendes says he was at home on his own on Friday night, and both Mendes and Johansson were home alone when Ramsay was murdered.'

Michelle grabbed a red marker and circled the four suspects' names on the whiteboard. Then she bracketed several and wrote *Sydney 2022*; after this, she drew a big black circle around everyone's name and wrote *M Huang* over the line before turning back to her team.

'And all of them, including the two deceased, were referred by Dr Lulu Huang. Mendes is also well-associated with this psychiatrist. She is not on the suspect list, but who knows, that could change. I'll assign two of you to visit with her later this morning,' said Gardiner. 'There's plenty to be done. You all have names to follow up, and I'll execute this warrant...,' she raised the document, '... with the forensic guys... plus you...' she looked around, 'Perkins... and you... Milford.'

Chapter 48

Jasper's Chronicles - Part 3

The Resurgence

My life has been one of learning. I admit mistakes have been made, serious mistakes, tragic errors of judgment. Unbeknown to me, the use of substances to enhance my abilities and improve my awareness became controlled by evil, which drove me to the point of excessive use and addiction. Now, I'm wiser, and should I take advantage of this option in the future, I will do so with the supervision of a cleansed soul.

One constant has been my duty to impair and, if possible, obliterate The Torment. This evil gained traction thanks to impure and misguided thoughts of the weak. It consumed the world for nearly two years and, even now, still lurks unseen among us.

My colleague, who has travelled with me and been there to collate and edit my words, has now assimilated with my core being. My writing has acquired a new urgency so that at some future time, it will be there both as a record and a powerful weapon for those who come after me and battle The Torment in whatever form it cloaks itself.

I've decided to go by a different name, one I will not commit to words on a page. Just like my trusted and now integrated colleague, I will, for the time being, remain nameless while my armoury strengthens.

My offspring are closer to me now, and I hope their earlier contamination has resolved. If they share my vision, understanding and aspirations, we may yet become a formidable force. I've been encouraged by recent events and have had a glimpse of this future. It has been heartwarming to see that my years as a guiding parent and the education imparted to the young have resulted in the development of astute minds. A recruit to our cause has been acquired, and others are in scope. Some, unbeknown to them, have already contributed to our plan. It is hoped this will be an area of growth. We must always think twice, plan methodically, and act decisively while remembering that nothing is a coincidence and that connections surround us. Their significance may sometimes elude us, but it awaits our discovery.

The battle lines are drawn, and the journey continues. Some souls have been saved, others have been lost, and some may need to be sacrificed as we move forward. Despite some setbacks, we continue with determined confidence and strengthened resolve.

Chapter 49

The Ocean Breeze

Caretaker Wally Goodall unlocked apartment twenty-three at the Ocean Breeze apartment building and stepped back as detectives and forensic officers filed into the Eduardo Mendes unit.

The three detectives wore shoe coverings, gloves and hairnets. In addition, the forensic investigators wore masks and disposable jumpsuits. Gardiner, Milford and Perkins waited inside the entrance as the others set themselves up. Alexander, a scientific officer, tore open a plastic sheet and flicked it over the dining room table. Another went from room to room, taking multiple photos of all the rooms without touching or opening anything. At the same time, a third lay two fat briefcases on the floor and opened them, revealing a plethora of jars, brushes, tape, bio-hazard bags, fingerprinting kits and other paraphernalia.

Georgina, the photographer, nodded to Michelle Gardiner, giving her the okay to proceed with the search. Gardiner asked her colleague, Milford, to wait near the door while she set off with Lucas Perkins and the photographer.

The trio started in the kitchen. Immediately, there was some success. Inside the dishwasher, apart from crockery, saucepans, and assorted cutlery, was a metal kebab skewer and an ice cream scoop with sharpened edges. Unfortunately, the cleaning cycle was complete, and the likelihood of finding further evidence was slim. Both items were bagged and placed on the plastic sheet in the dining area. Michelle opened the fridge and stood back while photos were taken, after which she and Perkins checked the contents, shifting items around. This was the procedure with every drawer and cupboard as they worked their way through the house. The next thing that caught their interest was found in the bathroom.

'This could be something,' said Michelle, looking into the middle drawer of the vanity. Georgina clicked away. 'Bag, please, Perkins.'

He passed her one of several he was holding. 'What are you thinking?'

'We know he does clowning, so the makeup here is no big surprise, but this item resembles something I've seen on some CCTV footage.' She held up a long-haired grey wig. 'And it's not something you'd expect a clown to wear.'

The search continued through the spare bedroom, where nothing of interest was discovered. In the main bedroom, they checked the bedside table and noticed a book on neuro-linguistic programming, a small bottle containing five Valium tablets and a King James Bible.

Michelle slid open the door to the built-in wardrobe. Georgina did her bit before the two detectives started shifting items aside and checking the shoes on the floor. They placed a pair of sandy sneakers into a plastic bag.

'Perkins, I need your tallness. Reach up here to the shelf. There are two urns, some shoe boxes, and other things. One at a time, pass them down.'

As he passed down the first urn, a single clack sound came from inside as it tilted slightly. 'Ooh… It seems that Francisco's not quite dead,' he laughed as Gardiner took the item. With the second one, he deliberately tipped it, and the sound repeated. 'Neither is Delfina!'

'Straight to the dining table with these. Then we continue looking.'

The urns were placed on the plastic sheet in the dining room. 'There's something in these that's harder than ash,' Michelle said to Alexander. 'If you could look when you've dusted for prints. Thanks.'

Back in the main bedroom, Lucas passed down the shoe boxes. Michelle placed them on the bed and eased the lids off with a pen. 'Photos,' she announced. She upended the three boxes onto the bed. Next, Perkins passed down some porn magazines and DVDs.

'There's a scarf at the back covering something,' he said. He pulled it free. 'Holy fuck!' He took a couple of steps back.

Michelle was on her toes but still struggled to see. 'What is it? Do we need a step ladder?'

'Georgina, reach up and take some snaps,' he panted. 'We've got eyes, boss. Three lots of eyes.'

*   *   *

The two silver urns had been opened. On the back of each was an engraved brass plaque with the full name of each person, Francisco Jose Mendes and Delfina Isabel Mendes, along with a list of their progeny, two girls and one boy, Eduardo.

'We won't do anything more with these urns until we're back at the lab,' said Alexander, the keeper of the evidence table. 'But you've seen the large marbles in both, so I guess you can draw your conclusions for now.' He sat on a dining chair and moved his masked face close to the three jars discovered under the scarf in the wardrobe. 'The eyes in the jar with the pickle label are significantly older than the other two. The fluid is cloudy, and some particles have come free and settled on the bottom. The other two are recent specimens. As for the wig...' he reached over and lifted the plastic bag, '... there is a dark stain at the base of a few hair strands. Could be several things, but residue from blood is one possibility.'

'Thanks, Alex,' said Gardiner.

*   *   *

Two hours after the search concluded, Eduardo Mendes was in custody and charged with two counts of murder. His fingerprints were found over all three jars and lids.

Gardiner had contacted Detective Harry Truman in Sydney and given him the heads-up. She was confident the DNA analysis from the pickle jar eyes would match that of "Randy Maybe", after which another charge would be added, most likely Improper Interference with a Corpse.

*   *   *

The planned visit to Dr Lulu Huang had been delayed due to her being called away urgently to review a private client who had attempted suicide at a private in-patient facility. The two detectives returned empty-handed after being turned away by Val, the receptionist.

'She said we should rebook,' said a female detective. 'I told her we could return this afternoon, but she said not to bother as the doctor was already over-booked.'

Michelle's eyes narrowed, and her mouth tightened. She turned to Perkins, sitting at his desk and halfway through a Whopper. 'Is the world conspiring against me, Perkins?' she yelled. He looked up at her with his mouthful and shrugged. 'Come on. We're going back there.' She grabbed her jacket and moved away, then turned back. 'Well, don't just sit there!'

'What? Like, now?'

'Yes, Perkins.'

'Not sure why we're doing this,' he said, squeezing his words out through a mouth half-full of food. 'We have the killer.' He got a few looks from his team. Milford smiled, moved his hand to his neck and pulled his index finger across his throat. 'We've got all the evidence and the murder weapons. What are you hoping to gain?'

'Perkins!' she yelled. 'There are questions that need some fucking answers. It is not case fucking closed just yet. So, drag your lazy arse off that chair, and let's go.'

Chapter 50

Lulu Huang

Detectives Michelle Gardiner and Lucas Perkins presented at the reception at level twelve. Dr Huang had returned and had already started seeing her afternoon patients.

'Sit there,' she instructed her colleague, pointing to a vacant seat in the waiting area. Perkins wasn't about to argue. He had already been listening to a barrage from the boss on the way over.

'We missed seeing Doctor Huang this morning,' said Michelle, trying to remain calm.

'Sorry, there was an emergency,' said the heavily made-up receptionist, with a name tag of Val. She looked over the top of her glasses at the detective. 'I could reschedule that meeting for you.'

'Certainly,' smiled Gardiner. 'If you could put me in next, please.'

'Oh, I'm sorry, but the afternoon is full.' She shook her head and looked at her monitor while tapping away at the keyboard. 'Wednesday afternoon would work,' she announced, looking up.

'That won't do. I said we could be next.'

'Sorry, that's not in order, my dear,' Val said firmly.

'It's not fucking *dear*, it's fucking *detective*, and there's been two fucking murders of the *dear* doctors referred fucking patients. Why don't I go in now? Thank you, Val.' Michelle headed off down the corridor. Perkins lowered his National Geographic and smiled but remained seated. *'Sit quietly, Lucas. Say nothing. Wait until you hear gunshots,'* he told himself.

'Detective! Stop! You hear me,' squawked Val as she scampered after her. 'There is a session underway.'

Michelle hammered on the door below the "Lulu Huang Psychiatrist - FRANZCP" sign on the door, then just opened it and marched in.

'Oh, my goodness gracious,' said Val as she arrived at the open door and placed a hand on her chest.

Huang, dressed immaculately in a cream collarless blazer and skirt, and her female client in thongs, jeans and a t-shirt, sat across a table from one another. The young lady was blotting her eyes with a tissue.

Gardiner took the patient by the arm. 'Up you get. Your session is over.'

'What on earth…' exclaimed the psychiatrist as she stood.

'You…' Michelle pointed at the doctor. '… shut the fuck up!'

The young lady reluctantly stood as the detective pulled on her arm. She looked about. 'What's happening? What's going on, Lulu?'

'You're leaving; that's what's going on. Keep taking the tablets,' said Michelle as she grabbed the tissue box and shoved it at the woman. 'Take these. Off you go. Come back next week.'

For a moment, the lady stood bewildered and motionless.

'Fuck off!' shouted Gardiner.

She left quickly, pushing past Val, who was still at the door.

'Close the door, please, Val,' yelled the detective as she gave a shooing away sign with her hand. Gardiner dropped into the vacated chair. Lulu Huang stood staring.

'It's my turn now,' declared Michelle.

'I don't care to be told to shut up in my own office, and I find this to be a very inappropriate intrusion,' said the psychiatrist.

'I'm Detective Michelle Gardiner, and I find murders much more so.'

Lulu closed her eyes briefly, took two deep breaths, and sat opposite Gardiner. 'How can I help you today, Michelle?' she said calmly.

Gardiner felt herself relax as if following the doctor's lead. She went on to detail all the names of the therapy group, dead and alive. As it turned out, Celine and Faith were private referrals, while the rest were seen at the mental health outpatient clinic and referred from there.

'I grant you it's unusual that all of them in the same group were referred by me,' conceded Lulu. 'I send many referrals there, especially from the outpatient clinic. Honestly, this is not a landmark event.' The psychiatrist was sitting cross-legged, leaning back in the high-back chair with her arms by her side.

'Hmm… I'm going to tell you something that is not as yet common knowledge. I expect it not to leave this room.'

'I'm a psychiatrist. You are in therapy with me, Michelle. It's all confidential,' she smiled warmly and leaned forward.

'Obviously, doctor, I didn't come here for therapy.'

'Perhaps not. But being in here with me has made you less combative. So, therapy or not, there has been some healing.'

'I can see why you have a full caseload.'

Lulu nodded. 'You were about to tell me something…'

'The eyes of both Myles Ramsay and April Armstrong were removed, most likely using a sharpened ice cream scoop. They died after being stabbed through the corner of their eye, deep into their brain.'

If the psychiatrist was surprised, she didn't show it. 'You tell me this, why? And I heard on the radio that an arrest has been made.'

'Eduardo Mendes.'

Lulu Huang took a moment to take in this new information before responding. 'That man is not a killer.'

'Evidence says otherwise - a lot of evidence. But I wanted to ask you what your thoughts are on that. What would motivate that style of killing?'

'Mental illness. A form of paranoid psychosis. It could even involve drugs. And none of that is Eduardo.'

'And if the killer substituted cat's-eye marbles for the eyes?'

'Oh... that is intriguing, Michelle... they still wanted the person to see. To be whole... at least in another life.'

Gardiner nodded slowly as she looked at the psychiatrist. She noticed the doctor's grey hair held in a bun towards the back of her head. Bizarre thoughts tumbled through her mind.

'A penny for your thoughts, Michelle,' said Lulu.

'Do you know where you were in early 2022?'

'Absolutely. I was at a mental health conference in Sydney. I was one of the keynote speakers.'

'Well, of course. It seems nearly everyone was there at the same time,' quipped Gardiner.

'I know Eduardo was too, because we attended many of the same sessions together. This was around the time he lost his job there. He assaulted a client's relative, although, as I understand it, it was self-defence. I told him we needed more good counsellors like him here at Broadbeach, and he should apply.'

'Do you know this man?' Gardiner opened Randy's folded sketch and held it up for the psychiatrist.

Lulu leaned a little forward. 'No.' She reclined again. 'Who is he?'

'We don't know yet. A person of interest, let's say,' smiled Michelle. 'How well do you know Mendes?'

'I'd say I know him better than most, but not as well as some. He did some pre-surgical counselling on a client of mine. I can't speak highly enough of Eduardo.'

'Have you been to his apartment?'

'Once, not long after he moved to the Gold Coast. It was a brief visit to make him feel welcome. We had a beer on his veranda.'

'I didn't pick you as a beer drinker.'

'It was a shandy, really. He didn't stock any Canadian Maple Whiskey,' smiled the doctor. Michelle nodded.

'We have some unidentified fingerprints from his place. Would you have any objection to giving us a copy of yours?'

'Happy to supply whatever you need.'

'Thank you… Tell me, what was your keynote address about?'

'I presented a paper. It was very well received and generated plenty of discussion.'

'What was the topic?'

'My paper was titled *Eyes: The Window to the Soul.*'

Chapter 51

A Mountain of Evidence

Early media reports said an arrest had been made, but the alleged perpetrator's identity had not been immediately released. Soon enough, though, the name Eduardo Mendes was all over the web, on TV and radio, and in the daily newspapers. Somehow, the details of the eyeless victims and jars of eyes being found had so far escaped the journos. Leaving them to note... *both of the victim's bodies were severely mutilated. The details have not yet been disclosed.*

The evidence against Eduardo kept rolling in. The dark marks on the grey wig were identified as blood and a DNA match with the deceased Myles Ramsay. The metal kebab skewer and a sharpened ice cream scoop from the Mendes dishwasher were consistent with implements used on the recent two victims. The ash particles from April's eye sockets were identified as the same as those in Eduardo's parents' urns.

The only unexplained mystery from the Mendes apartment was a set of unidentified fingerprints found on an empty glass in the kitchen sink, the bathroom vanity, and the polished wooden arms of a lounge chair.

While not completely called off, the search for Jerome was scaled back after his absent-minded grandmother finally recalled him saying something about heading to a friend's place at Tweed Heads. She could not provide the address but expected him to return in a few days.

*　　　*　　　*

Late that afternoon, Michelle met with her fellow detectives for a debriefing. Two had already packed up, shut down their PCs and were ready to go home. Two female and a male detective at the back of the open office moved forward and grabbed a chair. Perkins and Milford remained at their desks closer to the front.

'I've spoken with the Inspector, who, in his wisdom and despite my objections, has decided to release most of you from this investigation given the outcome of today.' There were a few nods, subdued cheers and some stifled applause. 'Finish whatever reports you need to, then you can pursue your other cases. That is except for Milford and Perkins, who will assist me in tidying up a few loose ends.' The two men looked at each other. Perkins sighed. Milford rolled his eyes. 'Yeah, guys, I'm not thrilled about it either.'

'How about a celebration drink?' said Milford. He looked around for support and got several gestures of approval.

'I think the Anglers Arms awaits us, guys,' agreed Michelle.

'You gonna tell us about your consult with the psychiatrist, boss?' scoffed Perkins.

'Sure,' she replied. 'It's not a pretty tale. So, that will be after a few ales. And just to let you all know, she was yet another person in Sydney in early 2022, and that ain't the best of it.'

Chapter 52

The Rosemeadow Building Site

Ten minutes after Jasper Johansson had fled the scene after wedging the carpet roll containing Cassie under the reinforcing and rocks, she made a sound.

Her head was closest to the framed border. She twisted and writhed, managing to push both arms past her head and outside of the rolled-up carpet. Her hands and fingers clawed at the rocks, shifting some aside. The metal reinforcing above her helped as she pulled against it, each time moving her body a few millimetres. When she was half out of her unwanted wrap, her head pushed against the timber boarding. For several minutes, she bumped at it, pulled at it with her hands, cutting her arms against the rocks. Eventually, the board bent over enough, and Cassie dragged herself out. She rolled over a few times and then lay on her back, panting and sweating despite the cold. Her face was scratched and cut. Her arms and hands bled. She turned once more, but something stopped her. There was a big pair of work boots. Cassandra looked up at the large profile of security guard Roscoe Romano.

'What the fuck are you doing here, lady?' he shouted. 'This is private property.' He shone a torch at the slab framing. 'Did you crawl out of there? Holy shit! Someone's done a number on ya.' The obese man squatted and searched roughly through her pockets but only found a small handkerchief. 'Who are you?' He looked at a trickle of blood near her eye. It was one of many bleeding areas.

Cassie panted, then finally managed to squeeze out two words. 'Faith… Delaney.'

'Faith Delaney… huh. Who did this to you?'

'Faith… Delaney.'

'Yeah, I got that. But who did this? You need to tell me,' he yelled at her.

'Faith… Delaney.'

'Are you a fucking brain-damaged bitch?'

'Faith… Delaney,' continued Cassie in a monotone voice.

Romano squatted and looked her over. He slid a hand across her shirt and squeezed her breasts. He then pushed his hand hard against the crutch of her jeans. She did not attempt to stop him and seemed unconcerned.

'Faith, Delaney,' repeated Cassie.

The security guard stood, took out his mobile phone, pushed several buttons, and waited.

'What do you want, Roscoe? I'm in the middle of something,' came the reply.

'You're going to love this, Randy. I got one for ya. She's a bit cute. Knocked off in the brain, I reckon. A bit banged up right now, but she'll be a great earner. Give her a bit of a clean-up, dress her fancy and point her in the right direction. I just gave her a touch-up; she couldn't have cared less. I'm pretty sure she's off the grid. She's got no ID, and someone must'a thought she was dead. Wrapped her in a rug under a slab waitin' for a pour.'

'Bring her over in the mornin',' snapped Randy.

'I'll be wanting a bit of commission on this one.'

'We'll see what she's like tomorrow, then we can talk. Gotta go now.' Romano hung up and squatted next to his prize.

'There you go, my love,' he brushed his fingers over her face. 'I Got ya a new job 'n all. But first things first. You're all mine tonight, sweetheart.'

'Faith… Delaney.' She blinked her eyes. Her gaze looked straight past the man to the stars.

Chapter 53

Trust

The morning after Eduardo's arrest, Faith visited her brother. She waited until after ten so he would've had time to have two coffees. When he opened the door, she stood there smiling and looking radiant with her long, curly locks gently waving in the breeze.

'It's not a happy day,' said Del grimly.

'And good morning to you,' said Faith. She almost danced past him and into the dining area.

'Eduardo has been arrested.' Del closed the door.

'Yes.'

'They say he murdered Myles and April.'

'Yes, so they say,' Faith pointed to the kitchen. 'Mind if I make myself a cup of tea?' she asked brightly.

'Go for it. The tea bags are probably a bit stale. Did those cops come to see you, too, then?'

She flicked on the kettle. 'Oh, yes. They were doing the rounds. Do you want a cuppa?'

'I rarely drink tea,' he said as he sat and faced the kitchen. 'Did you leak that online report you found?'

'No. A friend of Ted's did.'

'At your request.'

'That's the sort of thing that needs to be made public. Does that bother you?'

'The whole matter bothers me. Everything about it. And I now know more about it than I care to.'

'Oh, do tell.' Faith poured the hot water.

'Myles and April had their eyes cut out.'

'Oh!'

'The killer placed cat's-eye marbles in their empty eye sockets. Tom Bowlers.'

'And you know this… how?' She moved to the dining table with her tea.

Delaney went on to tell his sister about the visit, how one detective made him blackout, and how he used Jupiter.

'It's a wonder they didn't cart you off to the nuthouse.'

'If you don't mind,' said Del very politely. '… they seemed to have a degree of understanding and acceptance.'

'Were you a suspect?'

'Maybe,' he shrugged.

'Well, you knew both the victims. And you're the marble guru, after all. And you have those blackouts where you can't remember stuff. And you sent ground glass fragments into that boy's eyes back at school.'

Del stared at her. She sat there sipping her tea, still smiling.

'Really Faith. Are you suggesting I had something to do with their murders?'

'No, no. Of course not, silly. But this is why the cops would have you on their suspect list.'

'You blinded your foster father. I'm not sure which of us is worse. And they wouldn't have known about that kid anyway. No one knows but you and me. Do you think Eduardo is a murderer?'

'No, I don't, but what I think is unimportant. It's all about evidence, and from what I've seen on some confidential police reports, there is a stack of it pointing at the counsellor… but I came here this morning because I have some good news,' announced Faith, changing the subject.

'Well, that would be a change. Am I going to like it, or will I decompensate?'

'I think I've found Mum. And we need to go to Sydney.'

Chapter 54

The Road Trip

Faith told the Scriver-Bunts she would be away for a few days attempting to find her mother and would be taking the Audi Q7 SUV. She showed Gayle and Nadine the meals she had prepared and went through the freezer items that they could use in her absence. She marked on the calendar when Ted had his appointments; one was business, and one was medical. They had the second vehicle, so there would be no problems. The three members of her adopted family all wished her well and hugged her on her departure.

Del was unsure if he would still have his job on his return. The manager was unhappy that he was dropping three shifts and even less impressed when Del was unclear about when he would return.

'You don't need that job,' said Faith as the vehicle entered New South Wales. 'You can help me and look out for me.'

'Look out for what? Not that evil presence thing.' He shook his head. 'Because I don't think I'd be much good at that.'

'You have learned how to manage your anxiety. Granted, you still have episodes, and that is fine. We will work on that together. You must learn to deal with this wickedness, Del. Like me, you will learn.'

'Don't do this, Faith.'

'Do what?'

'Push my buttons.'

'This is important, Del. April was one of the wicked ones. I'm glad she's moved on.'

'There you go!' Del threw his hands in the air. 'Fuck! You'll need to settle down; otherwise, you can let me out now, and I'll go back home. And I didn't have any problem with April.'

'You would have. She would've got your address. She made you blackout at the centre. It was just a matter of time.'

'Jesus Faith! I'm glad you were dining out that night; otherwise, I would think you were the one that plucked her eyes out.'

'Hmm… do you think I'd be capable of that?'

'Right now, I don't want to think about any of that. So, stop all this disturbing talk.'

'Sorry. Just idle chat then.'

'Please.'

'We'll be stopping at Port Macquarie tonight. That's about halfway.'

'Super,' sighed Del. He focused on cars, houses, paddocks and hills out the window - anything to take his mind off his sister and her sinister claptrap.

Faith was good to her word and kept the conversation light for the five-hour drive until they checked into their Port Macquarie motel.

The accommodation was basic: one large room with a double and single bed, a large wall-mounted TV over a long bench with a built-in bar fridge and some small appliances, two small lounge chairs, and a tiny bathroom at the far end.

After unpacking a few items and freshening up, Faith went to the front window and stood there looking outside.

'Is everything okay?' asked Del.

'Hmm… seems to be.' She drew the curtains and chain-locked the door.

'You are a worry, sis,' sighed Del.

The siblings stacked pillows and sat beside each other on the double bed. The TV showed the gameshow Deal or No Deal, and the volume was on mute. Del was sipping on a Coke.

'About the same amount of driving tomorrow,' said Faith.

'And we are heading to a halfway house in Fairfield?'

'Yeah. To see Mum.'

'Maybe… we'll see, I guess.' Del sighed and drank some more Coke, then shook his head.

'What's up?' asked Faith.

'You, that's what.'

'Come on now. Spit it out.'

'It's like you are drip-feeding me, sis,' Del turned to her. She pulled her head back. Her eyes opened wider. 'You give me bits of information to keep me focused or anxious or something. I feel there's always stuff that you're holding back.'

'But if I say too much, I'm *pushing your buttons*, and you tell me to shut up.'

'No, it's not about that…' Del paused and thought. 'Honestly, I have a few questions. But I need honest answers. I need complete answers.'

'Sure. I love you, Del. I don't want to have any secrets. Ask me anything. I'll do my best not to cause you too much distress.'

'Okay, so you're this superwiz detective with your mate Ted. You guys are hacking stuff and getting secret files and reports and all that. You've been doing this for at least a couple of years. Here I am, living not so far away from you, yet it takes you two years or more to knock on my door. I don't get that.'

'I'm sorry that this has been troubling you…'

'And that's not all,' interrupted Del. 'You said Dad took a plane to the Gold Coast two years ago…'

'Hush, not so loud,' interrupted Faith.

'… Yet that's all you can tell me about him,' continued Del a little softer. 'It doesn't add up. This is what I mean…' Del moved his arms quickly. Some Coke flew out of the bottle, '… drip feeding me.' He rubbed the spilt drink into the quilt.

'You're right. I could have come to see you earlier. The truth is, I didn't want to until I was ready.'

'Faith, I was your long lost brother. How could you not make finding me a priority?'

'I needed to be reasonably sure you would be safe. For a long time, I doubted whether I could do that. I wouldn't want to put you at more risk than I could manage. Like Dad…' she paused and swallowed, then lowered her head and whispered, 'I don't want to say *Dad* or our *father* or his real name anymore. It sends out alerts to The Torment.'

'You sound like D…,' Del paused and corrected himself. 'You sound like him. You're going to have to do better than that. Where is he? Have you met him? Have you spoken with him? Have you actually seen Mum? Do you honestly believe she is alive?'

'I've shown you her pic on my phone.'

'Yes, but that's someone that bears a vague resemblance at best.'

'I haven't seen her,' said Faith. 'But this is her.' Faith held up her phone. 'You will see. She goes by the name Faith Delaney. That's proof in itself.'

'No, it's not proof, that's a coincidence. I could look up Facebook and find a dozen Faith Delaneys.'

'Coincidence doesn't exist. I thought you knew that.'

'Hmm… yeah, okay. I do believe that, but maybe there is an exception to the rule,' grumbled Del. 'What about he who must never be named?'

'I've seen him and spoken with him. At the Gold Coast and here in Sydney.'

Del's mouth dropped open. 'Fuck!' he yelled and threw his arms up.

'Delaney Jeffrey Johansson!'

'That's all your fault…' he pointed at her, '… me swearing.'

'We may be able to catch up with him while we're in Sydney.'

'You said he was on the Gold Coast now,' snapped Del.

'He lives there, and like us, he travels too.'

'What… so you two are like best crazy buddies now?'

'That's unkind and untrue.'

'Really?'

'You will see The Torment one day. Then you will be on board.'

'I don't want to see it. And I'm not boarding the crazy shuttle bus.'

Chapter 55

Loose Ends

'I want you to contact the Archbishop of Brisbane, Marcus Cole,' said Michelle to Perkins. 'Consider this as making up for your lack of diligence in researching the Mendes Angolan back story. 'I want some verification on that article that found its way into the news. I'm hoping the Archbishop has enough influence to help us.'

The trio were now in a smaller office for their continuing work. The whiteboards had been moved to their new location. All three detectives wore button-up shirts and trousers, the difference being that the two men wore ties.

'I'm not a Catholic, you know,' scoffed Lucas. 'How do I address this guy?'

'Your Grace is fine. Your Excellency is also okay. Maybe he'd even respond to his actual name,' said Michelle. 'Live dangerously, Perkins.'

'Milford, go see Jerome Gillard's grandmother again. See if she's had any contact with him yet.'

'You know she's a bit demented, right?'

'Does that bother you?'

'No. But whatever she says will be unreliable.'

'I don't care. I want information. And while you're there, check out his room.'

'What am I looking for?'

'Milford! Be a fucking detective. I can't be mothering you all the time. I'm cutting the apron strings. You gotta figure this shit out.'

'Before you both get on with it, we also need fingerprints from everyone associated with the therapy group. Obviously, we have Mendes, Armstrong, and Ramsay. I'll start on the others.'

*   *   *

The Gillard house was a cottage-style home with a loft. It was on the smallest allotment in the street and partly concealed by a large Illawarra Flame and a Golden Rain Tree. The other stand-out features were the sky-blue roof and the white picket fence.

As Detective Kevin Milford approached, some of the defects became more obvious. The gate needed some manipulation to open; the grass needed a mow, and much of the house paint was cracked and curling away from the timber. He pushed a door button, which made no sound, so he knocked and waited.

After more knocking, the door squeaked open.

'Good morning, sonny,' wheezed the white-haired Mrs Gillard. Her grey dress was soiled with some dribbles that looked like gravy. She was hunched over.

'I'm Detective Milford, good morning.'

'You still after Jerome?'

'We are. Is he in?' said Milford with some surprise that she would have remembered.

'No.'

'Is he still at Tweed Heads?'

'Why would he be there?'

'I thought he went to visit a friend.'

'I don't know anything about that,' she groaned.

'If it's not too much trouble, would I be able to see his room?'

'What's he done wrong?'

'I doubt he's done anything wrong, but he may have some connections with people we are concerned about.'

'Upstairs,' she moved aside. 'His room is in the loft. It's probably a pigsty. I can't get up there anymore. My hips won't tolerate these steps.'

'Much appreciated.' Kevin tipped his head and made his way up the stairs, which creaked under his weight.

The loft's ceiling was low and not the pigsty as Mrs Gillard had suggested. The detective could stand up straight, provided he avoided the light shade and stayed in the middle of the room.

He took a few pictures with his phone before ducking his head and having a poke around. Most of Jerome's clothing was neatly folded in three open cardboard boxes. A single mattress with a doona and two pillows were on the floor. A pedestal fan was nearby. Several hooks were on a low beam supporting a backpack, two belts, an iPhone ear plug set and a string-pull toiletry bag. Next to the mattress were two half-full water bottles and a glass. There was no TV, no computer and no phone.

Milford upended the toiletry bag and rifled through the clothes boxes, finding nothing interesting. He sighed and shrugged as he roughly shoved the toiletry items back in the bag and then hung the bag on the hook. As a final check, he shook out the doona and felt and banged at the pillows. Nothing but dust. He flipped the mattress and then stood staring. 'What the...' he squatted, pulled out his phone and took more pics. On the floor were four flat plastic containers with what appeared to be makeup inside, three small partly used tubes of super glue, a rectangular sharpening stone, a small squeeze bottle showing the words *LATEX - Liquid Rubber* and a book titled The Colour Atlas of Ophthalmology. As he leaned in closer, he saw several long, grey hair strands.

'You are the man, Milford,' he roared and jumped to his feet, hitting his head on the low ceiling. 'Fuck!'

*   *   *

The detective briefly excused himself, returning moments later with several plastic evidence bags.

On his way out, carrying the evidence, he met Mrs Gillard at the bottom of the stairs.

'You have a bit of a collection there, young man.'

'Do you recognise any of these things?' He held up the plastic bags in turn.

'No,' she shook her head. 'Who knows what you young'uns get up to these days?'

'I may need to come back again.'

'Yes, I know. He said the same thing.'

'Who?' said a puzzled Milford.

'You look a bit like him. A much younger version, of course. And perhaps a little heavier.' She looked the detective up and down and patted him on the arm. 'Don't want to offend you, young man.'

'Who do I look like?'

'The Angel,' smiled the woman. 'So wonderful.' She looked at the ceiling and sighed. 'If only.'

'What sort of Angel?' Milford instinctively looked up as if there might be something to see. 'Was this a real person?'

'He spent some time with me and Jerome. He was like a teacher. Giving us lessons. Jerome was really taken with him. What a lovely man.'

Chapter 56

Developments

Detective Milford was sipping his coffee the following morning, and Perkins was halfway through his bacon and egg roll when Michelle Gardiner walked in. She started clapping.

'Is that a good clap?' grunted Milford. 'Or a pissed-off slow clap?'

'Thank you, Milford,' she replied. 'You did a great job at the Gillard house. The hair strands match the wig we found in the Mendes' bathroom. The prints from the glass and the toothbrush you took as evidence match the unidentified ones from his apartment. The super glue is the same brand as what was used in the Armstrong murder.' Michelle parked herself at the third desk and turned on her desktop PC. She lifted a glass of water and raised it to him.

'Thanks, boss. And I'm thinking...'

'Superb!' interrupted Gardiner. 'I like it when you do that!'

'Yeah, yeah. Okay. I was thinking that this means either young Gillard and Mendes were working together or that Mendes could have been set up. I favour the working together theory for now. And while I'm about ninety-nine percent sure that the prints on the glass and toothbrush are those of Jerome Gillard, I'd like to be one hundred percent. And that can only happen when we get our hands on the guy.'

'But where is he?' She raised her open hands.

'The old dear knew nothing about the Tweed Heads friend. She indicated that someone else had been there. I'm unsure if it was to see her or Jerome. She said I looked like him... at least a younger version.'

'Like who?' asked Gardiner.

'She couldn't give me a name, but she said he was an angel. I had the impression it was some older guy. Mrs Gillard was light on detail.'

'An angel? Hmm…' Michelle pondered Milford's words momentarily, then moved on. She turned on her swivel chair to face her other charge. 'What about the Archbishop, Perkins?'

'Expecting a call back this morning. His Excellency said he would look into it overnight.'

'His Excellency?'

'Yeah,' smiled Lucas as he chewed. 'That be my mate, Marcus.'

'Okay,' grinned Michelle. 'I have some more news, guys. I went to the Scriver-Bunt mansion to get prints from Faith, only to find out she had gone to Sydney… and taken her brother with her. Some sort of family reunion.'

'I didn't think she had a brother, just a sister,' said Milford.

'Her brother is Delaney Johansson.'

'Shit!' exclaimed Perkins.

'Fuck!' said Milford.

'And she was adopted by the Scriver-Bunt family a few years ago. She was previously a Johansson.'

'And the cow chose not to disclose any of this,' said Milford, shaking his head.

'She spoke thoughtfully, as did her brother. Had it been known they were brother and sister, they would probably not have been permitted to attend the same therapy group.'

'Liars,' said Perkins.

'It was a withholding of the truth rather than a lie. But yes, given the circumstances, they could have been upfront. Today, I'll be chasing up more background on these two… but, gentlemen, there's more,' Michelle gave a cheeky grin.

'We're gentlemen, Kevin.'

'Who'd have thought,' added Milford.

'You guys are lucky I'm in a good mood this morning. Don't let it go to your heads.'

'What's the big news then?' asked Kevin, sitting forward. Perkins tilted his chair back.

'It was an attack with acid several years ago that caused Edward Scriver-Bunt's blindness. It was thrown directly into his eyes. No arrest was ever made.'

'Is that just a freakish coincidence?' asked Milford.

'Faith has ingratiated herself with the family since this accident. They depend on her now. She gets a generous allowance,' said Gardiner.

'What are you saying?' asked Perkins. 'That she is somehow responsible? For blinding her adopted father and who knows what else?'

'Don't know. I want answers. I'd like to chat with Dr Huang again.'

'Oh no!' exclaimed Perkins.

'It's okay, Perkins. I'll go on my own. Spare you any embarrassment.'

'It's not embarrassment,' added Lucas. 'It's another verbal assault from that bloody receptionist. I doubt the doctor will tell you anything about Faith Scriver-Bunt; that's all under the professional cone of silence.' He gave a quick demo with his hands over his head.

'We'll see. And there's still more news,' grinned Michelle.

'You're just full of it this morning,' joked Perkins.

'And you're full of it most of the time, detective,' she retorted. 'The DNA on the pickle jar eyes matches "Randy Maybe" from the stormwater drain. Someone's been hanging on to their souvenirs.'

*   *   *

Before heading up the road to visit the psychiatrist, Gardiner called Detective Harry Truman in Sydney. As usual, she was made to wait for twenty minutes.

'Hey there, Gardiner,' he eventually said. 'Sorry for keeping you on hold.'

'So far, I've managed to maintain my good mood, but it is still early,' she replied. 'You would know we have a match on the eyes.'

'Yeah, that's super. Not that we know his full identity.'

'The likelihood of his death being murder is very high now.'

'It is, but reopening the case is unlikely. Either way, he's still dead, and we have no one to charge for anything.'

'Not yet. This is where I need some more help from you, Truman.'

'Of course you do,' he grumbled.

She told him about Faith Scriver-Bunt and Delaney Johansson, the adoptions, their relationship, the blind adoptive father, the therapy group, their trip to Sydney, and details about April Armstrong. He started to chuckle.

'I didn't tell a joke. What's so amusing?'

'Coincidence. That's what.'

'Go on.'

'I worked on a coroner's case for a missing woman - Cassandra Johansson, their mother. You've got me interested now, Gardiner.'

'Holy shit! This case keeps on giving; unfortunately, it's mostly giving confusion.' She gave him all the details of the Audi SUV they were driving. 'You could track this car. Find these two.'

'I could. When they start driving, we can track them. Then what?'

'Shit Truman,' snapped Gardiner. 'You're sounding like Milford, my *wanna-be a dick* guy up here!'

'You are a very cruel person, Gardiner.'

'You haven't seen nothing… just talk to these two. Tell them a few of the case facts. See how they react. Find out who they're visiting and when they'll be back. If possible, get their fingerprints.'

'Yeah… well of course. I would've done all that.'

'You're a champion. Stay in touch.'

Chapter 57

Fairfield Sydney

The halfway house was a grand-looking old home with a wide veranda around three sides sheltered by a bullnose roof. The Audi entered the circular gravel driveway and pulled in alongside three giant lily pilly trees.

'You reckon that this is where Mum lives?' asked Del as he checked out the place.

'I guess it is. And I so hope it is. As I told you, I've only seen the photo one of the carers texted me. It looked like a much older and even skinnier version of our mother,' said Faith. 'I've never been to this place before.'

'Are you nervous?'

'My stomach is telling me that I am.' Faith looked at her brother as they sat in the parked car. Del's respiration rate had increased, and he was swallowing frequently. 'You going to be okay?'

'Yeah. This feels a bit different to my usual pre-passing-out anxiety episodes. So, fingers crossed.'

'We're going to see Mum, Del.'

'Yes. I hope you're right.'

'As I told you. Don't expect too much. They said she is quite damaged, and she might not even recognise us.'

Faith had told Del how she found their mother. It was after months of fruitless online research when she was randomly searching names on police reports that she came across a woman called Faith Delaney. This lady had been rescued from a life of abuse on the streets. She was in poor physical health and needed hospital care. The CT scan showed she had brain damage consistent with having had a lobotomy years earlier. It was not known if this damage occurred by intent or accident. Her identity could not be confirmed. She became known to everyone as Faith Delaney, as these were the only words she had ever spoken. She was discharged to the Fairfield halfway home.

Today, Faith wore her chunky rainbow necklace over a black button-up shirt. Del was in jeans and a grey Echosmith band t-shirt.

Faith gestured to his shirt. 'She should like that picture.'

'I think it was her favourite band.'

Faith smiled and nodded.

The siblings held hands tightly as they went up the six front steps to the veranda. To their left, an elderly man sat in a wicker chair, mumbling and smoking. Faith pushed a button on the front door, and a pleasant sound of bells chimed somewhere inside.

The large door opened to a smiling Indian man with a black goatee. 'Good morning, madam… and sir,' he nodded to both. 'How may I be of assistance?'

'My name is Faith Scriver-Bunt. This is my brother.'

'Ah, yes. We are expecting you. I am Kabir. How do you do?' The man spoke warmly, using excessive nods and gestures. 'Mrs Faith Delaney is in our guest room waiting for you. Follow me, please.'

Faith and Delaney walked down a wide hallway with polished timber floors. Their hand-holding tightened. They passed an activity room where people of all ages were engaged or disengaged with jigsaws, board games, artwork, and reading. One middle-aged man, with his shorts too high and mouth hanging open, stood alone and paced up and down in one spot.

'This is the guest lounge,' said Kabir, pushing open a slightly ajar door. 'Faith is having a good day today. There are times when she becomes a little irritable.'

A lady of slight build with long salt-and-pepper hair had her back to the three. She wore ill-fitting blue jeans and a baggy tracksuit top and had bare feet.

'I'm very excited to see if this is your mother and if she recognises you,' said Kabir. He remained standing at the door as Faith and Delaney stepped slowly forward.

'It's her,' whispered Faith. 'I just know it.' She glanced at her brother, who had tears flowing freely down his face.

'Mum,' sobbed Del.

'Hello, Mum,' said Faith.

'Faith Delaney,' said the woman, still looking out the window.

'It's us,' panted Faith.

'Ah… uh… huh,' uttered the woman as her head tipped from side to side. 'Faith… Delaney.'

'It's me, Delaney.'

'And it's me, Faith.'

She turned and saw them and started to tremble. Kabir took two steps forward. 'Faith… Delaney, she stammered.

They ran to her, hugged, kissed, and caressed her weathered face.

'Mum, Mum, Mum,' said Del through sobs and gasps.

'Mum. Oh my God. I knew…' Faith gulped in a breath. 'I knew… I always knew you were alive.'

Cassie continued trembling. Her eyes watered. She hugged her children back. 'Faith… Delaney.'

After many more hugs, kisses and tears, the brother and sister took their mother to the sofa, where they sat on either side of her.

Kabir came over, blotting his eyes with a tissue. 'This is a special moment. I'll leave you now and be back shortly with some tea.'

Chapter 58

Another Consult

'Oh no, not you!' exclaimed Val as Michelle Gardiner presented herself at the reception desk. 'Are you here to apologise, detective?' she asked with a tight smile.

'No,' said Michelle bluntly. 'I'm here to see Lulu.'

'Okay,' sighed Val in resignation. 'I'll squeeze you in for a few minutes before her next appointment. Please don't go barging in there.'

'That sounds perfect.'

'Take a seat. It shouldn't be too long.'

* * *

A thin man in shorts and sandals, blowing his nose, emerged from the hallway and stood at reception. Val was quick to greet Doctor Huang as she entered the waiting area. The receptionist whispered in her ear. The psychiatrist smiled and waved Gardiner in.

Once again, Lulu Huang looked striking in a dark blue pantsuit over a light blue, business-style shirt. The pair sat in the same chairs as their last meeting.

'Nice to see you, Michelle,' said Huang warmly. 'Another brief consult?'

'Brief... yes. I'm not after therapy.'

'Sure.' The psychiatrist leaned back.

'I accept you cannot tell me details of your clients, but I was hoping for some clarification on some matters. Faith Scriver-Bunt's adoptive father was blinded in an attack with acid. Given the recent killings that have occurred, this is one of several coincidences I don't like.'

'I was aware of that, Michelle. However, I'll neither confirm, deny, nor discuss any questions related to my clients' sessions with me.'

The detective took a deep breath and fired off a question regardless. 'I wondered if Faith had any involvement with this incident.' Gardiner watched her intently. Lulu Huang sat smiling, made no response, and did not indicate one way or the other on the matter. 'Okay, let's strike that line of enquiry. Do you still see Jerome Gillard?'

'I remember him. I saw him once. A troubled young man. I referred him to Eduardo's group. Is he okay?'

'Don't know. We can't locate him.'

'Oh, that's a bit worrying.'

'Yes,' sighed the detective.

'Your job is so stressful. Michelle, tell me what you do to unwind?' The doctor sat forward and opened her hands.

'I said before that I'm not here for therapy.'

'I ask out of care and concern. We all need outlets for our challenging feelings… like anxiety, guilt, frustration and anger.'

Michelle dipped her head, rubbed her temples and closed her eyes briefly. 'Please,' she looked at the doctor. 'It is these coincidences that concern me right now. There are so many references to eyes, marbles, and Sydney. Even your presentation paper at that conference. "Eyes: The Window to the Soul" - that hit me like a piece of four by two when you said it.

'The original title was simply "The Use of Eyes in Therapy." I changed it after chatting with one of my clients.

'What client?' Michelle fired back. Lulu sat for a moment, contemplating. 'Surely, telling me a name is no breach of duty.'

'It can be in some circumstances,' said the psychiatrist. 'Disclosing that someone is or has received mental health treatment can compromise them.'

'What about in this instance?'

'Under these circumstances, and as the individual is no longer under my care, it may be alright. I'm sure the man in question wouldn't mind. He's one of the kindest and most thoughtful men I've ever had the pleasure of meeting.'

'Yes… and…' said Michelle, hanging out for the name.

'I think I told you last time that when Eduardo worked in Sydney, he counselled one of my patients who was about to undergo cardiac surgery. This is the same man that I'm referring to. His name is Angel Abner.'

Michelle was momentarily lost for words.

'He was a lovely man before his surgery,' continued the doctor. 'But something quite rare happened after. There are many cases where patients suffer a decline in their mental health or have a negative change in their personality after such operations. With Angel, however, this had the opposite effect. It made a delightful man even more so. He became so engaging and confident. He even recognised this in himself. Quite remarkable, really…,' Lulu paused and looked at the detective. 'Are you okay?'

'You just hit me with another four by two.'

Chapter 59

Happy & Sad

Faith and Delaney spent three hours with their mother. Kabir had made a second pot of tea and rustled up some scones and sandwiches for lunch. They told her stories of their lives over the past ten years. Some editing of their tales was required when staff were within earshot. All three, and at times Kabir, had moments of tears and sobs.

'Faith... Delaney,' repeated Cassie many times as they spoke. For the most part, she spoke in monotone, but despite her two-word responses, she showed genuine emotion at times when she looked and embraced her children. It was unclear if she was understanding what they were saying.

Faith reached over and felt her mother's ribs through the tracksuit top. 'Mum, you are so thin.' She offered her a scone with jam, but Cassie ignored it. So far, she had only had half a cup of tea and two bites from an egg and lettuce sandwich.

'We encourage her so much,' said Kabir as he re-entered the guest room with a jug of cold water. 'But she eats very little - just enough to get by. She seems to like avocado. Unfortunately, we're all out at the moment.' He set the jug down in front of the three, all sitting snuggly on the sofa.

'We'll bring some back,' said Del.

'Yes, we'll come back in the morning,' added Faith. 'You have my number if Mum needs anything.'

Kabir stood in front of the family and placed his hands on his hips. 'Hmm... this is a most unusual situation. We have a lady we call Faith Delaney...'

'Faith… Delaney,' blurted Cassie.

'Yes,' continued Kabir. 'Her real name is Cassandra Johansson. A lady who was declared dead by the coroner. I feel the authorities need to be notified.'

Chapter 60

Jasper's Revival

January 2022

Jasper made his way along the path at a slow jog. He was on a five-kilometre route around the roads near Central Station Sydney and the adjoining Belmore Park. It had been ten weeks since his coronary bypass surgery. This was his eighth time on this route, and his pace was improving with each run. Today, as he had on his previous exercise outings, he hoped to meet a particular person. He had heard about a man who held some valuable commodities he wanted to get his hands on.

As some light rain started to fall, he stopped for a rest under the shelter of the old Central Station entrance. It was eight in the evening, and with daylight saving time, the sunset was still twenty minutes away. He counted eight homeless people who had already set up a space there. Some of whom he had already met, stopping to give them a few dollars and some muesli bars. There would be more as the evening wore on, especially if the rain increased.

As he stood with his hands on his hips, another man scampered into the area. Jasper checked him out. First, he tried to see his eyes but couldn't get a good look with the man's head down and angled to the side. The guy was untidy, with filthy jeans, a grey business shirt hanging out with two missing buttons, and a pair of Nikes. He had a leather man-bag over his shoulder.

The man brushed some water drops from his face, then turned and noticed Jasper.

'Hey mate,' he said in a husky voice. 'What's happenin'?'

Jasper saw his eyes. They were dark without being black. His pupils were oversized. Johansson immediately thought of drugs - cocaine, speed, ecstasy and others.

'What drugs do you take?' he asked bluntly.

'Fuck off!'

Jasper turned away, leaned against one of the pillars and started stretching his calves. The man stared at him.

'I can get you drugs, man,' he said more politely. 'If that's what you're into.'

'I have that matter already in hand,' replied Jasper. He changed to the other leg and pushed.

'I can do a better deal.'

'No thanks.'

'Hmm… I can sweeten the deal with some pussy,' he said in a deep but softer voice. 'I have 'em on hand at bargain prices.'

'You probably have them drugged to the eyeballs.'

'What do you care? You fuck 'em any which way you fucking like. I got a real cutie called Faith Delaney. She does anything and won't talk ya head off.' Jasper eased off the pillar and looked at the guy. He felt his heart rate increase. *Relax, Jasper,* he told himself. *The enemy is at hand. There is work to be done.*

Jasper touched his own lips as he checked out the guy. 'Do you use drugs and Botox?'

'Fuck, man! I've got naturally big lips. Do you want the fucking deal or what?' snapped the man.

'I might be interested. I'd need to see this broad first.'

'Hey, mate. No sweat. I got pics right here.' He opened his man-bag and took out a mobile phone. After scrolling a few times, he approached Jasper. 'Look.' He showed him a photo and then scrolled to the next and the next. 'See mate. She's a fucking gem.'

'What about meth tabs. You have them?'

'Of course. I got tens and fifteens.'

'I don't want any K or other shit mixed with those. They gotta be just meth.'

'Of course,' he nodded. Jasper sighed and sucked his lip as if thinking it over. 'I'm a man of my word,' continued the dealer. 'People around here know me. Ask around. My name's Randy. They'll tell ya my word is good.'

'Okay, Randy. Can you manage fifty tens?'

'Sure. For fifty skaters, you get a discount, big fella.'

'Really.'

'Four hundred plus a hundred for the woman.'

'Huh!' uttered Jasper with surprise.

'Are we on, my friend?' grinned Randy.

'I think we are.'

'What's your name, champ?'

'Steven,' lied Jasper.

'Okay, Stevie. Now, with the woman. There are rules - leave no cuts, leave no open wounds, no serious damage, especially to her fuckable bits.'

'Where and when?'

'Are you local?'

'Paddington.'

'Centennial Parklands, the car park near the homestead playground just off Grand Drive. Do you know it?'

'Run past it most days.'

'Midday tomorrow for the meth. Then I'll have to drive you five minutes to redeem your pussy voucher.'

'Drive me?'

'I figure a guy like you won't wanna be fucking a chick on a park bench or the fucking grass. I have a clean room. It's up to you.'

'I'll be there with the cash.'

'Sweet,' smiled Randy. Jasper did his best to hide his contempt. He shook Randy's hand, then took off, resuming his run.

Chapter 61

Centennial Parklands

January 2022

Jasper was dressed in running clothes and at the park two hours early. He jogged slowly around the parklands, the café and the information centre, down the narrow roads, across grassed areas, through heavily treed sections and past several waterways and small lakes. After an hour, he ventured beyond the parkland following an open stormwater drain. He ducked under some low-hanging branches and arrived at a high, barbed wire fence and a sign that read, *Danger: No Entry - Authorised Personnel Only*. Below the fence, where it crossed the drain, a heavy metal grate lay on its side, detached from the pole to which it was welded. The gap was semi-circular, with enough room for anyone to slide under.

*   *   *

Two minutes after midday, an old, white Corolla hatchback pulled up in the disabled parking space. Jasper was chatting to a young lady with long curly hair while doing his lunges. When he saw Randy, he stopped his exercises, gave the girl a few pointing gestures and hand signals, and then waved her off. The dealer gave him a *come here* with his head.

Johansson opened the passenger side door. 'Hey,' he said as he hopped in.

'Stevie, how's it going? Who's the young chick?' asked Randy as he watched the girl disappear past the playground.

CRAZY LIES & CAT'S-EYES

'Don't know. She wanted directions.'

'Fair enough. Hey, are you cashed up?'

'Yeah.'

'Lift your shirt for me,' said Randy.

Jasper pulled his t-shirt up, showing his tummy, chest, and a long central scar, still dark red.

'Been in the wars, have we?'

'A darkness took over my body, but I've been repaired.'

'What... like cancer?'

'Something like that.'

'Huh... lean forward. Let me see your back.'

'I'm not a cop, and I have no attached devices if that's what you're worried about.' Jasper bent forward.

'All part of my routine with newbies, mate. You're all good, Stevie. You got a phone on ya?'

'Course.'

'Turn it off.'

Jasper undid a zip on his shorts pocket with one hand while his other reached behind him into a back pocket. In an instant, he had a flick knife out and open at Randy's throat.

'What the fuck, man. You gonna rip me off?' Randy reached down the side near the car door and grabbed something. With his free hand, Jasper punched him hard in the face. His nose instantly poured blood. A pistol fell to the car floor. Randy covered his bloody face with both hands.

'Look at me!' yelled Jasper. There was no immediate response. 'Now, arsehole!' he roared. Randy, trembling and gasping, turned his head. Johansson looked into the dealer's eyes. 'Yes, it has taken you.'

'What the hell, man? Take the fucking drugs. Just fucking go.'

'It was partly there yesterday. Now, the transformation is complete. The Torment has you.'

'You've fuckin' lost it, Stevie.' He pulled his shirt from his jeans and held it to his nose.

Jasper slid the gun away from Randy's feet. 'Put both your hands on the steering wheel. One on either side. He pushed the blade harder against Randy's throat.

'Fuck! Okay, man. I'm bleeding everywhere here!' He did as requested. Blood from his nose dripped onto his lap.

'I'm putting my knife here on the dash. I'm going to zip-tie your hands to the steering wheel. Each time you become a problem, I'll cut off a finger.'

'Fuck, you came prepared. What's your fucking story, man?'

'Did you hear what I just said!'

'Yeah, yeah. Fuck ya. Ya going to chop off me fingers. Well, I'm cooperating, see. Not fuckin' movin'. So, tie me the fuck up and be fucking done with it.'

Jasper pulled a few zip-ties from somewhere under his shorts and secured Randy's arms to the wheel by his wrists.

'Now we have a chat. Truthful answers only or else…' he picked up the flick knife, '… chop, chop.'

Jasper asked lots of questions. He obtained Randy's full name, address, date of birth, housemate's name, a description of the inside of his home, and what Randy's room looked like. He also asked him about Faith Delaney. Randy said she was in a room built into his garage. He found out how she was found at Rosemeadow years ago. He got the name Roscoe Romano.

'Now we drive a short way.'

'What, like this?'

'You'll manage. It's not far.'

They drove for two minutes and then pulled off the road near an open drain. Jasper took the car keys.

'These your house keys too?'

'Yeah, but I don't keep drugs there. You're wasting your time with that one, buster.'

Jasper moved to the driver's side, opened the door and cut the zip ties. 'Now we go for a walk,' he smiled at the bloodied drug dealer.

The pair soon disappeared behind trees and bushes. Randy walked in front with the knife's sharp point at his back. After sliding through the drain, where the grate was broken, they arrived at a section where the shallow trench changed into a large tunnel as it continued under the road.

'Empty your pockets,' demanded Jasper. Randy pulled out a few crumbled receipts, dirty tissues, a Ventolin inhaler, a packet of cigarettes and a Zippo lighter.

'You haven't got a wallet or any ID.'

'No. I never carry them. Then the cops, or cunts like you, don't know who the fuck I am… having said that, the cops don't usually tie me up and smash my face in.'

'Where're the drugs I was buying?'

'In the boot. Under the spare tyre. Why don't you take them and piss off.' Randy looked at the drain ahead of him. It would be dark in there. Maybe he could get away.

'Huh… I'll be going to your place. If I find you're bullshitting me, I'll be back, and I'll remove more than just your fingers. I'm going to tie you again.'

'Bring me back a fucking beer, shithead.' Randy lunged forward away from Jasper. 'Fuck you!' he shouted. His foot slipped on the edge of the slimy drain as he tried to make his getaway. It shot forward, making him fall backwards. His head struck the concrete with a loud thud and crack. He lay there partly in the water. Randy took two quick breaths, then became still with his eyes open. His pupils became even more dilated.

*   *   *

Jasper unlocked the front door of a house in Norton Terrace, Kingsford, and marched in as if he owned the place.

'What the fuck!' yelled a dishevelled guy watching porn, smoking a joint and eating ice cream.

'It's okay, Neville. I'm Randy's mate. Although I prefer to call him Richard. He sent me to pack him a bag.'

'Where is he? Where's he going?'

'He's got a couple of new chicks he's checking out for some dude at Surrey Hills. After that, he said he wants to lay low for a few days. Some supplier shit, I dunno… is his room still down here at the back?' Jasper started to head down a hallway.

'Yeah, mate. Same place. Have we met before?' Neville stood.

'Course, a few times. You're using too much shit,' Jasper smiled and waved a finger at him. 'Fucking up your brain, Nev. I'm just gonna grab a few things for him.'

'Where's he going to hide out?'

'A place at Waverley. He didn't give me the address, which is probably for the best.'

'Yeah, sure… can I help with anything? Do you wanna bit of green before you go?' He held out his joint.

'Thanks, Nev, but gotta hurry along here.

'Some ice cream then?'

Jasper watched as Neville scooped out two rounded helpings and plopped them onto his plate.

'It's chocolate-chip?'

'Save me some. I'll pack Richard's stuff and be back.'

Minutes later, Jasper returned to the lounge with a small, packed suitcase on wheels and a rolled-up sleeping bag under his arm. Neville had an empty dessert bowl and spoon ready. 'There you go, man. Knock yourself out. I've saved you a bit.' Neville put his attention back on the naked threesome on the TV.

Jasper scooped out the last of the ice cream, then paused momentarily as he turned the metal scoop in front of his face. He grabbed the plastic container as well.

'You sure you don't want a toke, mate,' said Neville, offering him the joint without taking his eyes off the TV.

Jasper held up a hand. 'No thanks. Is that Delaney chick still in the garage?'

'Oh yeah,' laughed Neville. 'She's too fucking dumb to even try to leave.' Jasper waved the ice cream scoop at Neville's head and hissed through his teeth. Neville remained engrossed with the porn.

*   *   *

Jasper opened the unlocked side door to the garage. The room was hot and humid, with a putrid smell of stale urine. A lady sat slumped in a small lounge chair beside an unmade double bed. In front of her, a TV was on, but she wasn't watching it.

'Hello,' said Jasper.

'Faith… Delaney,' came the weak reply.

He moved slowly until he was standing in front of her. He kneeled as he stared at her bruised and dirty face. 'Let me see your eyes.' He took her chin and turned her head. 'Somehow, Cassie, the wickedness has left you. Perhaps this place...' he looked around, '... is even too forbidding and grotesque even for demons.' Her hair was thin and knotted. There were a couple of bald patches where some had been pulled out. Her arms had track marks and open infected sores. She smelt of decay. 'Come with me.'

Cassie stood, almost fell, then regained her balance. Jasper scooped her up. 'You have no weight. I'll get you help.'

'Faith... Delaney,' she breathed.

*   *   *

He parked the Corolla away from the hospital and carried Cassie to the emergency department. Jasper wore a broad-brimmed hat and kept his head low. Two nurses immediately arrived to help and escorted him to a curtained cubicle, where he laid her on a trolley.

'Excuse me,' he said. 'I'll be right back.' He left and never returned.

*   *   *

Back with the body of Richard Sadowsky, Jasper put on a pair of latex gloves, re-dressed him in fresh clothes and packed the blood-stained ones into a plastic bag. He lay the suitcase and the sleeping bag near the body. He flicked the lid off the plastic container and took hold of the metal ice cream scoop.

'Things happen for a reason,' said Jasper to the deceased Randy. 'There are no coincidences. I remember skewers were once called sewers, and here you are lying in one. I know there is another step here, and I apologise that I'm not prepared for that, but if possible, I shall return and rectify the matter as soon as I'm able. For now, though, I must do what needs to be done. I've been shown the tools I must use. May God have mercy on your soul.' Jasper knelt near Sadowsky's head, scoop in hand.

Chapter 62

Faith & Delaney Check-in

The Airbnb apartment in Ascot Street Canley Heights was only a short drive from the halfway house at Fairfield.

'This is a bit more upmarket than the motel,' said Del as he wandered through the two-bedroom apartment. 'I've even got my own room.'

'We'll be here a few days. Let's be comfortable.'

'At Ted's expense.'

'Of course,' smiled Faith.

The siblings unpacked and stocked the fridge with the few items they had purchased on their way there, including a few avocados for tomorrow when they would revisit their mother. Faith had an orange juice, and Del had an iced coffee. They moved to the veranda.

'Look, a barbeque,' said Del. 'What a place.' He sat in a well-padded, black rattan chair. A setting of four singles and a double surrounded a glass-top coffee table.

'Wow, what a day,' sighed Faith.

'Poor Mum,' said Del. 'How she even survived is a miracle. It breaks my heart to see her this way.' He put his hand to his head. 'Look, here I go, blubbering again.'

'She is way better now than she was.'

'What's to become of her? Can we ever be a family again?'

'Anything's possible.'

Del sniffed and looked at his sister. He waved a finger at her. 'Now, you promised to tell me when we got to the Airbnb. So, out with it. The whole story. The true story.'

'Okay,' she nodded.

'No more drip feeding,' he said a little louder.

'Yes, as I told you at the motel, I've seen him… remember we are not to use his name. Let's call him Uncle for now.'

'If you say so.'

'We've caught up a few times. He lives in a converted shed at the back of an old house at Burleigh Heads. Like me, he didn't want you exposed to risk by seeing you. He has a plan.'

'Of course he does. I don't buy the not coming to see me. That sounds like bullshit. If he genuinely cared, he would've come around.'

'I didn't… not at first, even though I knew where you were. Do you doubt my love for you, Del?'

'No. Not a bit.'

'Then you should not doubt Uncle's either.'

'You know I had a vision when scrying with Jupiter.'

'Okay.'

'I saw you… I saw…' he hesitated, not wanting to mention names, '… both my parents… and myself. It was unsettling. I felt it was a warning.'

'Yes, that makes sense to me.'

'It does?' said Del with surprise.

'Well, I've tried to warn you, but you don't pay much attention. You should heed Jupiter. It's a warning about The Torment.'

*   *   *

The two sat chatting, the conversation moving back and forth as they discussed their parents, their future, and the possibility of a family reunion. Del shifted the talk back to Ramsay and April a few times, but Faith refused to dwell on that and changed the topic.

The doorbell chimed,

'Huh… I wasn't expecting visitors,' said Faith.

'I'll go,' said Del.

*   *   *

Detective Harry Truman was dressed casually in jeans and a polo shirt. He sat in a rattan chair facing Faith and Delaney. 'Thank you for allowing me in, and thanks for the cold water,' he said, taking a sip.

'How did you know to come here?' asked Faith.

'Ah… yes… it's your car. I tracked it here. Got the car details from Detective Gardiner on the Gold Coast. She saw your adoptive father, Faith… Edward Scriver-Bunt.'

'That's a bit freaky,' said Del.

'It's common enough these days. Most newer cars can be tracked. I had to knock on three other doors here before I found you, though,' he chuckled.

'Is this about the murders from my therapy group?' asked Del. He swallowed hard, then checked his pulse rate from his wrist.

'Mainly that, yes. We've had confirmation that the report in the news about Eduardo Mendes… you know, all that stuff about him being a possible abuser in Angola. Well, it was fake. Planted on their servers by some clever hacker.' Truman watched the pair.

'Oh my God!' exclaimed Del. 'I always felt the whole thing was bogus.'

'We don't know that yet, son,' added Truman. 'There is still plenty of incriminating evidence. We'll have to see how it plays out.' He smiled and turned his attention to Faith. 'Edward Scriver-Bunt, I understand, is a bit of an expert on internet security and related matters.'

'That is true. Are you asking a question, detective?' said Faith calmly.

Del's eyes widened. His respiration rate increased.

'He became blind when acid was thrown in his face,' continued Truman. 'The offender was never apprehended.'

'Again, true. But I hear no question.' Faith turned to her brother. 'Del, maybe you should lie down. You're looking a bit pale.'

'I'm okay. Just give me a moment. Excuse me, officer, while I close my eyes and zone out for a few minutes. I get these episodes from time to time.' Del shoved a cushion behind his back and slid down in the chair. Faith looked at Truman. She placed a finger over her lips. 'Just a couple of minutes,' she whispered.

Harry Truman and Faith sipped their drinks and smiled at each other. Almost at the same time, they both checked their phones. Del breathed slowly and deeply. Some colour returned to his cheeks, and after five minutes, he opened his eyes and sat up straight. 'Thank you. I needed that. I should be fine now,' he said.

'Very good,' said Truman. 'So, you are both here... to see a relative?'

'Yes,' replied Faith. 'Our mother.'

'Really,' exclaimed Harry. 'Wow! She was declared deceased years ago by the coroner.'

'Obviously, that is wrong,' added Faith. 'She's living at The Fairfield Lodge, a halfway house in Fairfield. You should check it out.'

'I definitely will. Thank you. You know, I was involved in that case,' continued the detective. 'I interviewed your father, Jasper Johansson, with another police officer years back. What a coincidence that is!' Faith cringed when she heard her father's name.

'There's no such thing as coincidences,' said Del.

'Really?'

'Everything has an explanation and meaning,' he added. 'Connections are always there even though they may not be obvious.'

Faith stood and walked to the veranda railing, looking out into the street.

'Are you having an episode too,' scoffed Truman.

'No. I'm just getting some air.' She checked up and down Ascot Street and the area in front of the apartments. There was some movement across the road. Something caught her eye, a shape partly resembling a person, but then it disappeared behind a tree on the footpath. She walked back and looked at Truman. 'I'd like you to leave now. You've upset my brother. And I think you're trying to do the same to me with your ridiculous insinuations.'

'No worries,' said the detective. 'I'll be on my way.' He gulped the remaining water and stood. 'Tell your father... your real father, that I'd like to chat with him when you see him next. And I'm sure Detective Gardiner will want a word when you both return to the Gold Coast.' Harry Truman tipped his head and left.

Chapter 63

The Next Stage

'We know Eduardo was a conduit,' said Jasper. 'He had no knowledge that he was infecting people. He infected Myles Ramsay and April Armstrong. He needed to be taken away and isolated to preserve the innocence and the lives of others. Eventually, his eyes would darken, and his body would be lost to The Torment.'

'Yes, Uncle. I understand completely,' replied Faith into her phone. 'And, like you, I saw the darkness in those two. Myles as he ran through the park and April as she attacked me at the centre.'

'Is your brother gaining strength? Has he bore witness to the wickedness?'

'He believes what I see is real, but he resists seeing it for himself. To complicate matters, he's become very angry with me since the detective visited. He knows I set Mendes up with the hack.'

'If he becomes a witness, then he'll understand,' said Jasper.

'It's a slow process,' said Faith. 'We need more time.'

'Time is a luxury we no longer have. He needs to see it, feel it and be able to defend against it.'

'Please, give him a few more days.'

'Watch him, Faith. If he changes, it could come quickly. First in his words, soon after in his eyes.'

'Yes, Uncle. And, for what it's worth, Truman, the detective, wants to see you.'

'That's his issue. Not mine,' said Jasper. 'It is time to action the next stage of our plan. After I hang up, I'll be making the call to the young man.'

Chapter 64

The Confession

As Faith and Delaney visited their mother for the second time, a young man walked into the Southport police station and presented himself at the long reception desk. A uniformed officer was ticking boxes on a form, not paying him attention.

The young man, dressed in black jeans, a black t-shirt, a black cap and boots, stood quietly holding a plastic shopping bag.

*   *   *

Upstairs, Michelle Gardiner and her two offsiders were in a spin as more details about the Johansson family were uncovered.

'It was years ago,' said Perkins as he read from his computer screen. But Jasper Johansson has a history of attacking people's faces. He tried to gouge a doctor's eyes.'

'Well fuck!' exclaimed Michelle. 'And the bastard changed his name back in 2021. He now goes by Angel Abner… that bitch Faith knew that!' She looked at the ceiling, took a deep breath, and then focused back on her colleagues. 'Mendes counselled this guy; he was a patient of Doctor Huang and may have even seen Jerome Gillard.'

'The old woman just said *an angel*, not specifically saying that was his proper name,' said Milford.

Michelle glared at him. 'What then? Just another fucking coincidence?'

'Huh… probably not, boss,' he replied sheepishly.

'You got anything more on the brother and sister?'

Kevin Milford rifled through some printed notes. 'There was an incident where they barricaded themselves in a foster house. Police had to smash the door down. That was a long time back, though. They're a very clever pair.'

'Harry Truman reported having the same impression,' added Michelle. 'It's her more than him, I suspect. And I'd like to wager that it was her and her foster father that hacked the Angolan Catholic website.'

Gardiner's desk phone rang. She snatched up the cordless handpiece, 'Gardiner,' she answered. As she listened, she became restless in her chair. 'Oh... Oh...' she panted. Her head rolled side to side. Perkins and Milford stopped what they were doing. Michelle shoved backwards with her feet, sending herself and the chair backwards across the floor, crashing into the wall. She jumped up. 'For fuck's sake!' she bellowed.

*   *   *

Perkins watched through the one-way mirror as Gardiner and Milford, sitting across a fixed table, interviewed Jerome Gillard. They had taken his belt and boots and emptied his pockets. He declined representation. They questioned him at length about the murders. He knew every detail. They asked him about Mendes. He told them about the hack program he had downloaded from the dark web. He said how he had copied the master key and been in Eduardo's apartment, first stealing the jars and then returning them with the three sets of eyeballs included.

'I think you already have some items from my house. You'll find everything else you need to convict me of these crimes in the shopping bag. The real scoop I used to extract their eyes and the actual spike I used to pierce their brains and cause death, except, of course, for Richard Sadowsky, who fell and cracked his skull in the stormwater drain near Centennial Parklands in Sydney. I did go back and place marbles in his eye sockets, though.'

'Richard Sadowsky?' queried Gardiner.

'Otherwise known as Randy,' continued Jerome.

Michelle and Kevin looked at one another. 'We'll need to check on that,' said Milford.

'Of course,' said Jerome. He continued to disclose more information, including - his makeup routine, dressing up as an older man, finding a kid called Callum West in Sydney and exchanging the weed he took from Sadowsky's car for a Zippo lighter, and his extensive reading of ophthalmology texts.

'Why are you confessing to these murders and the abduction of this Richard guy, Jerome?' asked Gardiner.

'A demon possessed me. It controlled me. Gave me instructions and guided me. For the last two days, for reasons unknown, it has given me some respite and the opportunity to come forward and do the right thing.'

'And yet when we interviewed you at the community centre, you did not mention any of this.'

'It wasn't really me talking. It was the demon. I'm telling you I'm guilty and must be punished.' Jerome made fleeting eye contact as he spoke.

'It looks like you've punished yourself a lot over the years,' said Gardiner, looking at his scarred arms.

'I'm pleased to say all that is over now.'

'If what you say is true,' continued Gardiner, '... it is the demon that is the guilty one, not you, Jerome.'

'I did the acts even though I was guided. I knew it was wrong. I am weak.'

The detectives asked him questions about the therapy group, about Faith and Delaney and a man called Angel, who they suggested may have been at his house.

'I saw a demon in the shape of a man,' he said. 'He was definitely no angel. He visited my grandmother and me a couple of times. He was a conman trying to trick my nanna into parting with her life savings. I hope I talked her out of it. All I know about him is that his first name was Gabriel.'

Behind the mirror, Perkins looked at the evidence bags lined up before him - a master key, a stained metal scoop, a metal kebab skewer, a Zippo lighter with the initials R. S. and another key with a plastic name tag again showing R. S. and the address 867 Norton Terrace, Kingsford.

The two detectives continued, seeking more information about Jerome's time in Sydney. He never missed a beat in his responses.

'I'll be back shortly,' said Michelle. Both detectives stood. 'Can I get you anything?' she asked Gillard.

'Just more water, please.'

'You will have the pleasure of Detective Milford's company until I get back.'

As she left, she caught Milford's gaze. She pointed with two fingers to her eyes, then gestured with her head to Jerome. 'Right?'

'Right, boss,' nodded the detective.

She moved a bit closer to her colleague. 'Light banter only. Just make him feel comfortable,' she added quietly. 'I'll be back soon.'

Gardiner excused herself and joined Perkins to discuss their next course of action.

'I don't buy it,' said Michelle.

'Well, if his DNA or prints are on this shit,' said Perkins gesturing to the evidence bags. 'And if they are a match with those in Mendes' apartment, he is as guilty as all fuck.'

'And that, most conveniently, suits the Johansson's just fucking perfectly,' added Michelle.

'All we have on them is that they withheld information. Everything else is historical and circumstantial,' added Lucas.

'We were convinced that Mendes was our man. We had enough evidence to put him away. Now what? We're suddenly convinced Gillard is the guy? Maybe tomorrow, Celine Woods will confess she made Gillard do it by putting LSD in his biscuits, all because an evil cheesecake ogre took hold of her! Fuck me!'

In the interview room, Milford sat across from Jerome. He had engaged the young man in light conversation about football, surfing, and the weather while he waited for Gardiner to return. The young man coughed into his hand a couple of times, then sat forward, keeping his forearms below the table while listening to the detective prattle on.

Michelle looked through the window just as Jerome fell forward, his head striking the table. A pool of blood had expanded beyond his bare feet and up to Milford's shoes.

$*$ $*$ $*$

Kevin Milford was a mess, covered with Jerome's blood from attempting CPR and attempting to stem the blood flow. He sat in the staff kitchen with his head in his hands, sobbing.

Michelle came in, pulled a chair alongside him, and placed a hand on his shoulder. 'He had a blade secreted somewhere in his mouth. He spat it out when he pretended to cough. It's all on the recording. You weren't to know,' she said. 'All his previous cutting attempts were across his arms, mostly superficial, but this time they were long, deep and from his elbow to his wrist… I guess you probably already know that part.' She looked at his bloody clothes, then moved her hand to the back of the large man's neck.

'He planned this, Milford,' she continued. 'Right from the moment he walked in to confess.'

Kevin Milford could only manage blubbering noises and no clear words.

'You best go and clean yourself up,' said Gardiner. 'It's not a good look for a staff kitchen.'

Chapter 65

The Torment

That evening, Faith and Delaney shared a Hawaiian pizza on the veranda at the Airbnb.

'You've been pretty quiet today,' said Faith after ten minutes, during which neither had said a word. 'I thought Mum was a bit brighter. It was nice spending time with her.'

'Huh,' grunted Del.

'Okay, I know you're pissed with me for the hack on Eduardo.'

'You think!' snapped Del. 'You know what? I don't think he killed anyone.'

'He was a conduit.'

'Stop telling me junk, Faith. It's lie after fucking lie… fuck, fuck, fuck, fuck, and double fuck to you!'

'Uncle is coming around tonight,' said Faith, unphased by the barrage.

'You mean Dad, our father, Mister Jasper Johansson!' he yelled.

'Don't,' she stood.

'Mister Jasper Graham Johansson!' he shouted even louder.

'That's enough. It's Uncle that is coming,' she screamed. 'Uncle!' She threw down her pizza and hurried to the balcony's edge. It was night, but the area was well-lit with streetlights and the regular passing of vehicles. She strode up and down the railing, looking, then stopping to listen.

Faith dragged a rattan chair next to her brother and leaned forward. 'I am usually calm, organised, and systematic, Del, but this time, you are the one making *me* anxious. You have sent out an alert.

That isn't good, especially when Uncle is coming over. I'm becoming concerned that you, too, could be a conduit.' She grabbed his jaw and turned his head while studying his eyes.

'What the hell are you doing?' He pulled away. 'Leave me alone.'

'You have no clue what is going on. You have sent out a trigger. Something else, besides Uncle, is coming. Something evil.'

'Shut up, sis. Don't talk like that.' A cool breeze flowed over them, and they heard the screech of tyres. Del shivered.

'It's coming. We have to go! Leave everything. Come on.'

'Oh dear, oh dear, oh dear,' panted Del.

'There's no time for a fucking meltdown, Del. Get your shit together, or it's over.' The sky flashed with lightning. Five seconds later, thunder roared overhead.

Faith had her brother by the hand and dragged him down the stairs and out of the building. They ran up the road. 'Don't stop,' shouted Faith. Lightning struck somewhere nearby, and a deafening crack made them both squeal. Hail started pelting down, stinging their arms and faces. The wind intensified. Drenched, they kept running, soon finding themselves under an awning along a string of shops. They went into the laundromat, wet and panting. They hugged each other.

'Are we okay now?' gasped Del.

'I think so. I hope so.' Faith sucked in some deep breaths. 'Have you got your phone?'

'Yeah.'

'I need to call Uncle.'

Del panted and caught his breath as he watched his sister standing near the door, chatting on her phone. Had he witnessed The Torment or a fraction of it? Was that possible? Maybe it was simply a passing storm cell that happened at that moment – a coincidence. But he didn't believe in that. What did he believe? He was unsure.

*   *   *

The siblings had calmed and now sat close together in the laundromat, awaiting Uncle's arrival. An elderly lady was folding her clothes from the dryer into a laundry basket. Every now and then, she glanced at the pair with a sour look of disapproval.

'What's up with her?' said Del.

'Don't know. She doesn't seem to like us much. Maybe she just has a cranky face,' said Faith with a quiet chuckle.

'Tell me, sis. What is a conduit?'

'Think of it like someone who is carrying a virus. They go around spreading it to others without getting infected themselves… at least not straight away.'

'How long before they get infected?'

'Weeks, months, maybe years like Eduardo.'

Del took a deep breath. 'Am I a conduit?'

'No. You had me worried for a few seconds, but you're all good, Del. You are not… I promise.'

'So, how did you know that Eduardo was a conduit before you even joined the group?'

'Uncle told me. Eduardo provided counselling to Uncle in Sydney before his big heart operation.'

'And how did Uncle know?'

'Some conduits use certain words repeatedly. Sometimes, their eyes go dark without going black. Eduardo had words he liked to use. How often did you hear him say,' *Pass it on* or *share it around*?'

'Wow. Yeah, he said that a lot,' nodded Del.

'Yes, pass on the evil. Share the wickedness with others. That's what he was doing without ever really knowing it himself.'

'This whole thing…' Del shook his head. 'It's difficult to get your head around.'

'Absolutely.' Faith placed a hand on her brother's shoulder.

'Can people be infected with this wickedness thing and still recover?'

'Uncle has explained to me that this is possible under extreme circumstances. It requires a dramatic change - something so life-changing that it upsets the rhythm of The Torment. We hope this has happened for Eduardo. I believe it happened too for our mother, and maybe even ourselves when we were younger.'

Del sat up straight and looked at her. 'Holy crap!' he gasped.

Chapter 66

Case Closed

It was nine-thirty in the evening, and Michelle Gardiner and Lucas Perkins were having their fifth round of drinks at the Angler's Arms Hotel in Southport.

They had moved away to the outdoor area under an awning to avoid the crowds, the noise of the pokies, the tote gamblers and a contingent of overly loud, drunken older people celebrating a seventieth birthday.

'I hope Kevin's okay,' said Perkins.

'He'll be at home with a bottle of red and a pizza, crying to his girlfriend.'

'He should've come here. Could've brought her along.'

'He wouldn't have been much fun,' she shook her head. 'I tell you, Perkins, I've had enough bawling on my shoulder for the next fuckin' year,' slurred Michelle. 'What, with him and that bloody Mendes when we let him go?'

'That was a bit funny, though,' smiled Lucas. 'A big black dude, twice your size, crying on your shoulder.'

'I don't think I was laughing.' She took a mouthful of her drink.

'The poor bastard is rooted now. He knows it, too. He'll never get a counselling job again.'

'Yeah, sorry about that, Mendes.' She looked out into the darkness and sighed.

'You're a good boss, Gardiner,' drawled Lucas. 'You have your fucking moments, that's for sure. But you get the job done. Here's to you.' He raised his rum and Coke.

'The job's not fucking done yet,' she sighed. 'But thanks anyway.' They clinked their glasses.

'Forsyth has shut you down. You gotta leave it now.'

'There's a bug up my arse, Perkins,' slurred Gardiner. 'A big Johansson bug. Inspector Charlie fucking Forsyth doesn't get it. Doesn't wanna even think about it. Well, fuck him, I say!'

'Well, Gardiner, cheers to you,' Perkins said, lifting his glass again. 'Good fucking luck. You're gonna need it.' He emptied his drink.

'Harry Truman knows it's far from done and dusted. Cassandra Johansson's brain injury is the same as both Armstrong's and Ramsay's.'

'Except she's alive, or back from the dead or something,' drawled Perkins.

'I think Truman will work with me on this.'

'Not if he's got any brains… and it's your shout.' Perkins waved his empty glass.

'We'll see about that.' She stood and stretched. 'Same again?'

Chapter 67

The Family

A tall man with a square jaw and dripping rainwater filled the entrance to the laundromat.

'Uncle,' said Faith. She ran to him, and her feet swung in the air as he hugged her. Del stood and looked tentatively at his Dad, a man whom he now had to call Uncle.

Faith stood next to her father. They both looked at Delaney.

Jasper opened his arms and smiled broadly. 'Finally, my son. My wonderful son.'

Del erupted into tears, ventured forward and embraced his taller father tightly around the waist.

'This is a moment for the ages,' said Jasper, placing a large hand on Del's head. 'The time has finally come when we are strengthened as a family. The battle rages on, but we are renewed; our fortress is solid. We are resolute, formidable, and empowered…'

Del remained in his father's embrace as he listened to him speak about their future, about recruiting a vast army of supporters, vanquishing the evil converts and conquering The Torment. His voice was captivating, with the authenticity of a gospel preacher. His perfect emphasis on select words, phrases and syllables would be enough to secure him a role as a news anchor. This was not how he remembered his father.

Del eased back and looked at his father's face. 'You sound different… Uncle…' he stammered.

'Yes, my heart surgery changed me. The demons were cast from my body. I became a new man, revitalised with a clear direction and an unquestionable commitment. A spiritual master who assisted me for many years became one within me, lifting me to new heights, both intellectually and emotionally. I know I sound different because I *am* very different now.'

'Wow. That sounds like…' Del struggled to find the right words, '… like an amazing experience.'

Faith moved in closer and did her best to hug them both. 'My brother. My family.'

Del looked up at his father. 'Are we safe now… Uncle?' he asked, pausing to consider the word, which seemed wrong and insincere.

'We are never completely safe, my boy. But for now, I don't sense any immediate danger, but there is something…' Uncle tipped his head, listened and sniffed. 'This lady here,' he studied the elderly woman standing with a basket of folded clothes under one arm, waiting to get by the three blocking her way. 'She stares. There is a hint of darkness. You both wait outside. I'll engage her.' Faith and Del moved to the footpath and sat on a bench seat. The weather had eased to a slow drizzle.

'You are a woman with problems,' said Jasper. 'Great trouble is upon you, and you struggle to see your future.' The lady just stared.

'Take this,' he continued as he took her free hand, gently placed a cat's-eye tom bowler in her palm, and closed her fingers around it. 'This may help you. Treasure it. Keep it with you. Hold it to the light, and it will help you forsake the darkness.' With that, Uncle turned and left.

She opened her hand and looked at the marble. 'I've seen all sorts of fucked up people in my life. But this fucker gotta take the cake.' She headed off with her basket.

*   *   *

Thirty minutes later, the three returned to the Airbnb after Uncle had deemed it safe. The pizza on the veranda was soggy from the brief storm. Faith started preparing some toasted sandwiches.

Del took himself to the bathroom. Sitting on the toilet, he pulled Jupiter from his pocket, lined it up with the light, and gazed into the small glass orb. The white, orange, brown and red colours swirled as he moved it closer to his eye. There it was again - his family. Faith was still pulsating red, his mother a transparent white, his father black and changing colour to a dark red, then back again, and himself now looking smaller than last time and his colour a dusty brown.

'This is not good. If they think I'm a conduit, if they think I'm not on board, I'm pretty sure they'll pluck my eyes right out of my head.' He took a minute to relax before tucking Jupiter away and rejoining his family.

'You can call me Uncle Abner,' said his father. 'It may be easier for you than just Uncle. My first name is Angel, but Uncle Angel doesn't roll off the tongue as well as Uncle Abner.'

'You don't look much older,' said Del.

'There are times I look older, and there are times I don't. It is all contingent upon the battles I'm facing,' his father replied.

'I see,' said Del, even though he didn't. 'Will I need to change my name too?'

'Once The Torment sees you as a threat, yes. But there is some time before that will be necessary. The same goes for your sister.'

'Have you visited…' Del hesitated while he thought over his words. 'Let me say… have you seen… Auntie?'

'You mean Cassie,' smiled Uncle Abner. 'Yes, I've seen her.'

'She is a mess,' said Del.

'She was much worse before I rescued her.'

'You did that?'

'She was abused beyond belief and used as a prostitute by an evil man. Given drugs and mistreated, raped, beaten, enslaved, starved. I know the police showed you a sketch of a man. That was Richard Randy Sadowsky. I hope that I saved his soul, but I was not able to save his earthly life.'

'Oh,' uttered Del, trying to stifle a gasp.

'Here we are. It's a bit late, but dinner is served.' Faith placed the plate of toasted sandwiches on the dining table. 'What are our plans for tomorrow?'

'I'd like to see my mother again,' said Del. He grabbed a ham and cheese toasty.

'Yes, Delaney. We must do that,' said his father, taking one himself.

'What if that detective comes back?' asked Del.

'Be assured, my boy. The police no longer have an interest in this family,' chuckled Angel Abner.

Del's mind was filled with questions. *Have the police acquitted Eduardo? Why are they not pursuing the guilty? Who is the new fall guy?* For reasons of self-preservation, he chose to remain quiet.

'Later tomorrow, we need to find someone. I see you have your laptop, Faith. That's perfect. You can liaise with Ted if you wish. We will be planning a first for our family as a team. The liberation of a soul. The man's name is Roscoe Romano. He sold your mother to Sadowsky. I'd like to see his eyes.'

Another thought popped into Del's mind. *I'm going to need a new therapist.*

THE END

ACKNOWLEDGEMENTS

To my loyal readers, thank you for your ongoing support and encouragement. Without you, my books would not exist.

To my talented fellow authors and friends, Ian Laver and Robin Storey, whom I catch up with far too infrequently, thank you for your advice, encouragement, and feedback.

To my wife, Jenny, an avid reader, who gave this book its first read. Thanks for your comments and corrections.

To Stefan Proudfoot, who works closely with me and always steps up to produce an exceptional book cover.

I've read some popular novels and checked their acknowledgement sections, and in many cases, lots of people have contributed to their stories. Indie authors rarely have such a cast of assistants and contributors. It is a labour of love often completed in solitary confinement or in the company of Google.

ABOUT THE AUTHOR

Bob Goodwin has been writing for many years. He is a trained general nurse with psychiatric and counselling qualifications. He has worked in mental health settings for nearly forty years, and this experience has significantly influenced his work.

He's written novels, screenplays, short stories, short theatrical plays, and one-act-plays. Several of his shorter works are available on his website for free, as is a free self-help eBook for managing anxiety and stress.

While Bob writes drama and comedy, most of his work is in the suspense thriller genre. His eighth novel, "The Semblant," was a change from this and his first venture into Erotic Horror. "Crazy Lies & Cat's-Eyes" is his ninth book.

Numerous excellent reviews of his novels can be found online. Bob has managed the website StoriesAndPlays for over ten years.

Novels by Bob Goodwin:
- Strike Me Dead (2014)
- The 13th Black Candle (2015)
- Max Justice - Book 1 in the Max Judd series (2016)
- Max Justice: Turmoil - Book 2 in the Max Judd series (2017)
- Max Justice: Vengeance - Book 3 in the Max Judd series (2019)
- The Tree of Thorns (2020)
- Ezekiel: Madman, Mastermind or Messiah? (2021)
- The Semblant (2022)
- Crazy Lies & Cat's-Eyes (2024)